Iw

DEADLY ASSOCIATIONS

A CLAUDIA HERSHEY MYSTERY

LAURA BELGRAVE

An Imprint of The Overmountain Press
JOHNSON CITY, TENNESSEE

This book is a work of fiction. All names, characters, places, and events are either the product of the author's imagination or are used fictitiously. Any resemblance to actual events or persons, living or dead, is entirely coincidental and beyond the intent of either the author or the publisher.

This one is for Linda Liska Belgrave,
who gives new meaning to the words
"push, pester and prod."
Thanks, Inny—for that, and the endless reads.

ACKNOWLEDGMENTS

Writing fiction is a lonely and mildly neurotic business. While all the grown-ups are going to work at real jobs, there you are, playing make-believe on a keyboard with make-believe people in a make-believe world. Whole days can go by without the car leaving the driveway. But you know what? There are people out there who actually make writing seem perfectly reasonable. They'll bring you fresh coffee. They'll let you natter about the characters in your story as if your pretend people were next-door neighbors. They'll actually cheer you on.

In my world, those people are these people:

My husband, John Caramanica; my sister Leslie Curtis; my nephew Casey Curtis; my buddy Marlene Passell; the terrific people at the Florida chapter of Mystery Writers of America; and the clerks at 7-Eleven and Dunkin' Donuts.

To all of you, thanks. Again.

But wait! I'm not done. My gratitude likewise goes to the people who indulged my technical questions for *Deadly Associations* with patience and professionalism. Kudos especially to Judie Banks, public information officer and victim advocate at the Coconut Creek Police Department; Dr. Joshua Perper, chief medical examiner for Broward County; and David Knoerlein, forensic analyst with the Crime Scene Unit of the Broward County Sheriff's Office. These are busy people who took the time to help me get the details right. If I blew it—or took a liberty or two—holler at me, not them.

C H A P T E R · 1

THE WATER IN THE FISH TANK looked cloudy. That couldn't be good, although most of the fish didn't seem to mind. They glided tirelessly through the murk, occasionally darting left or right, or up or down, for no apparent reason. Maybe they were scavenging for particles of food invisible to the human eye. That's what the guy who owned the tank said. He said they had radar sharp as a bat foraging in the night for insects. Of course, that might not be true, because when the guy talked at all he leaped feverishly from subject to subject with no thought to connecting the dots for his audience. In a bar, it would merely be irksome and you'd sidle away. But this was the guy's family room and it was impossible to sidle anywhere, not with a gun trained at your head.

The tank wasn't huge—just twenty gallons. Claudia had learned that much, plus some of the names of the species in the tank. Platys. Neon tetras. Swordtails. Some kind of guppy with a colorful, fan-like tail. What she didn't know yet was the man's name or why he was holding four people hostage in his family room—five, if you counted her, and Claudia supposed she'd better. She wasn't bound and didn't have duct tape across her mouth like the others, but she'd been the only one hit on the head with the butt-end of his gun, a mean-looking 9-millimeter semiautomatic. If he wanted, it would take no effort to kill them all in less than ten seconds. The metallic taste of fear flooded her mouth.

"So, Detective Hershey," said the man, "what do you think of my house? Like it?"

"I haven't seen enough to form an opinion," she answered.

The man threw back his head and laughed, as though they were at a party and she'd just said something hilarious. That his laughter was out of context didn't scare her. But the sound did—a high-pitched bray that sputtered into a hiss like the *phssht* of a one-liter Coke bottle being opened. It betrayed him, revealing an anxiety that would probably take little to ignite into something far more dangerous.

"Maybe I should give you a tour. Would you like that?"

"I think what matters is what *you'd* like," Claudia said carefully. She adjusted her eyeglasses and exhaled. "Seems to me you're running the show here."

"True enough." The man shot to his feet and smiled down at her, then looked behind her toward the others. The smile faded. He scratched the side of his face with the muzzle of his gun. "You're all here because there's been a misunderstanding." He looked back at Claudia. "Actually, you're not here because of a misunderstanding. You had nothing to do with that. You're here because I needed someone with authority to help resolve the misunderstanding, which these people have demonstrated a distinct lack of interest in doing. Go ahead. You can get up and turn around, take a look at them."

When she'd first entered the family room, she'd had only the briefest of moments to see the captives and assess the situation. In the second that followed, when she simultaneously seized at her .38 and began to pivot back toward the man, he'd hit her with his gun. The blow, which landed clumsily on the bottom of her head and glanced off her right shoulder, wasn't hard enough to make her go down or draw blood. But it was enough to make her stumble, forfeiting any advantage she might have had. He'd put the gun just under her chin then, taken her weapon and handbag, and guided her to the floor, facing away from the others. He murmured something that might have been an apology. Claudia couldn't recall. Her head screamed from the knock, which quickly had morphed into a headache.

The hostages sat side by side on the tile floor, leaning against a long white wall. There were two men and two women. Each was bound at the hands and feet with duct tape. Smaller strips covered their mouths, but what they couldn't communicate with their voices they communicated with their eyes: terror. One of the men had wet himself.

"They're fine," said their captor. He paced, one hand gripping the gun, the other in his pants pocket, reflexively jostling keys and coins. "They're not in a position to play Twister, but—" He paused mid-sentence and glared at her. "You *do* know Twister, right?"

Claudia thought. "The game where people bend and twist all over each other, have to keep their feet and hands on the colored circles? That one?"

"Good, good! You're with me! I like that." He swiveled back to the captives. "I doubt *they'd* know that. I doubt *they'd* see the significance."

Significance? Claudia didn't press for details. She recalled Twister as a great game for hyperactive toddlers and drunken college students. She played once as an adult and threw her back out for a week. But the man was already moving on, muttering about his hostages.

"So my 'friends' here aren't comfortable! Who cares!" he said. "They don't deserve to be comfortable. I'm not even sure they deserve to live." His voice dropped to a conversational tone. "I suppose, Detective, that will be up to you."

Claudia's mouth felt like she'd been sucking on cotton balls. She cleared her throat. "Who exactly are these people?" she asked. "Who are you?"

"I'm just a simple homeowner. That's all you need to know for now."

He gestured with his gun, signaling her to sit again, this time against a wall perpendicular to his hostages. She sat, drawing her knees up toward her chest. Except for a straight-backed chair that the man used, a picnic cooler, a cardboard box, a small bedside lamp on the floor, the fish tank, and the cabinet upon which it sat, there was nothing in the room. Heavy drapes across a sliding-glass door were drawn, leaving only cockeyed illumination from the lamp.

"Moving in or moving out?" Claudia asked.

Once again, he laughed. "Neither. I've been here eighteen months and I'm not going anywhere." He pointed his gun at each hostage in turn and said "Bang, bang!" to each. If not for the restlessness in his posture, the gesture would've seemed almost playful. "Of course, they all wish I'd never moved here to begin with. Hungry?" He patted the cooler. "I've got sandwiches and cold drinks."

"No, thanks. I have dinner plans for later," Claudia replied.

"No you don't." He looked at his watch. "It's closing in on five-thirty. You're just starting your vacation, and—forgive me, I'm paraphrasing your daughter now—your plans are to do 'nothing but vegetate.'"

The terror Claudia had seen in the eyes of the hostages flared up her spine. He saw it and waved his gun dismissively. "Don't get excited. Your Robin and my Sandi know each other from school. I don't think they hung out together, but they wound up assigned to the same cabin for camp. Sandi mentioned it last week. She chattered about the camp, about the kids who were going, what they'd be doing, and somewhere in all of that she told me a little about Robin." He shrugged. "Kids talk about their parents. Robin talked about you. Sandi probably talked to her about me. I can't imagine parents are favored conversational topics for 14-year-old girls, but occasionally we come up. It just so happens that a throwaway comment by you to Robin to Sandi made its way to me. It was a fluke, but a convenient one. So how about that sandwich? We could be here a while." He looked disappointed when she shook her head. "All right. They'll still be good when you're ready."

The man leaned back on his chair, tilting it on two legs. He lapsed into one of his silences, the gun resting on his thigh but still pointed at Claudia. Physically, he was unremarkable in every way. She put him at his late thirties to early forties, maybe a hundred and seventy pounds, and a few inches shy of her own six-foot height. His hair, the color of a charred steak, hinted at the beginning of a widow's peak. But it was fashionably trimmed and he was clean-shaven. He looked like he'd be more at home holding a pencil than a gun.

The house had central air-conditioning. Claudia heard it cycle on, then shift to a steady hum. For Florida in the first week of August, it would run almost continuously to maintain whatever temperature the man had set. She guessed at seventy-four degrees—cooler than most people would set; maybe not cool enough for their captor. He wore pressed jeans and a crisp white shirt rolled at the sleeves, but the shirt was damp under the arms from perspiration. Another bad sign.

"So where are we going with this?" Claudia asked. "Obviously there was never a burglary—"

"Obviously."

"—which means the call you put in to the police station was just a stunt to get me over here for this, whatever 'this' is."

"I don't like the word *stunt*. It sounds like something you'd find in one of those gratuitous movies where pyrotechnic displays are more important than story. Bang-bang, shoot 'em up. That's all the film industry seems to produce anymore."

And then he was off and running again, leaning forward in his chair and lecturing about the decline of the film industry, then moving somehow, from there, into an animated discourse on the epidemic of drugs in the United States. He stopped in the middle of a sentence, sat back, and smiled. "Ruse. Let's just call it a ruse, and a damned clever one at that."

Sally had been on dispatch when the call came in to the station at four-thirty on the non-emergency line. The caller, who identified himself as Charles Gottu, said someone had walked into his house and stolen his stereo system. He said he was on his way out of town and needed a detective out now. No, he hadn't locked his door, but did that make burglary less of an offense? What? No, it couldn't wait. And no, he didn't want a patrol officer. His taxes entitled him to prompt and thorough investigation, which meant he deserved a detective. Surely the police department had at least one of those, did it not?

Of course it did. It had at least one. In fact, it had exactly one.

Claudia couldn't hear the man's end of the conversation, but she knew from Sally's rising voice that the most that was standing between "kiss my ass" and a hang-up was maybe thirty seconds. That wouldn't play well with the chief, so Claudia took the call, jotted directions to the man's house, and told him she'd be out shortly.

"What're you, nuts?" Sally had said. "This guy's gonna whine to you halfway into next week. You'll be starting your vacation with a headache."

"Nah. I'll catch him on my way home, take a report, and tell him to call his insurance company. Fifteen minutes, in and out."

"I don't think so. This guy's looking for a full-scale investigation. Until you have someone in handcuffs, he's not gonna leave his phone long enough to go to the toilet."

"Then I'll have to explain the facts of life to him, Sally. It just takes some people skills."

"You don't have people skills."

The phone rang before Claudia could frame a response. She made a face at Sally, then grabbed her jacket and handbag and headed out, little on her mind but seven glorious days of doing nothing. And now, an hour later, instead of peeling off her work clothes and feeding the cat, she was listening to the man carry on about how masterfully he'd baited her.

"The bit about my name—Charles 'Gottu'—that was an especially nice touch, don't you think? I mean, you *do* get it, right? Gottu? *Got you?*"

"I get it," Claudia said. She watched the man nod, satisfied, and it struck her that he wanted her approval, almost seemed eager for it. If she ever got the chance—a big if—maybe she could work it to her advantage.

"Don't take it too hard, Detective Hershey. What you fell into? It's all about human nature. Lacking evidence to the contrary, you trusted in the basic goodness of people—in this case, me. I called for help. You responded in good faith. You thought I was what I represented myself to be. That's the way it's supposed to work." He waved his gun toward his captives. "Of course, I'd have never gotten my 'guests' over here on a basis of trust. Them I had to lure with greed. It was disappointingly easy. Maybe one day I'll tell you about it."

"Why not now?"

He didn't answer. "They've turned me into someone I don't know," he said softly. "I've become more like them and less like myself. My own daughter wouldn't recognize me. She'd. . . ." He blinked and shook his head slightly, then, animated once more, he turned his attention fully back to Claudia. "Amazingly—even with all of this—I find that trust is still important to me. I'm not entirely willing to let it go, not yet. So let me ask you, Detective. Can I trust *you*?"

Somewhere here, there was a right answer. She didn't know what it was, who he was, what he wanted. If she said sure, he could trust her, he wouldn't believe her. If she told him no, he might admire her for her honesty but secure her like the others. Either way, there seemed no win-win in a direct answer, so she cranked her neck a bit and winced, giving him a little theater right back instead.

"That's not a fair question," she said. "You tricked me into coming here. You hit me on the head. You're holding a gun on me. Now, I'm prag-matic enough to recognize that you must have good reasons for what you're doing, so I'm *prepared* to trust you, but how about leveling the play-ing field?"

He smiled. "That's not an answer, but it's a good response."

"Best I could do under pressure." She smiled back, sensing that he wanted her to like him. "So? You ready to tell me who you are and what's going on? What you want?"

The man stretched. "Sure. Why not." He glanced at his hostages. "It's not like they don't already know." One of the men looked at him. The other captives studiously avoided eye contact. "Who I am is Steven Hem-mer, and what I want is to get my house painted."

CHAPTER · 2

NO ONE WOULD MISTAKE Indian Run as a vacation destination. That's not to say the town didn't have some impressive characteristics, of course. In its own quiet way, Indian Run put a lot of Florida towns to shame, what with its huge trees weighted by Spanish moss, wide-open spaces, a lake teeming with perch and bass, and a sky so free of pollutants you could almost see your reflection in it. But it didn't have sandy beaches or two-story shopping malls or even a single multiplex movie theater. No glitz. No glamour. None of that, not at all. What Indian Run had instead were cattle ranches, citrus groves, sod and vegetable farms, and light businesses that saw to their needs.

Oh, sure. There were some distinctions here and there. Indian Run was home to a dwindling group of psychics and mediums that attracted some attention back in the '70s—and then again in the late '90s when one of them got killed—and it also boasted one of the finest boot makers in the entire state, an enormous man whose custom work would embarrass competitors in Texas. Even so, it took little more than a glance at the Chamber of Commerce's outdated brochure to see that Indian Run was primarily about cows and corn and washboard roads.

Most of the town's 8,000 residents had actually been born and raised here, which always seemed to surprise the odd traveler who occasionally took a wrong turn into Indian Run on the way north to Disney World, just outside Orlando. Indian Run wasn't all that close to Orlando; it really wasn't close to much of anything. Still, the center of the state was vast and its roads less clearly marked than the superhighways in Florida's coastal areas. Getting lost wasn't easy but it likewise wasn't hard, and as long as mistaken visitors had their cup of coffee and then drove on, Indian Run's residents looked upon them with amused benevolence.

The same, though, could not be said of visitors who liked the quaint feel of Indian Run and came back to stay. Their numbers had grown, and in the previous six years Indian Run had seen a downright infiltration that bloomed into an exclusive community called Feather Ridge. The people in Feather Ridge didn't seem to understand just how unpopular they were, but that might've been because they insulated themselves from the very aspects of Indian Run that originally attracted them. They didn't raise cattle or corn in Feather Ridge. They raised a private airstrip and a private school, and they installed a lush golf course that hid many of their six-figure homes from prying eyes. They were happy. They worked up tans in the winter months, and when most of them retreated north during the hot summer, they enjoyed telling their friends they'd discovered one of the rare, still-pristine areas of Florida.

But as intolerable as Feather Ridge remained even now to many of the town's lifelong residents, it was nothing compared to the most recent insult—a gated community that in little more than two years had foisted 240 concrete-block houses on the opposite end of town. Florida couldn't get enough of gated communities, and a developer running out of space to build more of them in South Florida eventually discovered new potential in the central part of the state. He couldn't expect the same asking price for homes far from beaches; but he flourished anyway because land was cheaper, and so was construction labor. He gave Indian Run what he'd given South Florida: zero-lot-line single-family houses in mocha, peach, and off-white shades. What that basically meant were homes with virtually no yard, spaced about ten feet apart. He had no trouble selling any of them. People loved Florida, and they loved their gates.

The gates in this particular community, Willow Whisper, weren't really gates at all. They were nothing more than long, metal bars designed to stop vehicles, not unlike the bars that halted traffic at railroad crossings. To get past them, community residents were issued remote-control devices that could raise the bars to an upright position. Most homeowners kept the remotes clipped to their visors. Thieves had no such perks, which made their entry inconvenient, but not impossible. When Claudia made her way to Willow Whisper to take the burglary report at Hemmer's house, that was one of the possibilities she considered, especially because the bar at the entrance was currently stuck in an upright position. Apparently that happened a lot. It's what Hemmer was venting about now, telling her that for the eighty-dollar monthly maintenance fee he paid the homeowners association, he was entitled to reliable gates.

Claudia nodded. She knew little about gated communities or home-owners associations, but she could sympathize with paying for something you didn't get. She'd once had a skirmish with an air-conditioning company that billed her in advance for a routine service call and then made her wait all day for a technician who never showed up. She told Hemmer the story, hoping to nudge him into seeing her as a kindred spirit.

"So how did they resolve it?" he asked. "Did they fall all over themselves with apologies for the 'inconvenience'? Did they schedule another appointment and discount the bill for a whopping ten percent? Assure you it'd never happen again?"

"Something like that." As it happened, that's precisely what the company had done.

Hemmer smirked.

"But never mind," said Claudia. "It's nothing compared to what you've got going here. You said you wanted your house painted. What's the—"

Hemmer tossed a pen and a spiral notebook at her. "Here. You'll want to take notes." He paused while she flipped the notebook open. "I want my house painted. I also want the concrete patio slab out back replaced. And while we're at it, I want the gate fixed. I want all of it done now. Today. No later than the end of the weekend. The people in this room can make it happen. They already should've made it happen. Instead, they jerked me around, and now I'm out of patience. They do the job and they all live happily ever after. They don't do the job and you can guess the ending." He turned to them and did the "bang-bang" thing again.

The chill in Claudia's stomach had turned into a flame. She took a deep breath to fight back nausea, reviewing everything she had ever learned about hostage negotiation, knowing that what she knew was not enough. She tentatively put a hand on the floor to push up, testing him.

Hemmer was at her side in an instant, the automatic at her head. "Hey! What're you doing?"

"Whoa, whoa." Claudia froze. "I was just thinking about the tour you offered. I'll take that now. You can show me what you're talking about. Then you can tell me about the people you've got here."

He relaxed and took a step back but didn't lower the gun. "All right. Okay. But we take it slow, and you don't move unless I tell you to move. We're not buddies."

They started outside, Hemmer cautiously guiding her past the drapes and through the sliding-glass doors onto the patio. It had an eastern exposure and looked out onto a woodsy area, which wrapped the south edge of his property line as well. A chain-link fence choked with weedy undergrowth separated it from Hemmer's manicured yard. To the right, on the north side, a six-foot-tall privacy fence blocked his yard from that of his neighbor.

"Detective, did you know that in a development like this one, my corner lot is considered prime acreage? That and anything on a lake or a cul-de-sac."

Claudia shook her head.

"Sure, sure. It's all about the view or the privacy, and sometimes both." Hemmer laughed. "It's all an illusion, of course. Just like the security of an entrance gate." He waved toward the woods. "You see a gate there? A guard? Of course not. If people want in, they'll get in. I disabled my own alarm system first thing when I moved here. They go off when you don't want them to, and any kind of thief with an ounce of intelligence can breach them, anyway." He shook his head. "Gated communities. Security. I can't believe how gullible people are."

"So why'd you buy in here?"

"A divorce. A death. A daughter—mostly a daughter. It's a long story and none of it matters now. Point is, I didn't get what I paid for. Look at the patio."

The patio was nothing more than a concrete slab. Claudia guessed it to be about eight feet by fifteen feet. The only thing on it was a gas grill. A crack ran nearly the length of it, with spidery tendrils shooting off into a variety of smaller cracks. A tuft of grass poked out of the far end.

"I measured," said Hemmer. "The biggest part of the crack is over a half inch. And that's not the only flaw. The patio is buckled, too, mostly in the middle. See where it's stained?" He kept the gun on Claudia while he pointed. "See it?"

It would've been hard to miss. The discoloration was oval and darker than the rest of the concrete. Smaller patches crept toward the house.

"I get puddles you could water-ski on, and nothing I put out here sits level. I used to have a patio table and chairs, but they wobbled too much. Now I just keep the grill. The whole patio must've been put together by a couple of drunks, but the bastard developer flatly refuses to replace it. He says it's past the warranty period."

"Is he one of the people you have inside?"

"No. I wish he was. But all I have are his minions, one more stupid than the next."

Claudia thought she was starting to see where Hemmer was going with everything. "What's the story on getting your house painted?"

"The paint's fine. I just want a different color. What's on it now is called 'sea sand,' as if that makes it something other than beige. Here . . . wait." Hemmer used his free hand to grope in his pants pocket. He pulled out a card and handed it to Claudia. "You see anything obnoxious about that? Anything that isn't aesthetically pleasing?"

The paint swatch was of a dusky blue color. To Claudia's eye, it looked almost more gray than blue. She kind of liked it.

"It's called 'morning mist.' I let Sandi pick it out. She spent a lifetime finding just the right shade. That's the color I want on my house. Does it seem like a big deal to you?"

"No. So why is it?"

"Because of the people in my family room."

"In that case, maybe it's time to meet them."

He nodded toward the sliding-glass doors. "Maybe it is."

This time when he offered, Claudia accepted a drink from Hemmer's cooler. It held cans of Coke, Diet Coke, and Barq's root beer. In a pinch, any one of them could serve as a weapon, but Hemmer stood to the side watching, his gun held steadily on her. She selected a Diet Coke and slowly eased back to the wall. He watched her roll the can across her forehead, then pop the top and take a long drink.

"Hot as hell outside, isn't it?" he said. "I've been here a year and a half and I'm still not used to it."

Good. He was up for more conversation. "Where're you from originally?"

"Most recently Seattle. Stayed there longest, almost ten years. Before that, a whole string of places—San Diego, Denver, St. Louis, Boston. Moving around is the nature of my business. It was, anyway."

"What's your business?"

"Computers. Software, actually. I'm on my own now. What about you? I know you didn't start out here."

"No. Cleveland."

Hemmer brightened. "Oh, yeah. That's right. I read about you in the papers. City cop stuck in Podunk. But you just broke some big case, right? Something about an old guy out in Feather Ridge." He made a clucking noise. "I bet they thought they were safe there, too. Guess you proved they're not. No one is." He scowled at the hostages. "Right now, especially them."

Claudia took another swallow from the can. "And 'them' is . . . who?"

"No time for repartee, huh?"

"We've got to get some stuff done, Mr. Hemmer."

"Steven's fine."

"We need to get this thing resolved."

Hemmer began pacing. "That guy—the big one nearest the fish tank—that's Bill Bonolo. I think of him as Bill 'Assholo.'" Hemmer smiled at the flash in Bonolo's eyes. "He's more than an asshole, though. He's also president of our esteemed homeowners association, not to mention one of the smarmiest people you'll ever meet." He squatted in front of Bonolo and chucked the gun under his chin. "Think I don't know about you? What you really are?"

Claudia was too far away to make a play, not with Hemmer's gun at Bonolo's face. She watched the big man's eyes flare with fury. He squirmed against the duct tape.

Hemmer laughed and straightened. "Like the way I put them boy-girl, boy-girl?" He pointed at the woman beside Bonolo. "This is Gloria Addison. Far as I can tell, she's a kept woman. I don't know *who's* keeping her, but when she's around you can find her at the community pool with a gin and tonic she pretends is water."

Addison didn't react. But she held Hemmer's eyes until he turned away. "Anyway, Ms. Addison is one of three members of the association's property alterations committee. In the association newsletters, it's merely called the 'PAC.' Gotta love those acronyms."

Even with the tape across her mouth, Addison would be a magnet for men. She had flawless skin and thick tawny hair that cascaded to her shoulders. Her arms looked toned in the way that only religious devotion to a gym could produce.

"Next up is Kurt Kitner. He's also on the PAC. I don't think Kurt's all that bad a guy, actually. Trouble is, he doesn't know how to think for himself and he's fearful of his own shadow—or at least of Assholo there."

Kitner had closed his eyes and bowed his head, as if he could make himself invisible. But he trembled convulsively, and the stain at the crotch of his pants had widened.

"Kurt's an accountant. Rumor has it he has aspirations of being voted treasurer of the association." Hemmer shook his head disgustedly. "A dream come true, right, Kurt?" He got no response.

"Finally, we have Jennifer Parrish. She's a former elementary school teacher and now a housewife—excuse me, a 'homemaker.' What do you have, Jen? Three kids? Four? Anyway, Detective Hershey, she's the final PAC member. I don't know if she's particularly intimidated by the others, but she'd do anything to keep the peace. Keeping the peace means going along, so she always votes the majority way. Isn't that right, Ms. Parrish?"

Parrish nodded faintly. Hemmer sighed. "Silly goose." He turned to Claudia. "There they are, the characters in my little drama. Think I can get Spielberg to cast any of them for a movie version?"

Claudia pretended to listen when he lurched into a monologue about the nature of community. He seemed to be contrasting the peaceful coexistence of the fish in his tank to the lack of harmony in the Willow Whisper development. She stole surreptitious looks at the hostages whenever she could. The homemaker, Jennifer Parrish, appeared to be trying to signal something with her eyes. They darted to the left. The tank? Was she suggesting something about the tank? Kitner had opened his eyes, but he wouldn't look up. The other two, Addison and Bonolo, kept their eyes on Hemmer. Something had gone on in here while Hemmer was showing her around outside. Claudia didn't know what, but something.

". . . and you'll notice that the fish are only aggressive at feeding times or breeding periods. It's the natural order of things—very different than with people. You see the point, don't you?"

On some level she'd heard what Hemmer had said and she nodded. "I do. And I agree. But if we're going to get your house and patio taken care of, then we have to move past the philosophical. What has to happen?"

"You have a very practical nature. I like that." Hemmer sifted through the cardboard box and took out a file folder. He slid it across the tiles. "Take a look. Those are copies of the requests I've put in for property changes. Denied every time." He waited while she scanned the documents, then he slid another folder to her. "These are the forms we have to use when we want to change something. Homeowners fill them out and submit them to the property alterations committee—my good friends here. They review them. If a request doesn't threaten the structural integrity of neighboring property or harm the overall aesthetics of the community, the request is approved and the board signs off on it. But if the PAC thinks there's a problem, the request is denied. The homeowner can forget about it or change the request to try and make it more agreeable. The approval process can vary, but it typically takes two to four weeks."

Hemmer glared at the hostages. "That's how it's *supposed* to work."

He sent another folder to Claudia. "I got my hands on copies of some of the forms that *have* been approved for other homeowners. You'll notice the committee signed off on paint jobs from pale yellow to salmon pink, and on several occasions they've allowed homeowners to break up their patios so they could install new ones with pools. Now, what makes their patios different from mine, I'll never know." He wriggled his eyebrows at Bonolo. "Then again, maybe I will. But that would be pure speculation on my part, and it isn't the point of today. It's not the point of the here and now."

Claudia caught a glimpse of Bonolo rolling his eyes. "Okay," she said. "Let's assume you're right and—"

"I *am* right."

"Okay." She inhaled and told herself to slow down. She could make this work. "Okay," she said again. "Let's start by getting the house painted."

"My thinking, too. One last folder." The folder skidded toward her. "What you've got there is yet another completed form for the paint job. It's dated today. It includes the specs. It includes another sample card showing the paint color. Every detail is properly included. There's another completed form for the patio. Since the builder refuses to replace it, I'll do it at my own expense, which I've made clear to the committee on more than one occasion."

"A folder for everything. You're very organized."

"That, and considerate. I only brought downstairs what you needed to see." He nodded toward the folder in her hands. "What I want is for these jokers to sign off on both forms, make them official."

"And you want the work to begin now?" Claudia looked at her watch. "It's almost six-thirty."

"I have paint in the garage. We have light until close to nine o'clock. I have a painting crew on standby—a crew that's deliriously happy to work even in the dead of night for what I'll pay. All we need is a phone call to get started. The patio can wait until morning. Heaven forbid I should disturb the serenity of the community with drilling at this hour."

Hemmer retrieved a cell phone from the cardboard box. "I know the number by heart. Here. You can dial."

He liked to slide things, and apparently he liked to toss them as well. He pitched the phone toward Claudia. In the nanosecond that the phone hung in the air, she recognized the opportunity she'd been waiting for. She snatched at the phone and faked a fumble on the catch, slapping it toward the floor. It skidded in Hemmer's direction and he did what she hoped he would: He took an awkward step toward it and bent forward to stop the slide. It was enough. Claudia vaulted off the floor and kicked out, catching him in the ribs. His automatic clattered to the tile, and before he could react, she was on him.

Neither went down, and for one crazy minute they clung together like lovers, dancing like lovers, breathing hard like lovers. The room seemed to spin. It was like being sucked into a vortex. She couldn't get a grip. He couldn't get a grip. They grappled some more, their shoes squeaking on the tile, then collided into the fish tank. It went over, twenty gallons of water, gravel, and fish splashing everywhere.

Hemmer slipped. Claudia clutched him from the back, kicked him behind a knee, and straddled him the second he buckled to the floor. She put a knee on his back. She could smell him and she could smell herself—fear, fish, adrenaline. In a few minutes she would collapse in on herself, as overcome as the platys gasping for oxygen on the floor. With luck, she'd have him in handcuffs before that happened. Before Hemmer bucked her off.

But he didn't struggle. Maybe he was too played out. Claudia didn't care. She managed to get them both to their feet, one of his arms twisted behind him and locked tightly to her chest, one of her arms around his neck. She shoved him into the wall, pushing his face against it, near to the cabinet where he'd set her purse. Her handcuffs were inside, within easy reach, and she felt the bloom of confidence returning. In another minute, it would be over.

Hemmer's breath came in ragged bursts. "The gun . . . wasn't even loaded. How about . . . that? I bet you—"

Whatever he intended to say was lost in a blur of motion that Claudia didn't register until it was too late. From nowhere, Bonolo hurtled at them both, roaring and bringing them all down. Something flashed in the lamp light a second before Claudia's head hit the floor. Pain shot through her instantly, and when she looked up, she saw blood on the white tile, already puddling to pink in spilled aquarium water. At first she thought she'd cracked her head open or cut herself on a shard of glass. There wasn't time to think about that, though; someone was screaming. She wobbled to her knees and got her bearings. It was then that she saw the knife stuck in Hemmer's throat.

C H A P T E R · 3

THE STEAMY NIGHT shrouded Steven Hemmer's front yard in mist, giving it the gloom of a gothic movie. Claudia wondered what he would've had to say about that. A lot, probably. It wasn't a detail he would have missed. She shuddered and pulled the blanket more tightly around her shoulders. It wouldn't stop the chill, though, and it wouldn't stop the scent of blood settled in her hair, her clothes—in every pore of her skin.

"We'll get you out of here in another minute, Hershey. You don't look so good."

She glanced up from the patio chair someone had found for her. Blue light from a squad car flickered across the police chief's face. He stood with his arms folded across his chest, but the gruff posture couldn't conceal the concern in his voice. It wasn't something Claudia heard often, at least not directly, and never intentionally from Mac Suggs. She felt a thin layer of numbness slip away.

"I wish you'd gone with the paramedics, Hershey. One of the fellas told me your blood pressure was on the wrong side of the border." He grunted. "You'd think all those knocks on your head woulda put some common sense in that brain of yours."

This was more like it. Claudia shook a cigarette from the pack in her handbag. "Medical information's supposed to be private."

"You want private, you should be livin' somewhere else."

Old territory for them, and Claudia smiled tiredly. She lit her cigarette and blew a plume of smoke sideways.

"Those things are gonna kill you one day," Suggs said. He'd lost some weight in the past month, and he gave a hitch to his pants as he gazed across the yard. "They took Hemmer's body out a little while ago."

"Yeah. I saw."

"First time someone died in your arms like that?"

She nodded. It wasn't an image she would ever block. She took her glasses off and examined them. They were badly smudged and one stem was bent. It had all happened so fast. First the scuffle. Then Bonolo. Then Hemmer grappling with the knife, gurgling and pulling it out. She couldn't stop the bleeding. She'd put pressure on it with her hand, turned him away from gravity, held him. But she couldn't stop the bleeding, not that, and then not the convulsive tremors from shock. She could not stop anything.

Claudia took a drag of her cigarette, then stubbed it out. "Hemmer said his daughter's name to me, just before he went. He said something else, too—sounded like, I don't know—like '*dick*sharee' or '*dish*ree.'" She frowned, trying to capture the words. "He could hardly get any air. He was choking, and it was all so faint. He . . . I tried, but then he was just gone."

"Don't beat yourself up, Hershey."

"The gun wasn't even loaded."

"Yeah. We've verified that."

"He never meant to hurt anyone. He died for no reason."

Suggs sighed. "He had a reason, Hershey. It just wasn't one worth dyin' for. Sometimes—"

"Bonolo came out of *nowhere*. I already had Hemmer subdued. *I had him subdued.* It was almost over. We all could've walked away without a scratch."

"Bonolo says he didn't see it like that. He thought you were in trouble. He was trying to help."

"Right. A guy carries a knife wrapped around his ankle just to be helpful."

"Lots of guys around here carry knives, Hershey. Come on, you know that. Bonolo says he carries it for protection because he's on the road alone at night a lot. He says—"

"I know what he says." Claudia stood suddenly. She threw off the blanket and began to pace. "It was a matter of good luck and good timing. He happened to have the knife—that's the luck part. Then the timing. Hemmer and I go outside. Bonolo and Gloria Addison scoot around so she can get to the knife. It's awkward, but she manages to work it free and cut through his tape. We come back in. They pretend nothing's changed."

"It was an amateur job of taping."

She looked at Suggs. "Yeah. Just another bit of good luck."

"Call it what you want." He cleared his throat. "Bonolo's a little pissed that you knocked him on his ass. What he—"

"He was trying to get his knife back. Given what he'd just done with it, I didn't think it was a good idea. All I did was give him a little shove back."

"Uh-huh. Well, anyway, I don't think he's going to make noise about it, but—"

"Good, because I'm not about to apologize to that son of a bitchin' gorilla."

"It's late. We don't have to talk about it now."

"What does that mean? Wait—you already *did* apologize? On my behalf? You did, didn't you." Claudia shook her head and looked away.

"You need to go home, Hershey. You're gettin' all agitated. If you want, I'll have one of the guys run you back. Nothin' else to be done here now." He waited into her silence, then said, "You, uh, you got someone to stay with you? Just in case one of those bangs on the head concusses, or whatever."

"Yeah," she lied.

"Good. That's good."

A dog in the neighborhood started up. A second later another joined it. Hemmer's gated community was plenty awake and plenty excited. Neighbors had logged off the Internet and taken a pass on HBO to get as close as they could to the prime-time show right on their block. Now that they were there, they stood in small, quiet groups, feigning nonchalance.

Claudia watched them for a few seconds. "There's a girl who's fatherless tonight. It didn't have to be that way. It almost wasn't." She peered through the mist at Hemmer's house. Yellow crime-scene tape was looped around it, and a cluster of officers stood just outside the front door, talking in low voices.

Paint and a patio. It didn't seem that much to ask.

CHAPTER · 4

THE CHIEF had it all wrong. Bill Bonolo did indeed want to make some noise. He was making some noise—had begun making noise before the evening at Hemmer's played itself out. He'd cast himself as the savior of them all, contrasting his own aggressive actions against what he called the "surprisingly timid" response of the Indian Run police detective.

Claudia had watched him preen to neighbors at Hemmer's property, and by the time the press began arriving he had his lines well rehearsed for the most dramatic effect. He threw a few good quotes to a reporter from the town's twice-weekly paper, the *Indian Run Gazette*, but he sandbagged the best for the out-of-town TV stations and papers that either got tipped or picked up on events from their police scanners. The *Orlando Sentinel* had dispatched a reporter and photographer. They must have broken every speed limit, because they arrived in time for the photographer to capture a shot of Hemmer's body as it was being removed from the house. The picture, which ran in the morning paper, showed Claudia in the foreground, wrapped in the paramedic's blanket.

But that was then and this was now. Now she was on her couch in front of the TV, distractedly petting the cat and watching Bonolo run his mouth on the six o'clock news. He'd obviously had no trouble sleeping in the twenty-four hours since he'd stabbed Hemmer in the neck. His eyes were alert, his posture smug. The TV reporter had propped him in front of Willow Whisper's gates, where Bonolo somberly talked about how shaken the community remained from the previous night's violence. He called what happened "chilling" and said he was just relieved he could resolve the standoff before anyone got killed.

Right. Like Hemmer didn't count.

Claudia kept her eyes on the TV while she reached for the aspirin bottle on her coffee table. She looked like hell and felt like hell, and knew it showed. The blow to the back of her head from Hemmer's gun had settled down. But the knock to the front of her head from the floor still throbbed dully. She chased three aspirins with a cup of coffee gone cold.

The cameraman briefly panned on the reporter, a kid from Channel 3 in Land of Rivers. His name was Eric Morley, and Claudia had tangled with him before. She watched him adjust his expression to affect concern while he framed his next question.

"Mr. Bonolo," he said, "last night you made some serious allegations about the way Detective Lieutenant Claudia Hershey handled the hostage situation at Mr. Hemmer's house. What specifically troubled you about her response?"

The cameraman cut to Bonolo and slowly zoomed in. He had a square face with big parts—big nose, big lips, big chin, big ears—and a beige complexion that Claudia knew could mottle red with rage in seconds.

"Look," he said, waving a thick hand, "I don't mean to sound insulting. I'm sure Lieutenant Hershey is a fine police officer. But last night she had more than one opportunity to end things quickly. Hemmer was distracted a lot. And he was smaller than her. You'd think with her training she would've jumped on those advantages to disarm him."

"If our information is correct, she couldn't have known Hemmer's gun was unloaded," Morley reminded Bonolo. "Isn't it possible she was just responding cautiously?"

"Anything's possible." Bonolo shrugged in a way that made it clear he didn't think it was possible at all. "Look, my concerns are based on the totality of her response, starting with the way she let herself be conned by Hemmer before she was even in the door."

Totality. Claudia rolled her eyes.

"Our information," Morley said, "is that he allegedly conned everyone."

Bonolo smirked. "Yeah, well, the rest of us aren't exactly seasoned police detectives. We were just trying to be good neighbors."

The reporter nodded sympathetically and let it go. He already had a gripping story of heroics. Why screw it up?

The cat lightly jumped from the couch and began playing with Claudia's bare feet. She wiggled her toes for him while Morley laid out fluff about the "shattered serenity" of Willow Whisper. He mentioned the other hostages, intimating that all but Bonolo were still too shaken to go on camera.

Claudia guessed they might be more embarrassed than shaken. Hemmer had lured them over in half-hour increments, seducing each of them with outrageous promises of conciliation and a fat donation for the community. Jennifer Parrish was the first to arrive. He walked her through taping up each hostage in turn, then bound her with the tape when the others were secured on the floor.

Suggs had insisted on conducting the hostage interviews himself. The preliminary story he cobbled together showed Hemmer to be either extraordinarily precise or just plain lucky. "Hemmer was never even a grunt in the Army," Suggs had told Claudia. "Didn't matter. The way he got 'em in his house? The way he got 'em locked together like a bunch of Lincoln Logs? The fella operated like a military strategist." She hadn't bothered to point out the persuasive power of Hemmer's gun.

Morley was wrapping up. He asked Bonolo whether he had anything more to add.

Bonolo pretended to think, his simian face contorting with the effort. "I don't want to leave your viewers with the wrong impression, or make them think they can't trust the police to protect them. This Detective Hershey? What happened to her last night might've been a one-shot thing. From what the mayor told me, she was just tired. Battle fatigue, stress—call it what you want. The mayor said she'd recently finished a difficult case and was about to take a vacation. Maybe she should've taken it sooner. I'm sure she would've been more capable."

Claudia stared disbelievingly at the TV. *The mayor? The mayor had fed that to Bonolo?* She sprang off the couch and headed for the kitchen phone, furious. The cat hissed and sprinted out of her path. But just as she reached for the phone, it rang. She snatched it up and barked a hello.

"Mom, it's me." Robin choked on a sob. "Sandi's dad is dead."

Claudia felt her world shift with the pain in her daughter's voice. "I know, baby. It happened—"

"A camp counselor came into our cabin and woke her up last night and told her there was a family emergency. It was all hush-hush, but the rest of us in the cabin heard her tell Sandi everything would be all right, like there was no really big deal, like maybe someone just had a little heart attack or something. But it was a lie, Mom! Her dad was dead! *He was already dead.*"

"Robin, honey—"

"They knew and they lied. Now she doesn't have anyone, and they're making like her dad was a criminal. They said you were there. They said Sandi's dad had hostages and you didn't do anything to stop it."

Claudia closed her eyes. "Is that what you think?" she asked softly. She waited a beat. "Robin?"

"I . . . it's just . . . the kids here are all saying stuff."

Claudia heard her stifle another sob. "What they're saying doesn't matter. What you think does." She could hear Robin breathing and imagined her crouched somewhere with a phone, maybe in a camp office, trying not to be seen, trying to overcome the doubt that shaded her voice. The kids had already asked her to pick a side. Now her mother was doing the same. "Robin? Do you want to come home?"

When her daughter finally spoke again, the quiver in her voice was gone. "No." She repeated it more strongly. "I mean, if they want to be stupid and believe the first thing they hear, then that's their problem."

"You're sure?"

"You asked me what I think. That's what I think. If I left, they'd just assume everything they heard is true."

Translation: They'd think mother and daughter were both cowards.

They talked a while longer. Claudia tried to explain that Robin didn't need to defend her, but Robin didn't want to discuss it anymore. She wanted to talk about Sandi. Claudia already knew the girl's grandparents had flown in to take her out of camp. What she didn't know was that the girl's mother had died of breast cancer two years earlier. That's why Sandi had been living with Steven Hemmer. That's why he'd changed jobs. That's why he'd bought the house in Willow Whisper and why he wanted to spruce it up. He'd wanted what Claudia had wanted for Robin when she moved them from Cleveland. He'd wanted a stable environment in which to raise his daughter—in his case a daughter who had suffered not only the pain of divorce but had felt at too young an age the intractable sorrow of loss. Steven Hemmer wanted to fix things: his life, his daughter's life. The house, Claudia thought, must have come to represent a symbol of both.

"Will you check on her, Mom? Her grandparents are staying in a hotel just outside town. I think they figure they'll have to stick around for a couple weeks, and then I guess they're taking Sandi home with them to Maine. At least I think it's Maine. It's just . . . I didn't get to say goodbye. Will you do it?"

Claudia could think of a dozen reasons not to. She couldn't think of a single good one. She told Robin that sure, she'd try to see the girl before she left. Robin reeled off instructions: what to say, how to say it, what to bring—the old Pooh bear that she'd insisted she'd outgrown but until now would not give up. And then she grilled her mother about whether she was feeding the cat properly.

"Boo's fine," said Claudia, biting her tongue not to remind Robin that she'd been gone only one day, not enough time for her mother to starve the animal. "He eats more than I do, and he's still working on shredding the couch. I assume that means he's happy." She reiterated that she'd try to see Sandi, and then they hung up.

She stared unseeing at the kitchen counter, waiting for the calm that ordinarily followed a phone call from Robin on those rare occasions when her daughter was away. Nothing. She ate a hunk of leftover roast beef, giving it more time. Still nothing.

Boo had come out of hiding, so she gave him a scratch behind the ear, then dumped some dry food into his bowl. She brushed her teeth. She brushed her hair. She changed into jeans. She fooled with her oboe for a while. Still . . . nothing. A few minutes later she grabbed her purse and car keys to her police-issued Cavalier, and headed out the door.

The mayor of Indian Run stood five-foot-seven in lifts, and all his weight-training and jogging would never change that. To the never-ending amusement of the town's residents, he kept trying, though. Rumor had it that the mayor owned some kind of contraption designed to let him hang upside down, and that he used it for a half hour every morning and every night, the idea being that he would lengthen his frame while simultaneously improving blood circulation. Chief Mac Suggs was particularly fond of this particular rumor—and there were many such rumors about the mayor—but of course the chief would never give voice to such gossip himself. At least he wouldn't do so unless fueled by one too many beers and strictly in the company of those he trusted. The mayor held the chief's career in his hands, and though the mayor's hands were tiny, his power was not. If he wanted, he could sway the town council into disbanding the police department altogether and contracting law enforcement services over to the Flagg County Sheriff's Office.

For Claudia, the chief's fear and distrust of the mayor presented a dilemma. She wanted to look the mayor in the eyes and ask him about his remarks to Bonolo—and she wanted to do it now, right now, and unannounced—but she didn't want to put the chief in a situation that might compromise him and most certainly would piss him off. Even in Indian Run, there was a chain of command. On the other hand, if she told Suggs what she wanted to do, he would forbid it.

While she debated, Claudia sat quietly in the car as it idled in the driveway. She drummed her fingers on the steering wheel, half listening to a soft jazz station on the radio. She was not given to impulsive behavior in her professional life. Truthfully, she wasn't often impulsive in her personal life either, a factor that had created some of the ugliness in her marriage to Brian, a man who too often confused recklessness with spontaneity. Of course, Robin had been conceived in one such reckless moment, and for that Claudia was grateful. She was less forgiving about the reckless moments he'd shared with other women.

Go? Not go? She sat for another five minutes and had just about talked herself back out of the car when she heard Bonolo's voice again, this time during a news break on the radio. The newscaster was using a tape from its TV affiliate, keeping the story alive and reminding listeners to tune in for a talk show later on. He invited them to call in with comments on the "hostage fiasco" in Willow Whisper, then moved to a commercial.

Claudia drummed her fingers one more time. Then she gunned the engine and backed out of the driveway.

C H A P T E R · 5

AN ANNOYING SECOND THOUGHT nagged at Claudia while she stood at the mayor's front door, but by then it was too late. She'd already pressed the doorbell. Mayor Arthur Lane himself answered, opening the door to the festive sounds of a party going on behind him. They'd met only once before, and then only briefly, but the recognition in his eyes was immediate. He improvised a smile, the politician in him shifting into overdrive.

"Lieutenant Hershey! What a surprise!"

Lane's hand shot out and Claudia shook it. It was one of those wimp shakes that men sometimes reserved for women, as if fearful they might break something.

"Uh-oh. I bet I know what it is." Lane feigned a playful tone. "It's the noise, right?" He winked and thumbed the air behind him. "I invited just about the whole neighborhood so no one would complain, but you never know."

She looked at him.

"Of course, I can turn down the stereo." He flashed some teeth. "Not a problem."

Country-western music spilled through the doorway. Laughter rode above it. Claudia heard someone yell that the phone was ringing.

"It's a birthday party," Lane said. "Mine, as a matter of fact. Just turned 41, though I don't feel a day over 30." He smoothed back his hair, which was thick and wavy and carefully maintained with Grecian Formula. "Care to join us?"

"Happy birthday. No, thank you. Eric Morley interviewed Bill Bonolo about the hostage situation on the six o'clock news. I presume you saw it?"

Lane stepped into the humid night air and closed the door. "I saw it." He shrugged. "Bill Bonolo's a colorful character."

"He's also inaccurate as hell, and he's using you to lend credence to the outrageous version of events he's putting in front of the public." Claudia hadn't moved when Lane stepped forward, forcing him to inch close enough for her to see the pores in his skin. She smelled cheese and alcohol on his breath. "He quoted you as saying you believed I was 'tired.' Since you and I never spoke, I can't believe that's what you actually said, and I know it's not something Chief Suggs would've said to you."

The mayor cleared his throat and concentrated on her shirt collar. "You have to understand that when you're dealing with an excitable situation and excitable people, you sometimes have to mollify them any way you can so things don't escalate."

"So that *is* what you said."

"You're making too much of this."

"Is it a lawsuit you're worried about? Is that it? You're worried Bonolo will sue the town?"

"It's my job to head off potential litigation." He glanced up. "I *do* my job."

"Meaning what?"

Lane batted at a stray moth. "Look, this'll all die down. Trust me."

"It'll leave the wrong impression."

"You'll weather it."

"This isn't just about me, Mr. Mayor. It's about a young girl who woke up in the morning, excited about going to camp, and went to bed thinking that her father had turned into a brute so villainous that even the cops wouldn't try to protect him."

"Hemmer *is* the villain here," Lane said. "Don't forget that." He was spared Claudia's response when the door abruptly opened, thudding into his back. A face peeked out. "Artie? What're you doing out there?"

Claudia stepped back and Lane shifted into the spot she'd vacated. The door opened all the way and a petite woman said, "Oh. Sorry. I didn't realize you had company." She looked curiously at Claudia, but when it became apparent that introductions wouldn't be forthcoming, she turned her attention back to Lane. "Honey, I'm sorry to interrupt, but we're about out of ice. Also, the toilet in the guest bathroom is running again. I tried jiggling the handle, but I guess I don't have your touch."

Lane looked embarrassed. "Sure, sure," he mumbled. "Just give me a minute, Lorna."

The door began to close but then opened again just as abruptly. "Sorry," Lorna said. "One more thing. Boyd Manning called. He's on his way, but he said his truck had a flat and he'll be about another twenty minutes or so. Want me to reach him on his cell phone and see if he'll pick up the ice?"

"What? I . . . no. I'll go. Just let me finish up out here."

Lorna rolled her eyes. "Get two bags."

She vanished and Lane closed the door again. "As you can see, I'm pretty busy, Lieutenant."

"Right. A toilet to fix and ice to fetch."

This time the mayor looked up. His eyes flashed. "You're way out of line here, Ms. Hershey. This conversation is over." He pivoted and opened the door to go in.

Claudia heard the twang of a guitar from an old Ray Price song, and then the door slammed, leaving her alone with the rhythm of the crickets. There was nothing funny about the conversation she'd just had, but she smiled anyway, finding satisfaction in the image of that fatuous little weasel jiggling the toilet handle while his guests sucked up all his birthday booze.

In the time it took Claudia to swing by the 7-Eleven for gas on her way home, Chief Suggs had left two messages at her house. The mayor had apparently foregone his ice run to express his displeasure to Suggs, and the chief had wasted no time passing it on to Claudia along with his own. She was to call him right away, "before you pick your nose or even think about lighting the cigarette you probably have halfway to your mouth right now."

Claudia pondered the cigarette she had halfway to her mouth. She'd cut down to half a pack a day. This one would put her over her quota by two. She lit up and went in search of an ashtray, making a smoker's bargain to cut out two the next day. She prowled the refrigerator next and settled for another chunk of roast beef, the last of it. She chewed listlessly. If she called Suggs back while he was still raging, he might fire her. And what if he did? Indian Run had grown on her—sort of—but the town wasn't exactly the package she thought she was buying into when she and Robin settled into it some nineteen months earlier. Leaving . . . the idea was not without some merit. Unfortunately, getting canned right now would only lend weight to Bonolo's badmouthing. And that was something else altogether.

Claudia flossed a shred of roast beef from between her teeth, then wiped her hands on a paper towel. She picked up the phone and dialed.

She was as ready for the chief as she ever would be. But he surprised her. Either he'd burned through the worst of his anger or by now he'd calmed himself with a whiskey more fiery than his temper. That's not to say he was pleased. He skipped past a greeting and got straight to the point.

"I want you to listen, Hershey, and not talk," he began. "We're likely not to agree on everything that comes out of this conversation, but let's at least agree to that much."

"Okay."

"Now the way I hear things told, you're apparently on a mission to self-destruct. I find I can almost live with that. What I can't live with is you takin' me down with you, never mind the rest of the police department."

"That's a little dra—"

"Just listen."

"Right."

"The mayor says you interrupted his private birthday party so you could read him the riot act."

Claudia bit her lip.

"Now, I don't know what exactly you said to him, but I do know that showing up there at all was unauthorized as hell. It made you look bad. It made me look worse, which that silly little Napoleon was only too happy to point out."

"Did you hear the—"

"Shut up, Hershey. Just shut up." Suggs took a breath. "I spent ten minutes playing kiss-ass to talk him out of making me fire you. He enjoyed that, but in the end it wasn't my squirming that stopped him from ousting you. He stopped short of that because he's a politician and he was afraid that it might backfire on him with the press. The way he put it, it might be seen as 'capricious,' what with all the hero stories that've been done on you."

They weren't hero stories, not in Claudia's mind. They were straightforward media accounts of a few homicide cases she'd broken. She supposed the stories were flattering to her, but she didn't remember being called heroic. She did remember being called elusive when she refused an interview for a puff piece. Clearly, though, now was not the time to refresh Suggs's memory.

"The problem here, Hershey, is that you've become some kind of media darling—at least that's how the mayor sees it—and now, here we go again. You got the press back at our door, only this time he's in a Catch-22 with you. If he makes like you walk on water, like Bonolo is full of shit, then Bonolo's gonna go wild and keep the story alive. The press won't go away. But by—"

"I don't believe this."

"But by giving Bonolo his fifteen minutes of fame *and* explaining away the problem with his hero cop, Lane has himself some kind of middle ground. He gets to look like the good guy, like someone who sympathizes with everything you've been through and actually understands why you'd be worn out."

"I was *not* worn out. I'm not worn out now."

"Doesn't matter. That's the spin the mayor put on things, and he's not gonna change it just so your feelings aren't hurt. And you? You don't get a spin, Hershey. You get to keep your mouth shut and enjoy the damned vacation you were scheduled to take anyway."

"You *know* I wasn't worn out."

"Maybe you weren't when you went into that house, Hershey. Fact is, I woulda recognized it if you were. But the judgment you used when you took it upon yourself to visit the mayor? That says to me that you are now. Have your vacation."

"There's still paperwork to finish on the Hemmer case."

"I don't need you. We got everyone's statement, including yours. Face it. This one's a slam dunk. Hemmer made it that way himself."

"Someone ought to look at Bonolo for—"

"Forget it, Hershey. While you were stewin' in your ego, I talked with the state attorney's office. They're not thrilled with the way things went down, but Bonolo's got witnesses who say it was all about self-defense— and *your* defense. Like it or not, he's the hero this time. Not you. Live with it."

The phone went dead in her ear.

C H A P T E R · 6

SANDI HEMMER wasn't the kind of girl who would dot the *i* in her name with a heart or a circle the size of an M&M. Once, she might have been that kind of girl. She might've been the kind of girl who daydreamed doodles on book covers and wondered whether coloring her hair maroon would attract the boy she'd had her eyes on all summer. She might've been that girl once, a girl so young and spirited that her energy would kindle sparks in anyone who stood even in its shadow. Too much had happened for Sandi Hemmer to be that girl now. The face she showed Claudia on Sunday morning was that of someone who had learned too early the distinctions between sadness and sorrow, disappointment and defeat.

Claudia stood stiffly at the doorway of Hopper's Motel, where Sandi was staying with her grandparents. They had answered her knock, introducing themselves as Joseph and Phyllis Bayless—Hemmer's in-laws. They looked as wrung out as she'd expected. They'd been jarred from dinner with the worst kind of news, rushed to the airport by a neighbor, and finally shuttled in the middle of the night to a camp where their granddaughter had not yet been informed that her father was dead. Claudia didn't ask, but Phyllis Bayless told her that Hemmer's own parents had been deceased for years. Conversation lagged then, and they pulled the door shut so they could ask their granddaughter whether she wanted to speak to the tall cop at the door.

A moment later Sandi appeared, her expression devoid of curiosity. Claudia introduced herself and held out the ragged Pooh bear. "Robin wanted you to have this," she said.

Sandi barely looked at it. She pushed unwashed auburn hair from her forehead and said, "Tell her thanks. It's nice she thought of me."

Little of Hemmer showed in his daughter. In all the ways where he'd been merely average, she stood out. She had the tall, slender body of a dancer and skin so fair that her veins pulsed blue beneath it. Her eyes, though listless at the moment, were large and almost navy in color, attributes she must have picked up from her mother.

Claudia wanted to sweep the girl into her arms. "I'm so sorry about your dad," she said.

Sandi shrugged. "He tried to kill you," she said tonelessly. "Robin might be sorry. You can't be. You're probably glad he's dead. You're probably glad his fish are dead."

She spoke without accusation, but Claudia flinched as if she'd been slapped. "Sandi . . . it wasn't like that. It *isn't* like that. You need to know your dad didn't try to kill me or anyone else. He didn't hurt anyone. He *wouldn't* have."

Sandi looked away. "Yeah," she said softly. "Like you knew him."

"I didn't know him. But I was getting to know him. He . . . Sandi, honey? Look at me. Please. This is important." Claudia waited until the girl looked up. "Your father's gun wasn't even loaded—"

"I know all that. It's all over the news."

"He died in my arms, Sandi. The last thing he said was your name."

The girl didn't crumple. Her expression didn't change. But her eyes grew moist, and when she spoke again it was with a yearning that the single word she uttered could not conceal: "Really?"

Claudia nodded. "Do you want to talk a little? Maybe take a walk?"

Sandi glanced at the Pooh bear, then tossed it behind her onto a bed. When she turned back, a solitary tear showed on her face.

There wasn't much around Hopper's Motel. A gas station, coffee shop, and playground overgrown with weeds fronted it. Uneven rows of cabbage palms and yellow weeds blocked the back from a feeder road that paralleled U.S. 27. It was a stopover motel for people on their way somewhere else.

The hour hadn't yet reached noon, but already heat rose visibly from the asphalt parking lot. Claudia and Sandi crossed over it to the playground; neither of them spoke. A swing set with four vinyl swings, two of them broken, stood crookedly on parched grass that hadn't been tended for months. A sliding board and jungle gym were its only companion pieces, and they were in equally bad repair.

Sandi tested one of the swings with her hand, then sat. Claudia hesitated, then set her handbag on the ground and slowly eased onto the swing beside her. Her thighs pressed so tightly together that she felt like someone had just given her a wedgie. The swing set creaked with her weight. She would have struggled off immediately but thought she heard Sandi chuckle. She glanced over just in time to catch a half-moon smile on the girl's face before she swung out of view. Claudia stayed grounded. At 37 she had no interest in testing the durability of her tailbone if the seat collapsed.

A moment later Sandi skidded to a stop. "My dad was something else," she said quietly. "This swing could be hanging by a piece of lint and he'd probably kick off and try to make his feet touch the sun. He'd try anything. Sometimes he'd get too goofy and embarrass me, and I'd wish I could just snap my fingers and make him disappear. I never thought he ever would."

A lizard stood on the rusted crossbar of the swing, its throat expanded in a ruby display intended for a female a foot away. She skittered away, either unimpressed or playing hard to get.

"Your dad was trying to make the house nice for you," said Claudia.

"I know. He was like on this . . . mission or something." Sandi stopped swinging. She shook her head. "It didn't start like that, but it grew into this huge warlike thing when the homeowners association kept telling him 'no' about this and that. I told him, 'Dad, just give it up. These people just don't like you. For whatever reason, they don't like you and they're not going to do what you want.' But he said it was all about fairness, and he wouldn't let it go."

Sandi picked at a scab on her arm. "It's one of the reasons my mom divorced him. She used to tell him that he got too wrapped up in things. I heard her tell her friends that he was too intense. I was just a kid then. I didn't get what she meant. I do now."

She kicked off again, swinging a little higher this time. "I didn't even want to go to camp. Did you know that? I was only going because Dad thought I did and I didn't want to hurt his feelings. The camp is mostly about horses. Robin probably told you that."

"It's all she talked about," Claudia called out, trying to time her words with Sandi's swings. "She wanted to learn how to ride before school started again."

"Not me. I'm more into doing things like drawing, but Dad didn't seem to get that. He was even having some cowboy boots custom made for me. Turns out they weren't going to be ready in time, but that was fine by me. I couldn't care less about boots or horses."

"I understand."

"What?"

"I said I understand." Claudia sat astride a horse once, when she was four and her parents propped her on a pony's back for a birthday picture. She didn't remember the experience, but the picture showed her crying. "I like my feet on the ground."

Sandi slowed, then stuttered to a stop. Her hair was tangled and her face was streaked with perspiration, and maybe some tears. "Is that why you haven't moved an inch? You're afraid?"

Claudia tried not to read anything into the girl's question, but there it was—that word again—or if not the same word, an unsettling reflection of it: *timid*. Sandi's expression was guileless, though, so she answered as lightly as she could. "It's not about fear. It's about being too big for the swing."

"So what? So am I." Sandi kicked off again.

There seemed little point in calling attention to the difference in their sizes, so Claudia gave an exploratory push with her feet. She didn't swing so much as she rocked, but it was something.

"Your feet," said Sandi on a swing down, "are still on the ground," she said as she rose back up.

With a death grip on the rusted chains, Claudia pushed harder. When she felt something akin to liftoff, she began to pump. Her legs were too long and the swing too low for effective acceleration or height. The entire swing set wobbled, its legs rocking nearly off the ground. Claudia would have quit if not for the unmistakable pleasure in Sandi's expression every time she whistled past. She wasn't sure what she had given the girl, but something.

A few minutes later Sandi slowed to a stop, which was signal enough to Claudia that she could do the same. She longed to get off altogether in the worst way. But she waited, just in case Sandi had anything else she wanted to say. And she did.

"You tried to save him, right?"

"I did, Sandi. Yes."

She nodded. "I should go back in. Grandma and Gramps might start to worry."

"Robin tells me you'll be staying here for a while."

"I guess." The girl was gone, replaced by the somber young woman Claudia had first met. "There are details about the house. About Dad. Gramps wants to settle everything now. I don't think they can afford to fly back and forth. Anyway, they don't want to."

"Will you live with them?"

"I don't know. Them, or maybe an aunt." Sandi abruptly stood. "No one wants to talk about that yet. At least not to me."

Claudia worked her way out of the vinyl seat. Her hands were flecked with bits of rust from the chains. She wiped them on her pants. When sensation returned to her thighs, she jotted her home number on the back of a business card and handed it to Sandi. She told her to call anytime, for any reason, even if only to swing again.

They walked to the motel without speaking. Sandi didn't turn and wave from the door. Claudia sighed and headed home, knowing that Steven Hemmer's daughter would probably dispense with the business card without a glance. It was from an adult. Adults had let her down too often. Feet off the ground or not, Claudia was still one of them. Maybe the worst of them.

Among the woodwind instruments, the oboe was probably the least revered, or maybe just the most misunderstood. An oboe simply didn't have the sex appeal of a saxophone or the coyness of a piccolo. Never mind that it was an oboe player who sounded the "A" note before concerts so that the other orchestra members could tune their instruments. The minute the note flared, people craned their necks—not to spot the oboist, but to see the violin players and check out what the harpist was wearing.

Claudia didn't mind any of that. She played the oboe because its complex tones suited her. She also played because she could wring notes from the instrument in a way that gave her a sense of mastery like few things in life did. But almost no one ever heard her perform except for Robin, who endured the nightly one-woman concerts with surprising good grace. Even if she didn't, Claudia would play, anyway. The oboe transported her to a still place where the flotsam of a weary day could not reach, and she was always surprised when it failed her, as it was doing now.

Dusk had crept up on her, its phantom gray penetrating the house long after she'd given up on a tricky piece that should've been a delight for its challenging depth but had grown irritating instead. She knew what the problem was, or at least thought she did. The problem was the damned phone. Its shrill had interrupted her four times in two hours, but no one answered her hello any of those times.

Claudia pictured shooting the phone with her .38 the next time it rang, but when it did she merely barked "What!" in a tone she usually reserved for fleeing felons. She regretted it a second later when Sandi's voice came on, small and hesitant. Claudia assumed the earlier calls were from the girl, but feared embarrassing her by asking. She apologized for her gruffness and asked how she could help.

Well, Sandi said, she wondered a few things. Like was it true that Claudia was on vacation? Yes? Really? Well then, she wondered could Claudia maybe—because she was a police officer and all—could she maybe take her into her dad's house tomorrow? To get some stuff? And maybe stop by the boot place, too? Because, see, the boots should be ready now and her dad had paid in advance, or at least left a deposit or something. They didn't have to stay long. What? Oh. Her grandparents? Well, they'd probably do it if they absolutely had to, but they didn't say no to the idea of that police lady going instead. She wondered . . . was this something Claudia could do?

"I don't care about the boots, not really," said Sandi, her words still rushed. "I mentioned that on the swings, right? But I know Dad cares about them. He—" Her voice hitched. "He *cared* about them," she said softly. "He wanted me to have them."

There was nothing to think about. Claudia cleared the arrangements with Sandi's grandmother, then told the girl she'd pick her up at nine-thirty.

The phone didn't ring for the rest of the night.

C H A P T E R · 7

IN TERMS OF SIZE, the boot maker was a showstopper. His presence so consumed the small shop where he crafted boots that at first Claudia didn't even notice them lining the shelves on the walls. Four hundred pounds? Four-fifty? She put him somewhere in that range and automatically reviewed the CPR steps she knew in case he decided to have his coronary while she and Sandi were in his shop.

The place smelled of leather, deep and pungent and masculine. Tools Claudia couldn't identify lay atop a wooden bench where the boot maker worked, fussing with something that resembled a giant cookie cutter. He wore a sweat-stained bandanna around his bald head, and he sported a single ruby earring. He looked like a giant egg in clothes. So this was Buddy's Boots.

The boot maker caught her watching him and paused. "Welcome. I'm Buddy. Buddy Dunn. And this instrument you're looking at, it's called a die. It's what's used to cut out sections of a boot. Hasn't changed much since boots were made for a range instead of a dance floor." He hesitated between sentences, wheezing words as if from a worn bellows. "You folks looking to be fitted?" He leaned into his workbench to better see Claudia's feet. "I'm guessing you at a nine and a half, maybe a ten. I can probably get an accurate measurement in about twenty minutes."

Claudia shook her head, a little annoyed. Her feet felt plenty comfortable in a nine. "No. Thanks." She touched Sandi's shoulder. "We've come to pick up a pair of boots. Hemmer?"

Dunn's eyes signaled recognition. "Got 'em. Finished up just last night. Wish I could've had them sooner."

"Is it a problem that we don't have the receipt with us?"

"No. The boots were paid in advance. Four hundred dollars." Dunn labored off a stool and came around, wiping his hands on a towel. It did little to remove the permanent stain of leather and dye from his fingers. "You're Mr. Hemmer's daughter?" he said to Sandi. She nodded. "Thought so. You look just like he described you. I'm sorry for your loss. It's a hell of a thing, losing someone close. Your daddy seemed like a nice fellow."

He didn't wait for a response, turning instead toward a shelf just above his head. Four pairs of boots stood smartly on top, each spaced a few inches apart with military precision. He pulled the smallest boots off and handed them to Sandi.

"Here you go, young lady. They're calfskin, so they'll wear nice and long if you treat 'em good." He grunted. "Had to talk your daddy out of ostrich. No sense in a pricey skin for someone who's never worn boots at all. Especially no sense in 'em when all I had to go by for measurement were some old worn shoes your daddy snuck in when you weren't looking."

The vamps of the boots were mahogany colored, complemented by a deep cream shade inlaid to the collars with butterflies and yellow roses. The pull straps and piping picked up the mahogany again. Claudia didn't need to be an expert to admire the precision that had gone into the footwear.

Sandi held the boots as if they were as fragile as crystal. "They're beautiful," she said softly.

Dunn grunted. "Your daddy pretty much designed the pattern himself." He took another pair of boots off the shelf. He eyed them critically, then blew dust off the toes, his face pinking up with the effort. "See here how there's cactus and thistle running up the sides of these? Your daddy took a liking to the way that looked. He changed the colors some and then asked could I do butterflies and roses instead of cactus and thistle."

Sandi looked at the cactus boots wistfully. "Those are nice. I . . . if he'd just taken them, he could've had them for me in time for camp. That's what he wanted."

Faint perspiration lined the boot maker's upper lip like a thin mustache. He wiped it off and looked at Sandi sympathetically. "I don't get around much, but one thing I've learned even from my stool is there are a lot of 'ifs' in the world. Problem is, not a one of us can ever truly predict which way those ifs are gonna go. All we do is hurt ourselves trying." He blew on the boots again. "And anyway, if the fella who ordered these boots ever shows up to claim them, I'd be hard-pressed to explain that I sold 'em to someone else. He's only two payments away from calling them his own." Dunn chuckled. "Well, two payments and a year, give or take."

Claudia watched him return the boots to the shelf. "Annual payments on boots? That's some kind of layaway plan," she said.

"That's not what I meant. He was making weekly payments, regular as the sun rising. He just hasn't come by to finish them off in the last year or so."

"And you're still waiting on him?" She shook her head, incredulous. "Talk about patience."

"I'm a big man. I have a lot of it. Besides, the fella probably just fell on hard times. He'll be back." Then he winked conspiratorially. "What's more, he had small feet for a man, and one leg was a hair shorter than the other. Had to build a lift in. Truth is, it's not likely I'll be able to sell these to anyone else. Might just as well wait on him and let his boots sit on the shelf nice and pretty. They're not a bad advertisement."

So Dunn wasn't a saint. Just practical.

He turned his attention to Sandi. "Come on. Let's get you wrestled into your boots so you can take 'em for a test drive."

While the boot maker sat Sandi in a chair where he could fit her without bending over, Claudia wandered the shop. It was converted from the living room of a two-story wood-frame house. She assumed Buddy Dunn lived upstairs or, as a concession to his weight, more likely in a back room.

She'd never met the boot maker before, but it was impossible to live in Indian Run and not have heard of him. His custom work was well-known even outside of Florida; rumor had it that some of his boots ran upwards of $10,000. Hemmer had paid $400 for Sandi's boots. Claudia hoped Robin wouldn't want a pair if she ever saw them. It was hard enough to fork over fifty bucks for her daughter's Nikes.

She meandered, half listening while Dunn explained to Sandi the care and feeding of calfskin. Her mind, though, was already at the Hemmer house—their next destination. With luck, they would get in and out quickly. To begin with, Chief Suggs wasn't keen on her going at all. When she'd called him to describe what Sandi wanted, he'd bellowed disapproval and would have sent another officer in her place if he could have figured out a way to do it without looking like an insensitive clod. But Claudia had her own reasons for wanting to finish at the house fast. She craved distance from the Hemmer tragedy. And by now, whether she needed a vacation or not, she wanted one. Badly.

The door to the shop squeaked open and a man in black jeans entered, clutching a worn boot. Claudia didn't think she'd ever seen a genuine cowboy, but, from the hat on his head to the boots on his feet, she was pretty sure she was looking at one now. She stifled an impulse to ask him if he had a horse outside.

"Hey, Buddy," he said to the boot maker.

"Hey, Dix. How you doin'?"

"Good. But I'm in need of a new heel if you've got the time."

"Be with you in a minute."

"No rush. I'll just poke around."

Claudia had never heard a richer baritone voice. Then he turned and spotted her. He removed his hat, smiled, and remarked on what a hot day it was.

Now that he was looking at her, Claudia found herself struck not just by his voice, but by his eyes. And his curly hair. And his height. Whoa. A man taller than she was.

She thrashed about for something witty or perceptive to say. What came out was, "Florida. It's a hot state."

He looked amused. "Keep up with the Weather Channel, do you?"

An hour later she'd think of three perfect rejoinders. But that would be later. "The point is, it's too hot for boots."

"Hard to argue the perception. On the other hand, you're in the wrong place if you're looking for sandals."

"No, I . . . anyway, my feet are big enough in sneakers. They'd look like canoes in boots." *Where was this coming from?*

The cowboy studied her sneakers. "Oh, I imagine they'd look fine. Your feet are just sideways tall. They suit you. They suit you perfectly."

Claudia wasn't a blusher. She didn't blush now. But she felt a rise of something—some sort of man-woman chemistry thing—and stood stupidly mute in recognition of it. Dunn rescued her by calling the cowboy over and sending Sandi back to Claudia. She wasn't sure, but she thought he might've winked at her before he turned away. For a second, the heat of attraction flooded her again.

Sandi tottered around the small shop in her new boots, animation on her face for the first time since Claudia had met her. "These are a little weird," she confided on one of her sweeps. "But I think I could get used to them. I might even like them. It'll take a while to break them in, but. . . . " As her words trailed off, she looked where Claudia was looking. "Oh. That guy? Mr. Dunn said his name is Tom Dixon but that everybody calls him Dix. He owns a ranch here and breeds cattle or something. He's the real deal."

"What?"

"A cowboy, or at least close as you can get to one in Florida." Sandi looked disappointed when Claudia didn't respond. "I thought you'd be interested. You keep checking him out."

"I'm not checking him out."

"It kind of looked like you were."

"It's a small shop. It's hard to turn around without someone being in your line of vision." Claudia made a point of assessing Sandi's boots. "They look good on you. Are you supposed to—"

A door upstairs slammed, and an old woman spewing profanities clomped down the stairs. She stopped short when she saw Dunn's customers.

Dunn looked up, unperturbed. "Folks, meet my grandmother, Mae Dunn."

"Didn't know you had company," she huffed. "Place is downright crowded. Dix, I know."

"Hi, Mae," said Dixon.

She ignored him. "Who are all these other people?"

"Customers. What's got you all agitated, Grams?"

"I'm not agitated. I'm just annoyed. And it's HTML that got me that way." She looked at Claudia and Sandi in turn. "That's hypertext markup language. It's the code you use to make a Web page a Web page, and it's a lot worse than anything you mighta overheard me sayin' a heartbeat ago."

"Grams has this idea my shop should be on the Internet," said Dunn. "She's busying herself putting it together."

"You make it sound like I'm crocheting a doily, Buddy." She came around and made a beeline for Claudia. "You look familiar. Who are you?"

As accustomed as she was to blunt-speaking people, Claudia was nevertheless caught off guard by the woman who positioned herself six inches away and gazed up through eyes beginning to cloud with age. She was shorter than Sandi and thin, with skin blotchy from weather or medications or both. She had to be at least 80.

"I admit to being a little hard of hearin' now and then," Mae said, "but I would've seen your lips movin' if you'd answered me."

"Sorry. I'm Claudia Hershey."

"Hah! That's why you're familiar. I saw you on TV, bunched up under a blanket. This your daughter?"

"Grams. . . ," said Dunn from his stool.

Mae looked at her grandson sharply. "What? Just because I'm an old lady, I can't be curious?"

"It's okay," said Sandi. "My name's Sandi Hemmer."

Mae thought for a moment. "Huh. If you've been on TV I missed it. But you're a fine-looking girl, and you look even better in that pair of boots Buddy made you. He's an artist. It's why I'm tryin' to put him on the World Wide Web." She leaned in closer to Claudia and Sandi. "Buddy's a sweetheart, but he's clueless when it comes to business."

"I heard that, Grams," said Dunn. "I have all the business I can handle."

"It's not just about business, Buddy. It's about image." She shook her head and dropped her voice to a whisper. "He knows boots, is all he knows. And the truth is, he's afraid of technology. Now me, I'm not. Hah! I mail-ordered a digital camera and took great pictures of Buddy and his boots. I got a computer you wouldn't believe, and then I figured out how to get the pictures right into it. Simple! Everything I bought has all the bells and whistles." Her expression darkened. "It's just this HTML crap that's slowin' me down. Either of you know how to write HTML?"

"Sorry," said Claudia.

Sandi shook her head.

"Didn't figure you did." She sighed.

"Actually," said Claudia, "I might know someone who could help you. He helped me get my work computer up and running."

"Yeah? Does he work cheap?"

"I don't know. Probably."

"Then he's likely no good."

"He *is* good. He's just young."

"Well, why didn't you say that to begin with? Except for me, it's usually young people who pick computer stuff up quickly. Got his number?"

Claudia fumbled through her handbag for her address book. She heard Tom Dixon chuckling.

"When I was your age," Mae said, "I could give you every phone number I had by memory alone." She shifted impatiently. "Still can, most of 'em."

"I don't doubt it," Claudia mumbled. She paged through her book and read off a number. "His name is Booey Suggs."

"Hah! There's a name I won't likely forget. All the same, I wouldn't object if you were to write it down along with the number. No telling how much that HTML might've fogged my immediate recall."

Claudia ached to get out of the shop. She scribbled the information on the back of a business card and handed it to the old woman.

Mae didn't thank her, but she nodded, satisfied. "This works out, I'll see that Buddy gives you a five percent discount on a pair of boots." She disappeared up the stairs, chattering to herself.

A few minutes later, Claudia and Sandi made their exit. There was no horse outside.

C H A P T E R · 8

SOMEONE HAD BEEN BUSY. It's not the sort of thing you'd notice right off. Claudia wouldn't have noticed at all if not for Sandi's dispirited remark about the police not tidying up when they were finished at the Hemmer house. She wasn't talking about the family room; Claudia had deftly steered her past that. She wasn't talking about her own room, either. She'd moved swiftly through it, plucking clothes off hangers and stuffing them into a suitcase, then filling a purple duffel bag with music CDs, a jewelry box, and other remnants of the young girl she'd been when she left for camp.

Her complaint concerned the bedroom next to her own, which Steven Hemmer had converted into a home office. Sandi had paused in the doorway to take a last look, maybe to etch into memory better times. But just as she started to turn away, something caught her eye and she stepped farther into the room.

"Dad would have a stroke if he saw this," she said.

The office was decidedly cramped, what with two desktop computers and a laptop, but it appeared neat and organized, as efficient as Hemmer had described himself to Claudia. She looked at Sandi, perplexed.

"Dad never, *never* would've left his office junked up this way." Sandi scowled and pointed things out as a tour guide would, automatically repositioning a pencil cup on the edge of the desk. "Dad spent a lot of time in here. It's where I could always find him. We'd talk about school, his work . . . you know."

It bothered her that papers and file folders on her dad's desk were haphazardly stacked, that two file cabinet drawers were slightly ajar, and that one of the bifold closet doors stood partially open. She assumed the police had poked around as a routine part of their investigation, disturbing

Hemmer's carefully cultivated order. Little things, she told Claudia. They were just little things. But it bothered her just the same.

"Look at that," she said, pointing to a bookcase. "They couldn't even leave his books alone."

The bookcase was tall and narrow, with four shelves. Claudia owned a similar one, except the books on hers were mostly novels with no attention paid to the order in which they were arranged. Hemmer's shelves held nothing but nonfiction, most of them related to the computer industry. A dozen or so others were devoted to the film business, a few to social policy, and a handful to general reference. Claudia noted that Hemmer had the same fat dictionary she did, but it certainly didn't make them literary cousins. Hemmer's books were serious business—no *Dummies* titles here—and they were categorized by type and neatly aligned, their spines almost compulsively flush with each other, except . . . three books on the second shelf and another on the bottom jutted out, their spines out of whack with the others, as if they'd been hastily shelved after a fast reference check. Claudia examined the titles. They were upside down. One of them, a fat tome detailing the history of Hollywood, edged out from amid the computer titles.

"I know what Dad did at the end was awful," Sandi said, her finger tracing the edge of the bookcase, "but couldn't they have shown just a little respect for all the good things he did the rest of his life?"

Claudia barely listened. No cop had fooled with Hemmer's books. After the violence in the family room, one might've taken a fast look at his file folders, maybe even opened the closet for a look-see to ensure Hemmer the Hostage Taker wasn't also Hemmer the Secret Mass Murderer with garish photos of his victims tacked to the wall inside. So, sure. There would've been a cursory check. In and out. Wrap the case. Call it a day.

Somebody else had been here, though. Somebody nervous. Somebody in a hurry, trying to be careful but too rushed to make sure things were left exactly as found.

There was little point in alarming Sandi, and if the girl hadn't reached toward the bookcase to do some straightening, Claudia might have chosen a better time and way to explain why her house would have to be violated by strangers yet again. As it was, she barked "Hold it!" so sharply that Sandi flinched. Before she could straighten, Claudia was already apologizing and then explaining that it was best not to touch anything else in the room in case—just in case—someone other than a police officer had been in her father's office.

"Well, who would come in and. . . ." Sandi's eyes widened. "Wait. You mean someone like maybe a burglar?"

Claudia offered a vague nod.

"Dad's dead," she said, her voice wobbling. "Why can't everyone just leave him alone?"

Claudia had no answer to that, but when Sandi turned away to hide her tears, she pulled the girl into an embrace. Sandi didn't resist, and for a moment they stood like that, not moving, the girl weeping silently. Claudia felt her shudder a few times, but then Sandi eased away, her eyes as remote as the day before.

Once, not all that long ago, Claudia had seen the flame dim in her own daughter's eyes. The reasons were different, yet powerful enough to plague Robin with nightmares for months afterward. The flame hadn't died, though—not quite—and eventually it flared as brightly as before. Claudia looked at Sandi. Robin's triumph was something to hold on to for the damaged girl who followed her wordlessly back outside.

In exchange for the scorn Chief Mac Suggs typically displayed for the Flagg County Sheriff's Office, he received barely concealed contempt in return. That was a problem because he had no fishing buddies in the sheriff's office, no secret alliances, not even an annoying relative in the mail room or records department he could leverage for favors. When the chief needed something he couldn't provide through his own depart-ment—special patrols, crime-scene technicians, lab work, a canine unit—he had to call the sheriff's office for it and the town had to pay up. The arrangement wasn't unusual. Police chiefs in small police departments across the country relied on bigger brethren to get the job done. Plenty of them resented it, but few carried the hostility quite like Suggs.

Claudia didn't dwell on it, but when she saw the sheriff's crime-scene technicians pulling up to Hemmer's house a full thirty minutes late, she had to rearrange her face to keep her own resentment from showing. Nor-mally, she wouldn't bother. But she needed them; and before they'd even braked to a stop, she presented an amicable smile, as if she'd enjoyed roast-ing in the sun while awaiting their arrival. Of course, it hadn't all been wasted time. She'd called Suggs, talked to Sandi's grandmother, and arranged for a patrol officer to take the girl back to the motel. Even so, her patience was taxed, and her mood didn't improve when she saw the team the sheriff's office had dispatched.

There were two technicians, one male and one female. They strode from their vehicle with disingenuous apologies for the delay, blaming it on a high priority case they implied could not be solved without them. Claudia let it pass. They were young and they were civilians. They probably believed their own bullshit. She led them into the house, exchanging names along the way but refusing to give them the satisfaction of a reaction when they introduced themselves as Jack and Jill—no last names, of course, because who bothered with that anymore?

"So what've we got?" Jack said self-importantly once inside Hemmer's office. He already knew there was no body, but he peered beneath the desk as if he might find one anyway, or at least an intriguing sign of blood. "A burglary?"

"Don't get your hopes up," said Claudia. "Right now I've only got a possible illegal entry."

She ignored his expression and laid out what she needed. Jill fired up a camera, metered for light, and took pictures. Jack started working surfaces for prints. Claudia watched for a few minutes. They weren't on anybody's A-list, but they'd do. She wrestled on a pair of latex gloves and carefully circumnavigated the small room, looking, probing, peeking, examining. Now and then she gave Jack or Jill something to bag, her mind leaping ahead to possibilities she didn't like.

The pair filtered her out and talked shop while they worked. Claudia wondered what they did in their spare time, but didn't dwell on it for long, because within fifteen minutes of her own exploration she found something behind Hemmer's books that didn't belong. She pondered its significance, then moved on, not looking up until Jill pointedly cleared her throat forty minutes later.

"Claudia," she said, "we're—"

"Lieutenant is fine." The kids really needed a few lessons in protocol. "What's up?"

Jill shrugged. "What's up is, we're done."

"Yup," said Jack. "Good to go." He made a show of checking his watch, a digital too big for his wrist. "Nice meeting you and all."

"Hang on. Bag this." She handed Jack what she'd found. "Take the desk pad, too." She gestured at what looked like an artist's oversized sketch pad, its pages glued at the top and tucked into corners at the bottom. Not even a stray pencil mark showed on the first page. Claudia had already thumbed through the rest. Nothing on any of them.

"The guy wasn't much of a doodler," said Jack.

"Except that—"

"I know." He rolled his eyes. "A documents examiner might pull up some impressions. That it?"

"That's it. Except for the computers, of course. I need those brought in, too."

Jack and Jill exchanged disbelieving looks. No body, no blood, and they could kiss another half hour goodbye. Claudia turned away so they wouldn't see her smiling.

CHAPTER · 9

CLAUDIA KNEW A THING OR TWO about cows. They made milk. They made hamburgers. She suspected a few other things, chiefly that cows were probably every bit as stupid as they looked. But there had to be more to cows than that, because if not, she had no idea how she would hold an intelligent conversation with Tom Dixon if she ever ran into him again. The very idea that Dixon had breached her mind alarmed her. Even more alarming was that her attention had inexplicably drifted to him in the middle of the chief's cramped office, where theoretically she was explaining why the Hemmer case wasn't closed after all.

She felt the chief scowling at her and looked up from her notes, where she had jotted "cow" in a margin. She glanced at Moody and Carella, patrol officers who occasionally shed their uniforms for street clothes when an investigation threatened to loom out of control. Their faces were expectant.

"You gonna answer my question today, Hershey, or is today altogether too damned inconvenient for you?" Suggs cracked his knuckles and waited. "Well?"

It was early on in their meeting, but not early on in the day. Claudia had forfeited lunch to baby-sit Jack and Jill at Hemmer's house. She'd lost another hour making nice with lab techs at the sheriff's office, hoping to get the Hemmer case bumped up in their priorities—or even to get it *on* their priority list. Another hour and a half went to phone calls and playing catch-up at her desk. Calamity was descending. She didn't need Suggs to remind her of that.

"You're talking about the video I found," she said.

He looked at her, exasperated. "Hell, yeah, I'm talkin' about the video! Right now it looks like it's the only thing *worth* talkin' about, and from what I can see it doesn't exactly support the high-voltage direction you're tryin' to take us in. Fact is, all it does show is that Sandi Hemmer clearly did *not* know her daddy as well as she thought she did."

"It's . . . a problem," Claudia conceded.

The chief made a rude noise and glared at the video, which now sat on his desk as innocently as a police-training film, but depicted the kind of pornographic production not available on even the most liberal pay-per-view stations. They'd all watched it in uncomfortable silence, fast-forwarding past a grainy segment involving Shetland ponies. No question that it was a black-market film. You wanted something like this and you had to actively seek it out; it didn't jibe with the man Hemmer had presented himself to be, but most assuredly it came from his bookcase. Claudia wished she hadn't found it. Without a doubt, it was a complication. Carella caught her eye and nodded toward Moody. His ears still bore traces of red from their private screening.

Suggs abruptly stood. He turned toward the wall, where a thirteen-pound bass mounted for eternity hung slightly askew. He nudged it straight, then looked at Claudia.

"It's not just the video that's a problem, Hershey. The mayor doesn't even know about that yet. But he knows you been back to Hemmer's house with the girl, and that's enough for him to conclude he needs to take a 'personal interest' in our investigation."

"He's already been in touch?" asked Moody. "Unbelievable."

"You just get off the boat?" Suggs growled. "Come on! Lane's got spies everywhere. And hell, yeah, he called the second they checked in with him. He told me he's very 'troubled.' He's troubled that Indian Run's ace detective was out and about with the Hemmer girl instead of being on what he called a 'much needed' vacation. He's troubled that Indian Run's ace detective is tryin' to turn an open-and-shut case into a 'dubious situation.' And he's troubled that Indian Run's ace police chief is 'rudderless' when it comes to running a department."

Suggs sat back down. He unfolded a sheet of paper on his desk. "I even took notes. The mayor—"

"I think—" Claudia began.

"Don't think yet, because I haven't even got to the best part, which I didn't need to write down at all. What the good mayor said next was, 'Settle this down fast, or I'll see to it that someone else does.'"

Ribald laughter floated into the office from the multipurpose room. A phone rang. Then another. Beneath it all was the ever-present sound of the dispatch console. Officers checking in, asking for case numbers, going 10-40 for burgers and fries. It had been the backdrop to Claudia's police career for more than twelve years.

"Hershey? You listenin' to me?"

She came back. "Yes. Of course."

"Okay, then." Suggs straightened. "Want to know what I said to the mayor? I said, 'Yes, sir.' I said, 'I understand, sir.' That's what I said."

Claudia nodded. She didn't look at Moody or Carella. She was pretty sure they weren't looking at her, either.

"But it's what I *didn't* say that matters, and what I didn't say is what I'm gonna tell you now, and it better not leave this room." Suggs leaned forward and lowered his voice. "I don't like Mayor Arthur Lane. Bigger, though, I don't respect him and I don't trust him, not one little bit. I wouldn't let him walk my dog if I was laid up to the point where I couldn't move and the dog'd crapped all over every room of my house. Now you, Hershey, I don't always like you, either. Truth is, it kinda comes and goes. But I do respect you and I do trust you. Carella? Moody? Both of you, too. Any of you, I'd hand you the leash, take a nap, and know the dog would get walked and the stink in the house would be gone when I woke up."

Most of the time Claudia could anticipate what the chief would say. This wasn't one of them.

Carella found his voice first. "Guess we can't ask for a better vote of confidence, because the way I remember it is you have a big dog. A *really* big dog."

Suggs snorted. "A Rottweiler. He gets in your face and his breath alone could knock you out. Forget the dog, though. Point I'm tryin' to make is that whether Hershey here is draggin' us into quicksand or not, Lane's *not* gonna call the shots. If he thinks he can close us down without us takin' a proper look at the Hemmer mess, then he's gonna find that his 'dubious situation' is gonna get even dubiouser. I've played his way too long and on too many things." He cleared his throat. "Hershey, your coffee's gettin' cold. Take a sip and then run this by us one more time. Persuade me that I'm not about to trash my career for nothin'."

Claudia picked up her cup. "Rottweiler, huh?"

She laid it out seamlessly, bringing them back to the hostage crisis at Hemmer's house. A man with no history of violence had seized five people. Her take? No doubt about it; he'd gone over the edge. But he'd made the leap with an unloaded gun, which suggested that he had no intention of killing anyone.

"The guy whacked you on the head, Hershey," said Suggs. "The blow could've killed you."

"And if it had, no one would've been more surprised than he. I think Hemmer measured that risk and took it to prove he was serious. And to seize the advantage from the beginning."

"It worked," said Carella.

No argument there. Claudia still had a lump on the back of her head. "We could let everything be if not for the fact that someone broke into his house *after* he was dead, *after* everyone bought into him being a whacko, *after* Bonolo was made into a hero, and *after* the press already had a terrific story that would've died down in another day or two. Why would—"

"You don't know for a fact yet that anyone really broke in," Suggs said swiftly. "You got the girl sayin' her daddy's stuff was messed up, and you got your own speculation. Worse, you turned up that video, which don't exactly support the notion that Hemmer was a choir boy. So once again, Hershey, *here's* where I need to be persuaded."

"Two things," said Claudia. "First, Hemmer had some neatly organized folders in the family room where he held us hostage. He told me he'd only brought downstairs what I needed to see, implying that he had other files with additional information related to his dispute with the homeowners association. He was a meticulous man, so I tend to believe him. But crime scene didn't turn up anything, and neither did I—not a single document or even a scribbled note. My thinking is that however it was done, someone got into the house to take those files before Sandi's grandparents could unearth them, which would've happened when they boxed up Hemmer's possessions and closed up the house for sale."

She took a breath. "And the video? I think whoever took those files *might* have planted the video to reinforce Hemmer's 'bad guy' image, to make sure no one ever had reason to even begin to think differently about him. The porn doesn't sound like Hemmer, but even if it did, hiding it practically in the open doesn't. Do the arithmetic. Take the video and add it to some missing files. Now add things being out of place. And finally, add his daughter's observations. We have more than coincidence."

"Uh-huh. So where's the hard evidence?"

"We'll get to it."

The chief sighed. "Look, I'm not hedging, Hershey. We're goin' forward with this thing. I'm runnin' full tilt on blind faith and your history of ferreting out crookedy little details that make the case in the end. But it'd be of considerable help if you'd give me one of those crookedy little details sooner rather than later. Please—tell me you're sandbaggin' on *somethin'.*"

Now Claudia sighed. "I wish."

Carella hummed the opening to "When You Wish Upon a Star." Nobody smiled. "From Disney's *Pinocchio* movie," he said. The silence lengthened and his voice trailed off with, "A 1940 release. . . ."

"Maybe the lab'll give us something to go on," said Moody. He pulled at his mustache. "Prints? Clothing fibers? A lead on the source of that video?"

"I should get a report on prints before the day is out," said Claudia. "Some of the other stuff we gathered, it'll probably come in piecemeal."

"We can't wait on piecemeal," said Suggs, "so what do you propose we do in the meanwhile? I *know* you got a meanwhile, Hershey."

She rolled her pen between her fingers. "Meanwhile, we revisit the people who pissed Hemmer off enough to make him step off a cliff. We begin there and see where it takes us, because there was nothing random about Hemmer's files going missing."

"The people who irritated him. . . ." Moody ticked them off on his fingers. "Bill Bonolo. Kurt Kitner. Jennifer Parrish. Gloria Addison."

"Pipelines to the town hall," said the chief. He stood and looked at Moody and Carella, then settled his gaze on Claudia. "I'd say you've just shut the door on your vacation for now. And all of you—you'd best work fast. I won't cave on this, but I can't guarantee I'll keep my job long enough to see it through."

CHAPTER · 10

SYDNEY STIHL'S REMARKABLE CAREER as a photographer was launched the day she immortalized on black-and-white film the horrifying crash of a twin-engine plane, which unaccountably spiraled out of control and plunged nose first into the ground between two houses in a quiet residential neighborhood. Sydney Stihl was 16 years old at the time. The plane carried her parents, and one of those houses was theirs—and, of course, Sydney's.

The crash occurred on a brilliant morning, not long after the sun burned the dew off the grass. Sydney knew the plane would be flying over. Her father had told her to watch for it, that he would tip a wing in greeting and then continue on his way. Sydney was new to photography and excited about shooting from a challenging angle. She planned carefully, choosing a vantage point from a modest distance that would allow her to frame both the plane and the house in one shot. From the moment the plane came into view, she was ready.

Her first shot showed the plane against a sky empty of clouds, the sun glinting off the fuselage like a starburst. Even for a professional photographer it would have been an impressive shot, but what people would whisper about later were the other shots—for even though Sydney surely could see through her lens what was coming, she continued to shoot. In twenty seconds, maybe thirty, she managed twelve pictures. When neighbors ran to her after the plane thundered into the ground, they had to pry the camera from her hands.

One way or another, the local newspaper managed to acquire three of the photos, including one that showed the wreckage between both houses. The pictures ran in a sequence, along with a riveting story about the ironic tragedy that produced such captivating images. Weeks later the paper ran another story, this one with investigators' conclusions that pilot error was to blame.

Sydney was 37 now. She owned dozens of cameras and went nowhere without at least two. Hers was not a household name, but within photography circles it carried star status. She received critical acclaim for much of her work, which embraced everything from photojournalism to fashion photography to coffee table books. Even now, when most photographers were turning to digital photography, Sydney's preference remained black-and-white 35-millimeter film, which she'd used for some of her most compelling and occasionally haunting images.

Claudia owned one of Sydney's coffee table books. Wrapped in plain brown paper, it was kept on the top shelf in her bedroom closet. She'd looked at it once. She intended never to look at it again, or even to think about it, and might have been able to keep that vow if not for Sydney Stihl's voice on her answering machine, calling to say she was in town and could the two of them get together? She left her cell number—repeated it twice—and then simply hung up. "Goodbye" was a word she never used. Not since the plane went down.

Claudia's finger hovered over the delete button on her answering machine. The hour had long since slipped past midnight. Since the meeting with Suggs, Moody, and Carella, she'd logged most of her time chasing details on the phone or computer. The work was tedious, and for every new thread she turned up, half a dozen others unraveled. Now her back ached and her eyes burned from lack of sleep. The only voice she craved was Robin's, but it was too late to call her. The last voice she wanted to hear was Sydney's, because Sydney meant distraction and she meant pain, and if not for the quirk of genetics that brought both of them into the world from a single egg, Claudia would have less of each.

For a second, she put her finger on the delete button. She wanted to press down. She wanted to throw away the package in her closet—now, immediately. She did neither. She went to bed instead, and hoped that sleep would claim her before the images from her twin sister's book did all over again.

For Florida in August, when rain usually meant wind-whipped gushers that swallowed whole streets in minutes, the drizzle that rode in with dawn on Tuesday was an embarrassment. It qualified as mist more than anything else, and it clung to an air so still that every scent stood out sharply enough to be almost visible. Claudia caught a powerful whiff of cow on her drive to the station. She immediately thought of Tom Dixon, whom she'd met only once but who inexplicably had the staying power of a bad song.

She flashed on a time when she'd heard the jingle for a hot dog on the radio upon rising one morning. For the rest of the day, she couldn't quite ditch it: "Oh, I wish I were an Oscar Mayer wiener. . . ." She hummed it, she sang it, she whistled it. The more she tried to banish it, the worse it clamped down on her. Tom Dixon was becoming a little like that, and she shook her head, annoyed, because she could no more avoid cows in Indian Run than advertising jingles on the radio.

Then again, thinking about the cowboy was preferable to thinking about her sister. She turned on the radio to drown out both and had just about succeeded by the time she parked her car and reached her office.

Mitch Moody was ready for her. He wore a charcoal suit, a remnant from his flirtation with law school. He'd exchanged suits for a police uniform when he realized that he could be more effective dispensing the law on the streets than trying to salvage it in a courtroom. The suit was dated, but Claudia said nothing. Most of her clothes were, too.

"Good morning, Lieutenant," he said. "Want some coffee before we head out?"

"I'll pass. Where's the chief?"

"Dodging the mayor."

"Lane's already put in another call?"

"Not yet, but the chief was leaving when I was coming in. He says it won't take long before Lane figures out how to react to the initial crime-scene report, so he's trying to buy us some time by making it tough for Lane to reach him."

Lab technicians had called in a preliminary report. They'd turned up exactly what Claudia thought they would: nothing. There were no fingerprints that didn't belong in Hemmer's office. No unusual footprints around the house. Not even subtle indications that anyone had fooled with a door or a window to get in. Results on the desk pad and computers would take another day or two. At the moment, all that stood out as a curiosity was the lack of prints—any kind of prints—on the video.

"Carella in yet?" she asked.

"In and out."

"You're joking. It's not even seven-thirty."

"He's showing off. This is the third time he's played detective with you. I think he's itching to get bumped up a notch permanently. He's already off to see the crew at Discreet Services over in Flagg."

Discreet was death's janitor, a cleaning service that specialized in crime-scene cleanup. Sandi's grandparents had been given a list of three such services after the scene was cleared by police. They didn't dwell on it. They chose the name at the top.

"You're not expecting anything from this, are you?" Moody asked.

"No. An officer baby-sat the premises while Discreet did its thing. But there's no point in leaving it to question. If the Hemmer case gathers steam, the mayor certainly won't."

"Got it."

"All right. Give me five minutes and then we'll roll, see if we can stir anything up."

Claudia headed into her office, a cubbyhole situated just off the multi-purpose room. It had been converted from a utility closet and still held a dingy sink, which saw a lot of traffic from people looking to refill the coffee carafe. She snatched a fresh pen and notepad from her desk drawer, then angled out in pursuit of Sergeant Ron Peters. Peters took care of administrative functions with the practiced efficiency of a soccer mom in a van full of 10-year-olds.

"Hey, Sarge," she said. "Anything I need to know that can't wait?"

"Nope. It's blessedly peaceful right now. With Moody and Carella off the streets, we need it to stay that way."

"The chief filled you in?"

"Yeah. He said we're playing the Hemmer investigation low-key, which I take to mean that only half the town knows about it by now."

Claudia smiled. "Give it another hour. The rest will catch up." She turned to go.

"Oh, hey. Lieutenant? I almost forgot. You got a call just before you walked in." He handed her a message form. "I was about to leave it on your desk, but now I can save myself those whopping ten steps to your office."

Sydney. Claudia jammed the note in her pocket.

"I don't recognize the name," he said, "but I'll do a call-back if you want."

"Not necessary, Ron. I'll check in later."

"Okay. And good luck out there."

She didn't hear him. The jingle was back in her head.

CHAPTER · 11

WHEN HEMMER DECIDED TO TAKE HOSTAGES, he had picked Jennifer Parrish to arrive first. He obviously perceived Parrish as the weakest lamb, both physically and emotionally. She wouldn't try to fight him. She would tape the others up as ordered. She would do whatever it took to get home safely to her kids and husband. Claudia figured that what worked for Hemmer would work for her as well.

With Moody buckled in beside her, she steered her Cavalier through the entrance to Willow Whisper. A repairman was working on the gates, mindless of the drizzle, and paid no attention when they drove by. Five minutes later she braked to a stop in front of a two-story house and turned off the ignition. The engine shuddered and announced its age with rude sounds that prepubescent boys would find hysterical.

The Parrish house was nearly twice the size of Hemmer's. The driveway was paved and anchored by queen palm trees. Thick grass so green it looked artificial bore a variety of insufferably cute lawn ornaments: Elves holding lanterns. Fawns. Pink flamingos.

"Check out the flag on their house," said Moody.

Claudia looked up. The flag displayed huge daisies with smiling human faces, but just now it hung limply, as if embarrassed by its childish spectacle.

"I feel like I just entered the Magic Kingdom," he said, matching her strides past a spritz of periwinkles to the front door. A TV and a crying baby sounded from inside.

Claudia rang the bell. "Maybe if we're lucky she'll give us the keys."

Jennifer Parrish opened the door a few moments later, an unhappy baby on one hip and a dishcloth in the other. She blanched.

"Good morning, Mrs. Parrish." Claudia nodded pleasantly, enjoying the moment. "You know, you really ought to make a practice of using your peephole. This is Officer Mitch Moody. We need a few minutes of your time."

Moody had already begun cooing at the baby, easing himself in.

"I . . . it's pretty early and—"

"We won't be long," said Claudia. She wasn't a natural with babies, so instead she edged closer and peered inside, remarking on what a beautiful house the woman had.

"It's . . . thank you."

The baby was about eight months old. He regarded Moody through wet eyes, then hiccupped. Moody hiccupped back. The baby chortled and wriggled in his mother's arm. Two other children, one about three and the other a year or two older, peeked around a corner. Moody feigned being startled, clutching his chest and sliding down the door frame. The kids laughed like they'd never seen anything so hilarious in their young lives.

Claudia hid a smile. They were in.

Jennifer Parrish escorted her visitors to chairs in the living room, shooing the older kids into the family room, where she could still keep an eye on them while they watched cartoons. She excused herself for a minute, then returned with a bottle of apple juice. She sat on the couch, propped the baby on her lap, and stuck the bottle in his mouth.

"There's a lot of commotion here in the mornings," she said, trying to appear nonchalant. "First it's Daniel getting off to work—Daniel's my husband—and then there's the whole routine of getting the kids fed. It's a lot of commotion."

Moody nodded sympathetically. "Takes a lot of energy. What're your kids' names?"

"Oh." She jostled the baby slightly. "This is Donny. That's Dolly and Denny in the other room."

"Donny, Dolly, Denny." Moody inclined his head. "Must get confusing sometimes."

"Always." She pushed aside a lock of errant hair. "The *D* thing with their names, that was my husband's idea." Parrish was warming to Moody. "He's kind of a playful guy. When our first arrived, he—"

Claudia stood so abruptly that Parrish nearly dropped the bottle. "Mrs. Parrish, guess what? Someone broke into Steve Hemmer's house. We're not sure why yet, but it's an interesting twist. Tell me, why wouldn't the Property Alterations Committee sign off on a new paint job for Hemmer's house? Why wouldn't they do anything about his patio? Why *really*?"

Parrish's mouth dropped open. Claudia moved closer and took a gamble. "We've seen all the files by now. You must know that." Parrish tried to look toward Moody, but Claudia was blocking her view. "We know what got approved in Willow Whisper and what didn't, so don't try to think this through. Just tell me why Hemmer's requests were repeatedly spurned."

Little Donny squawked threateningly. In another moment, he'd start crying all over again. Parrish rocked him for a second, then mumbled she should put him down for a nap. Claudia shot a look to Moody. He moved swiftly to the woman's side and reached for the baby.

"Here, Mrs. Parrish, let me," he said. "I'll keep him and the other kids entertained. You ladies can talk."

"Oh, no, I . . . I couldn't." But she was helpless between them and didn't resist when Moody gently eased Donny from her arms.

"You a cutie, yes you is," he crooned. He took the bottle from Parrish's hand and half-walked, half-rocked into the family room. Parrish watched until he and the kids were out of view, then folded her hands in her lap and stared at them.

Claudia settled onto the other side of the couch. She draped an arm over the back and crossed her legs. "Did you really care if Hemmer painted his house blue-gray? 'Morning mist,' I think he called it. Did you care?"

Parrish shrugged.

"Did you really care if he tore out his patio and put in one without cracks?"

"Why does it matter?"

"Just answer. Did you care?"

"Okay, no. I didn't care. Not personally."

"But you voted like you did, like what he wanted would violate community standards. They didn't, though, did they?"

"Standards can be hard to define. They're—"

"Not that hard. Yes or no?"

"I . . . no. Not essentially. But—"

"So why vote against what he wanted?"

"I wasn't the only one who did."

"But you *were* one of them. Why?"

Parrish swiveled toward Claudia. "What is this? Why are you even asking me? Hemmer was a monster. He proved that himself! He was *worse* than Bill told us he was!"

"You mean Bill Bonolo?"

She shook her head irritably. "Yes, yes. Of course. What other Bill is there?"

"You lost me. Bonolo told you Hemmer was a monster *before* Hemmer even took you hostage?"

"Oh, come on. You know what Hemmer was about."

"Pretend I don't."

"The porn stuff! The porn stuff!" Parrish's eyes flashed. "He was a pervert! He kept it. He traded in it. He sold it. Before long he might've started going after kids. It's how these things develop. You *know* they do. But Bill gave us the heads-up and told us the only way to protect the community was to tire Hemmer out, get him to move away. See, if we tried to go after him criminally or civilly, we'd tarnish the whole community, and anyway, it would take years—and even then we might not be successful. I can't *believe* Hemmer's record wasn't brought up in those newspaper stories."

"Let me make sure I got this right. You were on a systematic harassment campaign to make Hemmer move. You figured he'd get frustrated and just go away. That about it?"

Parrish grew defensive. "You make it sound like something downright slimy. Slimy would've been if we'd exposed him to the whole community, the whole *town*."

"That was *your* thinking?"

"Bill laid it out. It seemed to make sense. Who could've guessed how far Hemmer would take things?"

Claudia shifted gears. "Hemmer's record. You didn't actually see it, did you?"

"Personally? No. But Bill has connections. He'd seen it."

"It keeps coming back to Bill Bonolo."

"He's president of the homeowners association."

"But he wasn't a member of the PAC. He didn't vote on property changes."

Parrish looked unhappy. "That doesn't mean we didn't respect his opinions."

"Did he share his opinions on everyone who requested a property change? Or just Hemmer?"

She looked away. "Other people didn't come up the . . . same way. They were ordinary. I . . . only Hemmer had a record."

"Uh-huh." Claudia stood. She turned and gazed through a window behind the couch. The backs of the lawn ornaments faced her now. The elves looked less like mischievous fairies and more like malevolent trolls. But maybe it was the mist. Claudia shook it off and turned back to regard the woman on the couch. "Hemmer didn't have a record, Mrs. Parrish. He didn't have so much as a parking ticket."

For a long moment, Parrish said nothing. Then her mouth opened, closed, opened again. When she finally spoke, Claudia had to lean in to hear.

"He took us hostage, though." Her voice trembled. "That tells you something about the man, doesn't it? I mean, it shows you. . . . Look, we're not bad people. We were just trying to—"

"Spare me," Claudia said flatly. "If you want absolution, go talk to a priest. If you want understanding, go talk to a shrink. I'm a cop, and the way I see it you and your twisted committee held Hemmer hostage long before he took you as one."

High-pitched giggles sounded from the family room. Moody's laugh resonated above them all. When Parrish finally did talk, her voice was so unexpected that it almost seemed loud, though she spoke barely above a whisper.

"Bill Bonolo has a . . . commanding presence," she said listlessly. "You couldn't challenge him on anything. Kurt tried once, in his own way." Her eyes darted to Claudia's face, then away. "It was when Hemmer's record first came up, when Bill said he'd seen it and we needed to take measures to protect the community. Kurt didn't exactly dispute the idea, but he suggested we get a copy of the record and keep it on file, just in case things got nasty. I thought that made sense, but. . . ." She studied her hands.

"And?" Claudia prodded. "Mrs. Parrish? Stay with me now."

Parrish didn't lift her eyes, but she continued. "Bill shot Kurt down before I could even open my mouth. He accused Kurt of calling him a liar. He got loud and red in the face. Kurt let it go, and after that, we all just let things sit."

"So Bonolo intimidated the whole committee?"

"In retrospect, I think . . . well, I know that was true of me and Kurt." Parrish wrapped her arms around herself. "I don't know about Gloria Addison. When the Hemmer thing came up, she got kind of . . . intense. She backed everything Bill said, and I thought she honestly *did* believe what he was saying. But that was the only time she seemed to care about anything the committee did. The rest of the time, she seemed . . . bored. I don't know why she even wanted to be on the committee."

"Why did you?"

"Why did I what?"

"Want to be on the committee?"

Parrish's eyes fell back to her hands, her anchors. "I . . . thought I could make a difference in the community."

And that you did, thought Claudia. She ran the woman through a few other lines of questioning and then tore Moody away from the kids. They were out of the Magic Kingdom by nine-fifteen.

They expected that Kurt Kitner would already have left for work and were startled when he opened the door to their knock. Nothing in his expression showed surprise. Either he was more security conscious than Jennifer Parrish and had looked through the peephole, or he already knew they'd be coming. Claudia bet the latter, and Kitner confirmed her guess before she had a chance to say anything.

"Jennifer called the minute you left her. She's only three-quarters of a mile from here, but she had time enough to tell me why you'd been there." He opened the door wide but retreated before Claudia could introduce Moody. They looked at each other and shrugged, then followed him into a house steeped in gloom.

Kitner led them wordlessly past a small combination living room and family room, which held a sofa and love seat, a coffee table and one book-case. The walls appeared to be some sort of deep blue, but the blinds were closed and Claudia couldn't tell. She looked for a TV or stereo—any-thing that might hint at real human habitation—but there was none. Everything ached with stillness.

Kitner ushered them into his kitchen. Like the other rooms, it was small but sufficient to hold a round table and four chairs. If the blinds had been open, it might have been pleasant. He gestured for them to sit.

"I'm an accountant, and ordinarily I would've been at the office at this hour, but I've taken the rest of the week off. It's not every day that one encounters a tragedy such as what occurred at Steven Hemmer's resi-dence." He spoke evenly but without inflection, and he had yet to make eye contact.

Claudia murmured a sympathetic response, then introduced Moody. Kitner nodded perfunctorily, but she got the impression he wasn't really listening. Then abruptly, tears pooled in his eyes.

Moody reacted first. "Mr. Kitner, are you all right?"

He blotted his eyes with a tissue. He nodded. "It's been . . . difficult, though." He swallowed. "I'm sorry."

"Don't be," said Moody. "Mr. Kitner, what happened to you was unspeakably terrifying." He shook his head. "Even as a police officer, I've never run into anything remotely like you did. You're entitled to your emotions."

Kitner found Moody's eyes. "Thank you."

Not for the first time, Claudia marveled at Moody's nimble ability to connect with people. He could quiet an emotional outburst as smoothly as a prestidigitator pulling a scarf from his sleeve, and yet everything he said or did resonated with sincerity. That, of course, was why she'd brought him along. She wasn't surprised when Kitner offered to make coffee. Moody said he'd love a cup.

"I don't drink coffee very often myself," he said, "but I buy an imported brand that's highly rated for its richness. I like to keep it on hand for guests who come by."

Claudia wondered how often that happened. She couldn't remember the last time she had met someone so formal in manner, speech, and appearance.

"Detective Hershey, would you like a cup as well?"

"Sure," she lied. Anything to relax him.

He moved around the kitchen methodically, taking pains to measure the coffee just so, to fill the carafe precisely to the right line with cold bottled water. None of that tap water stuff for company. Claudia watched him turn a routine task into ritual while he talked politely with Moody about the weather and then fluctuations in the stock market. He was a diminutive man with thinning hair and rounded shoulders; she could picture him bent over ledgers and computer printouts, more comfortable in an office with a calculator than in his own home with a television. She wondered how he'd been drawn into a committee that dealt with property aesthetics.

When the coffee was finally brewed, Kitner served it in china cups on saucers and took a seat. He inhaled, and for a moment Claudia worried he might begin to tear up again. But he didn't. He folded his hands on the table and spoke in a voice as measured as his coffee.

"I'm not a man of courage," he said softly, "but I always thought myself to be a man of honor and integrity. On Friday I learned that I am neither of those, and because I'm not, a man is dead."

"Whoa. Mr. Kitner, don't beat yourself up," said Claudia. "No one—"

"Please. If I may finish? This is difficult enough for me."

"I'm sorry."

He paused to sip his coffee. "From the beginning, I let a schoolyard bully kick sand in my face. I. . . ." He hesitated, collecting his thoughts. "Bill Bonolo is big and confident and arrogant. He doesn't walk into a room. He *swaggers* into it, and he can diminish a person with just a look. Perhaps for that reason I tried to challenge him only once." Kitner nipped at his lower lip. "It was about Mr. Hemmer's purported police record, and my challenge was so feeble that even before events escalated, I felt ashamed. The truth is, it wasn't my lack of action Friday night that demonstrated everything I'm not. It's my lack of action *before* events spiraled out of control. I saw a speeding car headed in Mr. Hemmer's direction and I helped push him in front of it."

"Most people are less forgiving of Hemmer than you are," Claudia said.

"Most people don't know the truth. I did—at least some of it—and though I can't change what's already happened, I can do the right thing now. It's not enough for the little girl who lost her father, and it won't restore my integrity—"

Claudia tried again. "You're confusing fear with integrity."

Moody added, "A very legitimate fear."

Kitner tapped his fingertips together. Then he looked up, locking eyes first with Moody and finally with Claudia. "Bill Bonolo talked me out of what I really felt. Please don't you do it, too, even to be kind. I bear a lot of responsibility. I'm trying to take it. I need to. . . . Look, just ask me anything you'd like. To the degree that I can answer, I will. Fully and honestly."

Rarely did police investigators get an open invitation like that. Moody had set the stage; Claudia leaped on it. She started with the break-in at Hemmer's house—ostensibly her reason for visiting Kitner at all. Of course, because Parrish had already alerted him to the break-in, he'd had at least a few minutes to consider his response. But he seemed genuinely mystified and almost apologetic that he couldn't help with more than speculation. He wondered aloud if the break-in had been the work of an opportunistic thief. Anyone who watched TV or read the newspapers likely would have expected the house to be vacant after the hostage situation.

"We're exploring that possibility," Claudia said carefully.

"But you're also concerned that perhaps one or more of the hostages had involvement?"

"We have to look at everything."

She changed the subject, broadening her questions to the committee, the structure and history of the homeowners association, Hemmer's requests, Bonolo's lies. Kitner reiterated much of what Parrish had said, and filled in a few gaps. Once, he left the table to retrieve association papers he believed might be useful. He smoothed the top of a file folder before handing it over, like maybe he could press out a wrinkle or two.

"Detective, I know you've taken notes of our conversation, but I'll also write and sign a detailed statement; maybe more will occur to me. I'll get someone to witness my signature." He shrugged lightly. "That's the CPA in me. I . . . well, anyway, I can drop it off at the police station later today or early tomorrow. Would that be of some help?"

Claudia nodded, hoping her face didn't reveal the exhilaration she felt. *A volunteered statement? Written?* Kitner was full of unexpected treasures. But then, the guilt he felt was almost palpable. She looked at him and saw Sisyphus, forever damned to push a boulder uphill.

"Thank you," she said simply.

He nodded—came close to smiling—and then, just when she thought he'd given her everything he could, he gave her something more: validation of her own actions at Hemmer's house.

"You've been maligned in the press and maybe other places; I don't know. But I've gone over that evening dozens of times, and from what I could tell, your actions were without flaw. I'll add that to my written statement as well. I should have spoken up when I was interviewed immediately afterward, but . . . well, even then I couldn't find the courage to go up against Bonolo."

"You'd just seen him kill a man," said Claudia.

"You're doing it again," he said mildly.

"I . . . all right." She looked to Moody for help, but he said nothing. "Sorry. And thank you for your assistance."

Moody shook Kitner's hand and closed with a few more pleasantries as they walked back through the gloom to the door. Claudia almost asked Kitner why he didn't open his blinds and let in some light. But she thought she knew why already. Light offered hope and optimism. Kitner had neither in reserve, nor the strength to seek them. She hoped he would get help.

Their luck ran out with Bill Bonolo and Gloria Addison. Neither was home. From what Claudia had learned about Addison, the woman could be guzzling gin and tonics with lunch somewhere in Indian Run, or for that matter, anywhere from Tallahassee to South Miami. She owned a fast car, and when she wasn't polishing her tan at the pool, she used it to race from one impulse to another. How she managed all that without a job, no one seemed to know.

Bonolo logged a lot of miles on the road, too. He worked for a bottled-water company that had aggressively expanded into Central Florida and was keenly peddling its newest product, flavored water. Theoretically, he was a distribution manager. But it was a glorified title, because Bonolo mostly spent his time troubleshooting accounts in a competitive market unforgiving of errors. If a store didn't get its delivery on time, he was there. If a store got the wrong delivery—there again. He toted cartons of bottled water in an oversized pickup truck with a grill persistently clogged by insects. He'd held the job for eight months and he hated it. He hated sucking up to customers. He hated the asshole salesmen who put him in the position of sucking up because they made promises they couldn't keep.

Claudia had learned some of Bonolo's current history through discreet background checks. Kitner had supplied the rest; Bonolo routinely favored board meetings of the homeowners association with colorful descriptions of how he'd spent his time saving someone's ass. You'd think the guy put in sixty-hour work weeks. Kitner thought he must. Claudia had already discovered otherwise. Bonolo's job was on the line. He'd taken to missing appointments, and he was padding his expense reports. Right now, he could be with a client in Okeechobee or Bartow—or not.

The thought made her smile. She loved inconsistencies, and this was one of them. Too bad it would have to wait.

CHAPTER · 12

CRINKUM-CRANKUM. If it was a bona fide word, it wasn't one Claudia had ever heard before. Neither had the chief, who figured it for some kind of fancy spice or maybe even one of those sissified herbal concoctions you'd hear about practically every day. Carella said nah, it was probably an obscure crossword-puzzle word. His wife worked the crosswords every day and ranted about how they were loaded with words you'd swear were bogus. Moody pictured crinkum-crankum as something out of a fairy tale or movie for children; it had a fantasy sound to it. A story about witches maybe?

Suggs didn't bother to conceal a yawn. It was late and they'd just about beaten crinkum-crankum and the rest of the Hemmer case to death. They were tired and hungry. Worse, the bloom of optimism they'd felt after the Parrish and Kitner interviews had been replaced with the nagging sense that a long day had actually produced little more than continued speculation. Crinkum-crankum was just more of the same, and even Claudia found it hard to work up genuine enthusiasm for it. That a forensics analyst at the sheriff's office had managed to distill the word from Hemmer's desk pad through digital imaging was interesting, yeah, but so what? The word didn't exactly shout "clue" like bloody handwriting on a wall would.

She hid her own yawn. The Hemmer case had started thin. It was still thin. Neither Bonolo nor Addison could be found. Kitner hadn't dropped off his statement yet. The sheriff's office had given them crinkum-crankum but wouldn't put Hemmer's computers on a priority list.

Claudia had two choices. She could retrieve the computers and get a big-ticket private firm to explore Hemmer's hard drives, or she could wait her turn. That could take weeks.

"Could be we need a foreign-language dictionary," Suggs halfheartedly said.

"Pardon me?" she said.

"Crinkum-crankum, Hershey. Crinkum-crankum." He frowned. "You still with us?"

"I am."

He grunted. "Okay, the reason I'm thinkin' about a foreign-language dictionary is because this *crinkum-crankum* could be Italian. Lots of vowels in it."

"Could just as easily be Welsh," said Carella. "Lots of consonants, too."

Claudia had looked the word up in her office dictionary—English language, of course—but wasn't surprised not to find it there. The book was paperback, old, and so worn it looked like the Yellow Pages at a public phone booth. She'd also run a search with the spell check on her word processor, but the closest it came to crinkum-crankum was *crinkle*. Maybe she'd fare better with her hardcover dictionary at home. She said she'd try that.

The discussion faded like vapor, and she caught Moody discreetly eyeing his watch. She looked at her own. Eight-fifteen already.

"The hell with it," said Suggs. "Let's bag it for the night." He squirmed in his chair and gave Claudia a sour look. "Last time you involved me in one of your cases I got an ulcer. If I keep my ass in this chair any longer for this one, I'm gonna wind up with hemorrhoids."

Carella snickered, and everyone stood. They filed out of the chief's office, wishing each other a good night, anxious to get home where someone would have the lights on and maybe a hot meal waiting. Claudia wistfully watched them leave. With Robin still at camp, her house would be dark and bleak. She thought about it, then doubled back to her own office to catch up on work unrelated to the Hemmer case.

She was behind on everything. Peters had left shift reports from Monday night and today. She scanned them, then thumbed through two days' worth of incident reports. Indian Run had been blessedly dull, with little more to show for it than call-outs on loud stereos, trespassers, a domestic disturbance, illegal drag racing, fender benders, a disorderly conduct, and two-bit bar fights—nothing that required her involvement. Peters had left another message from Sydney, which she crumpled and tossed, and the chief had routed a memo bellyaching about people letting food go bad in the refrigerator. She tossed that, too, then stuffed files and notes into her briefcase. A few minutes later she slid into her car and cheerlessly headed for home, still brooding on the Hemmer case.

For reasons not yet clear, Bonolo wanted Hemmer out of Willow Whisper. Through old-fashioned intimidation and lies, he'd enlisted the property alterations committee to help. In the short term, his tactics failed, not because the committee didn't go along, but because Hemmer didn't react predictably. But in the long term, Bonolo still got what he wanted because Hemmer was dead, killed on a stage he himself had set. Best yet, Bonolo emerged a hero after taking him down personally.

So why wasn't that enough? Why continue the smear campaign by planting a video? Why—

Claudia swerved to avoid an armadillo scuttling across the road. She swore out loud, then glanced in her rearview mirror in time to see the witless creature shuffle into shadow. Somewhere, she'd heard that armadillos were the only mammals besides humans that were vulnerable to leprosy. Booey, no doubt. Yeah. It had to be Booey who'd told her that. He kept thousands of factoids parceled off in some obscure part of the brain that was beyond the reach of average people. But then, nothing about Booey was average.

Claudia braked for a stop sign and sighed. She could go whole weeks and not think of him. She liked it that way, partly because he was the chief's nephew and partly because he made her nuts. Here he was, though, on her mind for the second time in two days. That hardly qualified as an omen, but it sparked an idea. Carella knew computers better than anyone in the police station. Booey knew computers better than Carella. If she had to guess, he could probably hack into a Swiss bank and access the names of all the account holders. Not that she would ask. Not that he would do it. But maybe he *could* do for her what the sheriff's computer guru wouldn't.

She pulled into her driveway and turned off the engine. There it was, the dark house. She let herself in, snapped on a light, picked up the phone before she had her purse off her shoulder, and made arrangements. So all right; it wasn't a big deal. Still, momentum was momentum, and she was surprised to find that in nudging the investigation forward even a little, she felt more restless than satisfied.

She looked around sourly. It was just shy of nine o'clock. A man was dead. He shouldn't have been dead. There had to be more she could do than make phone calls, something that would put her in motion and burn off the restlessness that plagued her the more she thought about it. Thirty minutes and one cigarette later, she had an inkling of what that might be. She retrieved her purse and headed back out into the night. This time she left a light on.

The gates at Willow Whisper were working. To get in, a visitor had to stop at a mounted panel that contained an electronic listing of names and telephone access codes for each house, locate the name of the desired homeowner, and dial the corresponding code on a keypad. The homeowner's phone would ring, and after a tinny conversation to verify the visitor's identity, the homeowner could open the gate by tapping in a designated number on his own phone.

Claudia didn't need to fool with any of it. Police officials maintained emergency access codes for gated communities, and she was privy to the code for Willow Whisper. She punched it in and the gate rose like a practiced salute. As whims went, this one showed promise. She smiled and glided through, then guided the Cavalier toward Bonolo's house. If her luck held, he'd be less elusive at night than during the day.

She passed Hemmer's house, which looked even more forlorn than her own, then took a left and finally a right onto a street that ended in a cul-de-sac. Not for the first time, it struck her just how deserted Willow Whisper appeared at night. Garages dominated the houses to which they were attached, effectively concealing living areas in the back. The only visible signs of life came from the occasional glow of light spilling from the rear of houses. Paradise was all about privacy, and Willow Whisper had scored a home run with that one.

Bonolo's house was the last of eight two-stories on the cul-de-sac, which wrapped around a circular fountain and allowed only one-way traffic. Claudia had barely entered the cul-de-sac when she spotted Bonolo's truck backing out of his garage. By the time she completed her circle around the fountain, he was headed in the opposite direction. She could accelerate and pull him over. She could wait for him to return. Or she could tail him and see where the son of a bitch was going, because he was a son of a bitch—of that she felt certain. Never mind that he had no police record, no liens on property, no lawsuits past or present; something about him gave off the stink of malevolence.

Traffic was never heavy in Indian Run. On a nondescript Tuesday night, it was practically nonexistent, so when Bonolo left the development and cruised south through town, Claudia gave him plenty of space. The whim that brought her to Willow Whisper had given way to resolve. Wherever he led, she would follow.

* * *

Bonolo surprised her. Given the hour, she figured his destination for a bar or a house, either of which might hint at his associations. Instead, he swung onto U.S. Alternate 27, only to abandon it ten minutes later for State Road 60. He headed east, and Claudia's heart sank. You didn't take 60 in search of the nearest bar. You took 60 for a journey. She glanced at her gas gauge. Better than half a tank. If she didn't lose him in traffic, it should keep her on him for a good long time.

Bonolo drove fast, which on 60 meant he was doing nothing more than keeping up with traffic. She stayed with him, holding her breath every time they passed a truck where the highway narrowed to two lanes. By day, the road was picturesque, both sides of it lined with citrus groves and cattle ranches. At night, the same landscape brooded in shadow, rendering most of it indistinguishable. Claudia paid it no attention, her eyes locked on Bonolo's taillights. They'd driven just over forty miles when he surprised her again, this time turning onto the turnpike at Yeehaw Junction. She swore when he took the southbound ramp, because if State Road 60 was a journey, then the turnpike was a quest. Bonolo could be headed as far south as Homestead.

She didn't have time to think about it. She took a toll card at the booth, then merged onto the turnpike behind him and lit a cigarette, giving him a wider lead this time. He goosed his speed to seventy-five and stayed there. Claudia glanced at her instrument panel. Seventy-five on the turnpike wasn't much of a risk for Bonolo's truck, but it could be a ball breaker for the Cavalier, rarely accustomed to pushing more than forty-five. She hoped the gods were with her.

They whisked past exit after exit, Bonolo slowing only when lanes dropped off in occasional construction zones or when the speed limit fell to sixty in more densely populated areas. Fort Pierce, St. Lucie, Stuart, Jupiter, Palm Beach Gardens, West Palm Beach, Lake Worth . . . with every exit they passed, Claudia became increasingly aware of her bladder and hoped Bonolo would have to stop for the same reason. But except for a brief pause at the Lantana plaza to relinquish his toll card and pay up, he was of single-minded purpose. Before long, he'd led her out of Palm Beach County and into Broward. By the time he finally exited at Sample Road, they'd traveled some 124 miles on the turnpike alone.

Bonolo wasn't finished driving. He took Sample east a few miles, then continued his southern route on I-95. They'd been on the road nearly three hours. Claudia would've bagged it if she hadn't already come this far.

She checked her gas. The gauge showed just under a quarter tank remaining. She laughed at her plight. Everyone knew the last quarter went a hell of a lot faster than the first quarter. No reason. It just did. The bastard better *not* be destined for Homestead.

The traffic on I-95 moved steadily and in an orderly fashion, a phenomenon this far south, and they passed only one wreck. It was recent enough to jam things up for a few miles, but not so new that the Florida Highway Patrol wasn't already on it. Claudia sped up, closing the distance between her and Bonolo. He'd taken to weaving around cars, making it harder to keep him in sight. She didn't think he'd spotted her tailing him, but there was no way to know for sure. Maybe he just had to pee, too.

Finally he exited, swinging east all the way to Biscayne Boulevard and then past it, across the Julia Tuttle Causeway and over the Intracoastal Waterway into Miami Beach. Claudia forgot about her bladder. She didn't know the area, and it took all her concentration to stay with Bonolo. They were on Arthur Godfrey Road, and when he took two lights on caution, she was forced to follow through on red. Apparently that was the accepted practice on Miami Beach. On both occasions cars sprinted through after her.

Bonolo made a right on Collins Avenue, narrowly missing a pedestrian. A convertible blaring rap music snaked in front of her, but she could still see Bonolo's truck without difficulty. And unless he intended to drive straight into the Atlantic Ocean, he had to be close to his destination. Claudia's spirits hitched a notch. She couldn't remember the last time she had to pee so bad; and almost as appalling, she'd run out of cigarettes on the turnpike. But they'd driven more than 200 miles in about three and a half hours, and she'd never lost sight of him, she still had gas, and in moments she'd know more about him than she did before. She gave a small whoop of satisfaction, then slowed for yet another traffic signal, her mark stuck at the same light.

While they idled, she gazed around. It was after midnight, but Miami Beach was impervious to the hour. Throngs of people gathered in front of bars that spilled music onto the street. Lovers threaded their way through traffic, crossing to the beach side. Claudia thought maybe she'd bring Robin here sometime—not this late, of course, but not so early that she missed the magic of a city known for its night pulse. She tapped her fingers on the steering wheel, picking up on a reggae beat from somewhere. Nice.

The light changed and traffic began to inch forward. Bonolo moved.

The convertible moved. Claudia rolled with them, and then . . . nothing. The Cavalier simply stopped. It didn't sputter. It didn't shake. It just pooped out. She swore, pushed at the pedal again, harder, but the car wasn't going anywhere. Horns blared impatiently. Two or three vehicles lurched recklessly past her. She ignored them all and watched helplessly as the taillights of Bonolo's truck receded, gutting the buoyant feeling she'd enjoyed just seconds earlier.

There wasn't time to brood. One way or another, traffic was making its way around her, and a trio of young revelers appeared at her window. A girl wearing an eyebrow ring leaned in. "Want a push?" she asked.

"Yeah. Among other things," Claudia muttered. But she was grateful for the gesture, and in another minute the kids put their shoulders to the task and managed to bump the Cavalier onto the sidewalk, which was marginally more advantageous than the street. Claudia got out of the car, but before she could thank them they were already moving on. A minor hiccup on Miami Beach.

She glared at the car, then rooted in her handbag for her cell phone. It wasn't there. She closed her eyes against the headache that threatened, picturing the phone anchored to the recharge cradle on the kitchen counter.

Stupid, stupid, stupid.

All around, people went about their business, which mostly involved wandering in and out of bars. Claudia hardly noticed. She slumped against the traitorous vehicle, furious at the whim that had brought her onto one of the most desirable streets in the continental United States under one of the most undesirable circumstances she could imagine.

Traffic never slowed. She glared at the cars sweeping past and tried to push aside fatigue long enough to evaluate her options. Once, she opened the hood of the Cavalier and studied the engine. But of course she had no idea what she was looking at and slammed the hood down a few minutes later.

"Looks to me like you could use a lift."

The voice was familiar, but out of context. Claudia straightened and sought the source. And there stood Sydney.

·

CHAPTER · 13

REAMS HAD BEEN WRITTEN about identical twins. Scientists studied their gene structure. Psychologists studied their emotional makeup. Hollywood filmmakers and marketing moguls studied their moneymaking potential. And twins studied each other. They had their own annual conventions and festivals, one in Twinsburg, Ohio—so close to Cleveland that you'd think Claudia and Sydney would've attended at least once. They hadn't. The duplicate chromosomes they shared intrigued Sydney for six months, Claudia for about five minutes. It's not that they went out of their way to distinguish their individuality. It's just that neither much cared if on any given day their striking appearance made others do a double take. Nature versus nurture aside, they were sisters first, twins second. The bond was strong throughout their childhood and even after Sydney captured the drama of their parents' death. There were any number of ways to explain that. But the book—that coffee table book still in Claudia's closet—that was something else.

Claudia's mind flickered to the book at the same instant she registered Sydney's face on crowded Collins Avenue. Except that Sydney was thinner, sun-tanned, and wore her hair short, she could've been looking in a mirror.

"So?" said Sydney. "Do you want a lift or not?"

"What are you doing here?"

"You know, for a second there I thought you might actually be happy to see me. My vehicle works. Yours doesn't."

Sydney toted a heavy satchel with a multitude of bulging pockets, but she slung it easily from one shoulder to the next. She wore a sleeveless denim shirt that revealed triceps hard as iron. She'd always been the more athletic of the two.

"I'll ask you again. What are you doing here, Sydney?"

"Same old Claudia."

"That's right. Now why?"

"You're not good at returning calls."

"I'm not—so . . . what? You *followed* me?"

"You should check your rearview mirror now and then."

Claudia blew out a pocket of air, too spent to summon fury.

"It wasn't my original intent, okay? I was just pulling up to your house when you were leaving. I followed on a whim. When you—"

"You followed on a whim."

"You telling me you never acted on impulse?"

"I . . . never mind."

"When you went into that development, I almost bagged it because I couldn't get past the gates. I idled for a minute or two, thinking, being pissed off, but then you surprised me and came right back out. Picked you up again and . . . well, here we are."

"How resourceful."

"Expedient, Claudia. That's all. Apparently, you'd let my hair go gray before you'd ever call me back. Of course, I might've opted for that if I knew you were on a marathon."

A man in a red bow tie passed by, hawking flowers. He sized up Claudia and Sydney, then moved on to friendlier prospects.

"A quest," Claudia said tiredly. "Not a marathon."

"You mean the big hairy guy?"

Claudia looked up, surprised.

Sydney shrugged and pulled a camera from her satchel. "You were following his truck. It didn't dawn on me until we were exiting I-95. Then I couldn't figure out why it took me so long." She patted the camera. "Anyway, I got the guy on film. After your car died I took out a few pedestrians to get past you, and then I stayed with him. He didn't go much farther up Collins. Went into a beachside condo. I bailed then. What he is? Bad guy? Ex-lover?"

"So following me wasn't good enough. You had to play cop, too."

"Just trying to suck up a little, see if I can dent your armor."

Claudia didn't smile.

"Look, don't make more of this than is there. He seemed important to you, so I followed him. That's all. It's late. You want that lift or not?"

The whole night had turned into a Salvador Dali painting. Claudia met her sister's eyes. Sydney held them. Neither looked away, not even when someone called out, "Hey, look! Twins! You guys are twins, right?" Sydney offered a one-finger reply, but her eyes never wavered from her sister's face.

Claudia gave up. "I don't suppose you've got a cell phone."

"Why? So you can call a taxi?"

"No."

"In that case, I have one."

"Oh, man. You really are a—"

"I know."

Another second went by. "I'll need to use it," Claudia said levelly. "Then I need a bathroom. A cigarette. Aspirin. A tow truck." She shook her head. "And . . . yeah. A lift home."

"Good call."

"Like there's a choice involved."

"There are always choices."

"Something you'd know about."

"Something we both know about."

They got back to Indian Run before dawn, but not much before. On the way there, they made the polite noise of strangers, sharing an occasional cigarette and sipping from bottles of water, knowing that whatever needed to be said dare not be said until they were free of exhaustion. Sydney glossed over her reasons for being in Indian Run, saying only that she was working on a new coffee table book depicting small towns battling for survival. Indian Run qualified. Claudia didn't buy it, but she let the challenge die on her lips, and both of them lapsed into silence.

For miles, the only sound was the hum of tires on the road and the occasional swoosh of another vehicle passing them. There weren't many of those. Sydney drove like a fleeing felon, her red Jeep turned into a muscle car. Under other circumstances Claudia would've pulled her over. She said nothing, though, so consuming was her need to be home. When they finally arrived, she pointed her sister to Robin's vacant room, then set her alarm to go off in two hours and collapsed on her own unmade bed. She couldn't afford to be as tired as she was, but she couldn't shut down her mind long enough for sleep to claim her fully.

Images from her past fused with events of the week in a nocturnal fog, as if she were drugged. One minute, there would be Sydney's face at the age of 12; the next, Hemmer's body leaking blood on white tile. The kaleidoscope would turn. She'd see herself breathing in Robin's faint baby hair the first time she held her, the memory inexplicably dissolving into a vision of the cold interview notes she'd written at Jennifer Parrish's house the day before. She saw her first car, then the abandoned Cavalier; her mother shaping meat loaf, then the mayor's face, splotchy with anger.

Claudia kicked off her covers and vaulted out of bed. She showered, dressed, made coffee, and called for a patrol officer to pick her up. While she waited, she flipped through her dictionary for a definition of *crinkum-crankum*. Big surprise; it wasn't there. She paced idly, wishing it weren't too early to call Robin at camp. Once, she peeked in on Sydney. Her sister slept without moving. She watched for a minute, struck again by the sameness of their features, even these many years later. Then she quietly closed the bedroom door. On her way outside, she put a spare house key on the kitchen counter and scribbled a note: "Food in the fridge. Coffee in the pot. Follow me again and I'll kick your ass."

CHAPTER · 14

CLAUDIA DIDN'T THINK ANYTHING could blow the sand out of her eyes sufficiently enough to jolt her into wakefulness, but the sight of the chief's nephew pacing in the police station's multipurpose room did the job. It wasn't that she had forgotten he would be there. They'd made plans to meet the day before, and Booey set his watch by the U.S. Naval Observatory. Of course he would be there, and of course he wouldn't be late.

What she didn't expect was that he could possibly look any more dramatic than he ordinarily did. In his natural state, his hair was the color of a red hibiscus flower in glorious bloom under full sun. It announced him and defined him and permanently etched him into the memory bank of anyone who met him, and even if it didn't, the energy field that clung to him like a second skin did. The last time Claudia saw him, just over a month earlier, he'd hated all of that about himself. But the gangly manchild she now saw before her apparently had dispensed with those issues. In fact, he'd embraced what previously embarrassed him and even added his own little spin to it. His hair was still red enough to give off sparks, but now it sported an uneven streak of silver the shade of aluminum foil. Worse, though his hair had grown some in the last month, it hadn't grown enough to justify the ponytail he'd created from it. It stood from the back of his head like an abscess.

Claudia wondered why his new appearance surprised her. Booey had never subscribed to the theory of "less is more." His new look just offered more evidence. Still, she hoped he wouldn't ask what she thought, which of course he did the moment he spotted her.

"Lieutenant!" he said, his smile so broad that it shuffled the freckles on his face. He bounded over. "Long time no see. What do you think of my makeover?"

Roll call for the morning shift had just finished, but two uniformed officers lingered in the multipurpose room, facing away, making like they were busy. Booey's infatuation with Claudia had become legend. One of the officers snickered.

She took in the changeling before her. "It's . . . distinctive."

Booey beamed. "I knew you'd like it."

"I need some coffee."

"Partly it's about image, my new look. I've definitely decided to become a filmmaker. This could work for me, don't you think?"

"I don't know much about what goes into the movie business, Booey."

"It's a cutthroat industry."

"Ah."

He stayed in her shadow, chattering about coming to grips with his insecurities, giving her full credit for awakening his newfound sense of self. Claudia rued the day she'd rescued him from a tree. If she could, she'd put him back up one right now. But that was another story, and not one she cared to rehash—now or ever.

"Let's talk about computers, Booey," she said while she filled her coffee cup. Sergeant Peters had retrieved Hemmer's three PCs from the sheriff's office. They were crammed together on a long folding table that sagged under their weight. She led Booey toward them, briefing him on the broad elements of the Hemmer case. "I need to know what's in those computers; and if anything's been deleted, I need to know what. Is that doable?"

"It depends on a lot of things," he said, eyeing the computers one at a time.

Claudia knew slightly more than zip about how computers worked, and her brain numbed when anyone tried to enlighten her. But she tried to show interest when Booey launched into an animated monologue about the not-so-hidden nature of deleted files. Deleting a file didn't actually deep-six it from the computer hard drive. It only erased the information that pointed to the file's location.

"See, to a casual computer user, the file might *look* like it's gone," said Booey, "but really it's just invisible—the emperor without clothing." He carried on about contiguous sequences of bytes, directory hierarchies, and file attributes.

Claudia occasionally nodded, which Booey mistook for interest.

"Of course, how *effectively* files can be recovered," he continued, "depends on how much the hard drive had been overwritten since the files were trashed, or if a security program had been used to truly delete files.

Some of those programs are pretty sophisticated and they open up a whole new challenge."

Claudia nodded. *Snooze.*

"But the good news is, there are also programs specially made to recover deleted files, even if the hard drive has been overwritten multiple times. Now if—"

"Yeah, yeah. Booey? That's all great. Fascinating stuff." She tried to defuse her impatience when she saw his mouth turn down at the corners. "I . . . this business about contiguous bytes, for instance—"

"Sequences. Contiguous *sequences* of bytes," he clarified.

"Right. Anyway, that's something, uh . . . especially interesting, but right now, Booey? I have too much on my plate to pay proper attention. How about if I let you alone and you just do your magic. You can tell me how you did it later."

"*If* I can do it."

"You're Booey. Of course you can do it."

He blushed.

Claudia turned to leave, then paused. "Say, Booey, have you ever heard the word *crinkum-crankum*?"

"I've never heard anyone use it in an actual sentence."

"But you've heard it? You know what it means?"

"Sure. It's a noun. It means 'something full of twists and turns.'"

"Huh. It wasn't in my dictionary."

"It probably got squeezed out to make room for more contemporary words. See, there's a whole process for updating dictionaries and—"

"Thanks, Booey." She'd mull it over later. Once again she turned to leave. Once again she paused. Was that a hole in his earlobe? She asked him.

He colored again. "Normally I wear a small earring," he confided. "It's nothing ostentatious—ostentatious is definitely *not* me—but even so, I thought an earring might be a little over the top for a police station. Know what I mean?"

Claudia smiled. Yeah. She knew.

An hour dragged by, then another. While Booey hunched over Hemmer's computers, Claudia met with Moody and Carella. She glossed over her Miami Beach misadventure, grateful that neither man probed for details. The chief likely would, but he hadn't surfaced yet. Moody told her Suggs was out on a public relations mission, playing Officer Friendly to a bunch of 8-year-old kids at a day camp. They all smiled at the image, then got back to business. Claudia struggled not to yawn as she assigned new tasks and guzzled coffee.

Later, she plowed through paperwork and made phone calls. She learned that the Cavalier was on its way back, pulled by a tow truck like a dead fish behind a trawler. The car's engine was shot. Maybe it could be fixed, maybe not. Unfortunately, Indian Run's police department didn't have a motor pool, so she made arrangements to rent a clunker for short-term use. Someone could run her over to pick it up later.

Annoyed and dispirited over the inertia of the Hemmer case, Claudia wandered into the ladies' room. Inspiration could occasionally strike in the least likely places. It didn't, but a few minutes later when she emerged, something else did.

Contrary to all expectation, Gloria Addison walked into the station. She sashayed toward the front desk, her hips rolling beneath a skirt so short that it looked like an extension of the tube top she wore. Her clothes were too tight to rustle with movement, yet she was resonant with swishes and jangles from the bangles liberally draped from her wrists and ears. For the second time that morning Claudia came fully awake. So did the handful of officers writing reports. They smiled stupidly when Addison favored them with a hello, pretending that she hadn't spotted Claudia in her peripheral vision.

Claudia watched her play the game out, chatting up Sally, asking where she could find "that woman detective" who she'd heard had been trying to get in touch. When Sally pointed Claudia out, Addison slowly perambulated in her direction, stoking fantasies for each man she passed.

Claudia extended her hand. "Ms. Addison. I'm glad you stopped by." The woman's handshake was firm, but moist with a hint of nervousness. "You look recovered from last week's trauma."

Addison shrugged. "That was then," she said lazily. "This is now. I'm over it."

Right. Just another day on Mulberry Street.

"Well, good," said Claudia. "Glad to hear it. Can I get you some coffee?"

"No, thanks. I heard you were looking for me. There's been a burglary at Hemmer's place? I stopped by to tell you that I don't know anything about it."

"Let's talk in my office," said Claudia.

"Right here is fine. I can't stay long." Addison's eyes settled on Booey. She waved a pinkie, immediately turning him to stone. When she brought her hand down, she frowned at her fingernails. Fuchsia. "I have an appointment coming up."

"Manicure?"

Addison's eyes narrowed. "As a matter of fact, that's right. I need to leave in five minutes." She looked at Claudia's hands. "I'd be happy to give you a referral. My manicurist does wonders with challenging nails."

Claudia resisted an impulse to shove her hands into her pockets. Instead, she said she'd be grateful for a name. With luck, Addison's manicurist might be a gossip. The Hemmer case didn't even have much of that at the moment. A second later, the idea morphed into another wild whim.

"You know what?" she said to Addison. "Why don't I go with you? Maybe they could squeeze me in, too."

"You mean now? *Now* now?"

"Sure. You're in a hurry. We can talk there."

"I . . . my manicurist is always swamped. I'm sure you'd be wasting your time. And there's not much to talk about. I don't know anything about a break-in."

Claudia held her hands up. "My daughter's always after me to get my nails done. Let's give it a shot. You're on your way there, anyway, right?"

"Yes, but—"

"Good. Let me grab my purse. This could be fun."

"I need to make a call first."

"You can make it from your car. I'll bring my cell phone."

"My . . . you're going to ride *with* me? I thought you'd just follow."

"My car's in the shop," Claudia said gaily. "I've ordered a rental. Actually, maybe you can drop me at the rental place when we're done."

She watched the effervescence bleed out of Addison's demeanor, and wished there was a reason to shake hands again. She bet the woman's palms were slick as Crisco.

CHAPTER · 15

ADDISON DROVE an Alfa Romeo Spider with the top down. The Italian import could probably do a hundred miles an hour in under ten seconds, but Addison stayed within the speed limit, which was still plenty fast enough to blow Claudia's hair into the shape of an untended hedge. The car wasn't made for someone with her height or her wallet. She wondered how the woman afforded it.

Finally, Addison pulled into an upscale plaza and parked in front of a salon graced with palm trees and a fountain. "We're here," she said flatly. She hustled inside before Claudia could unfold her legs from the car.

The salon interior had a high ceiling and was decorated with chrome and expensive mirrors, making it appear larger than it looked from outside. You had to really like yourself to spend hours here, which Claudia imagined most customers did. The salon was more than about nails. It boasted every permutation of indulgence, from hairstyling to facials to massage, but if there were signs displaying prices, she didn't see them.

Addison was already at the front counter, tapping her nails impatiently while an officious woman behind the desk studied an appointment schedule on her computer screen. She looked up blandly. "I'm sorry, Ms. Addison. I don't have you down for anything today."

"Well, look again," Addison demanded.

Though the monitor was angled at a way so that Claudia could see Addison's name didn't appear, the woman feigned another careful study of it.

"I'm very sorry," she said. "Perhaps I can schedule you for this afternoon? I've had a cancellation for three."

"No! I had an appointment for eleven. I made it days ago. I'm not leaving until I get my nails done. You people get a lot of my money. A *lot* of it.

I should *not* have to tolerate this kind of screw-up."

"I understand, but—"

"But nothing. I want my nails done *now*." She cocked a thumb at Claudia. "I've brought a friend along for her nails, too. Is *this* the image you want to show prospective clients? That you can't even keep appointments straight for long-standing customers?"

People were staring. The woman studied her monitor once more. "You know, although I really don't have anyone available for manicures right now, I *do* have openings for a pedicure. Two, in fact. I can get both of you done instantly—and of course, yours would be on the house. A gesture for your inconvenience."

Addison immediately began to shake her head, but she stopped abruptly. A smile played at her lips. She looked at Claudia, then back at the woman. "That would be acceptable."

"Wait a minute," said Claudia. No *way* was she putting her feet in some stranger's hands. "I don't think—"

"It won't take any longer than if you got your nails done," said Addison. "Some other time."

"Why? You're here now. You *wanted* to come. Feet, hands . . . what's the difference?"

"Well, then!" said the desk woman, happy to serve as Addison's ally if it would deflect a scene. "I insist you try us. In fact, because we had a mix-up—and I *am* so very sorry about that—we'll give you an introductory special of thirty percent off our aromatherapy pedicure. It's a *very* good deal."

She beamed and Addison smirked, and Claudia recognized she was stuck. If she wanted to learn anything from Addison or about her, then she had no choice but to go toe to toe with the younger woman. At thirty percent off.

It took fifty minutes, each of which Claudia would remember long after the polish on her toenails wore off. Before they even got started, she had to forfeit her slacks and knee-highs for a silvery gown, but she couldn't abandon her jacket because it concealed her revolver. She felt ridiculous with her lanky legs and long feet poking out from beneath the gown; and air-conditioning aside, she was hot. The combination gave her new incentive to wipe the sneer off Addison's face.

They sat side by side in plush chairs, their feet in whirlpool foot spas filled with seaweed water and something sweet smelling. Their pedicurists were Asian women, who smiled and nodded and asked in broken English if they'd like coffee, spring water, or wine. Claudia said she'd take the water. Addison accepted a glass of Chablis.

"They're Vietnamese," Addison confided when the women went off to fetch their drinks. "The Vietnamese, the Taiwanese . . . they have a lock on the manicure business. They adore the work and they're suited for it."

Claudia bit back a response, because although Addison's bigotry came as no surprise, the flagrancy of it reinforced her impression that the woman's bag of tricks didn't include intelligence. That could be useful.

"You work?" she asked.

"Not at the moment. Is that important?"

Claudia smiled. "Not at the moment."

Their pedicurists returned. They handed the drinks to Claudia and Addison, along with expensive cocktail napkins embossed with the salon name. Claudia thanked them. Addison said nothing, immediately too busy with her wine to acknowledge their existence. She drained her glass and demanded another. When her pedicurist returned with it, she took one more swallow then relaxed into her chair. She waved both women off, explaining to Claudia that their feet had to soak for a while. "But of course, you knew that," she said.

"Every salon is different."

"Right. So look, Detective. What is it you really want? You're not here because you have all the time in the world or because you want to be my new best friend. We have nothing in common."

"Seems to me we have Hemmer in common."

"He's dead. We should be grateful. *You* should be grateful."

"How'd you know Bonolo had a knife strapped to his ankle?"

"What?" Addison didn't see the question coming. She took a pull on her wine. "I thought you wanted to talk about some supposed burglary."

"I'll get to it. The knife?"

"Oh, please. I was stuck to him like glue. Remember? It would've been hard not to know."

"You're clairvoyant?"

Addison rolled her eyes dramatically. "Honestly, I really don't follow you."

"Then I'll make it easier. Your mouths were taped. How'd you know about the knife? He couldn't have told you."

"I . . . well, Bill signaled to me."

"Ah. Body language."

"That's right." She thought for a moment. "And I could see the bulge under his pant leg."

"The knife didn't make a bulge. I would've seen that myself if it did."

"Oh, really? It sure looked like there were some things you didn't see at all."

The pedicurists moved into view and pulled their hands into synthetic gloves. The woman attending Claudia tapped her ankle. "Done with soak. Let feet dry now." She eased Claudia's feet from the spa one at a time, gently patted them with a white towel, applied a lotion that smelled faintly of almond, then tucked them into blue foam slippers. "There. I come back soon. You want more water?"

"No, thank you."

Addison's pedicurist had done the same, though of course she was instructed to fetch another glass of wine. "Sorry, madam," the woman said. "Two glass is limit. Salon rule. You want water?"

"No, I don't want water! I . . . forget it." She waved the woman away and muttered something about never bringing her business to the salon again. "You know, this feels almost like harassment," she said to Claudia.

"They're just doing their jobs."

"I don't mean them," she snapped. "I mean you. I voluntarily came into the station because I'd heard you were looking for me. Now all you want to do is talk about Hemmer. Hemmer this and Hemmer that. You have some kind of agenda here?"

Claudia smiled. "We can talk about the burglary. If that's what it was."

Addison twisted to look at her. "What are you talking about? What does 'if' mean?"

"All I want to know is whether you've seen anything unusual, or heard anything through the neighborhood grapevine. We're asking everyone the same thing."

"That's not how I hear it. It sounds to me like 'everyone' really means just the people Hemmer held a gun to."

"You're being paranoid. If you'd bothered to check with other neighbors, then you'd already know we're knocking on just about every door." Lies, lies, and more lies. But Addison backed off.

"I'm not into gossip," she said. "Whatever happened, I can't help. I hope you're enjoying the pedicure, but you didn't have to buddy up to me to pry that out of me."

They lapsed into silence. Addison fidgeted with her empty wine glass and sighed elaborately. Claudia felt another powerful wave of fatigue sweep over her. She tried to concentrate on the salon's piped-in music. Finally, the pedicurists returned.

"Feet dry now," Claudia's attendant announced. "Feet soft for next step." She put on fresh gloves and held up a pumice stone and yet another tube of cream. "You too tense. Lean back. Relax." Claudia complied. "Good. I work on feet." She examined the bottoms of Claudia's feet and muttered. "Feet much rough. You too much in shoes, I think. But no matter. For you, I go gentle. Enjoy."

A cartoon image of a trapdoor opening beneath her flashed invitingly through Claudia's mind. She could handle the boot maker's observations about her feet. And all right; true enough that she felt an absurd ping of pleasure when Tom Dixon zeroed in on them. This, though, this was something else; and anyway, what was the woman doing down there, because damn, it *hurt.* She stiffened and glanced down, but her pedicurist merely issued another instruction to relax.

Addison snickered. "No pain, no gain."

Claudia didn't flinch, but she angled around to face Addison.

"You're into pain, are you?"

"Not as much as I'm into gain. They go together."

"I take it you've had practice."

Addison laughed huskily. "Honey, every woman *better* practice. You might carry a gun, but it's still a man's world. I've learned how to move around in it, and the pain is *nothing* compared to the gain."

"Is that a strategy or a philosophy?" she asked.

"Both."

Claudia smiled inwardly, because there it was, the opening for which she'd been enduring the pedicure.

"No pain, no gain," she mused. "No wonder you gravitated to Bill Bonolo. I should've guessed as much."

"What?!"

"Joined at the hip. I can't believe I missed it."

"Are you insane? Me and—"

"All this time it was right in front of me. I missed the significance."

Addison's eyes blazed. "You don't know what you're talking about. Who's feeding you this crap?"

"Tell me—I mean, okay, I get the 'pain and gain' thing—but tell me, *Bonolo* is the best you can do? What's he do? Keep you in liquor? Buy you fancy clothes?"

"This is outrageous! It's outrageous and *you're* outrageous, and I don't have to put up with another word."

The pedicurists had stopped working to listen. Claudia ignored them and she ignored the tingling in her feet, her eyes locked on Addison.

"See," she said, "the thing I couldn't figure is how you, of all people, could be cowed by Bonolo into going along with that lame plan to drum Hemmer out of Willow Whisper. The other members of the property alterations committee have families to protect. Jobs to protect. But you? You don't have either. Fear alone wouldn't make you roll over. Not *you*. The thing about gain, though . . . wait." Claudia paused, feigning growing comprehension. "Wait, wait, wait. Is he the one who actually *keeps* you? He is, isn't he. *That's* how he manipulates you. *That's* how you gain. I never would've—"

"That pig does *not* 'keep' me and he does *not* manipulate me! *I'm* in control! I manipulate *him*."

"You're telling me the harassment campaign was *yours?* It was you calling the shots?"

"No! I . . . you're twisting things around."

Claudia pounced. "Then untwist them, because you can't have it both ways. Either Bonolo came up with the plan and he manipulated you into going along, or *you* concocted it and made *him* fall in line. Make a call, because unless there's some phantom mastermind yanking *both* your chains, it's got to be one or the other."

Addison blanched. She reached for her wine glass, then remembered it was empty. Finally she looked at Claudia. The flash was gone from her eyes, though, and when she said "Screw you," her voice trembled. She jerked her foot from the pedicurist's hands and twisted free of her chair.

The pedicurist looked alarmed. "Lady! Not done!"

Addison shot her a look. "Shut up." She slipped on the tile while fumbling for her sandals, but managed to struggle into them without falling. She didn't look at Claudia again. She didn't look at anyone. In seconds, she was gone.

CHAPTER · 16

ORDINARILY, the Indian Run bowling alley did a good business on Wednesday afternoons with daytime leagues, but the lanes had been closed all week for resurfacing and general maintenance, an annual ritual that made bowlers howl and threaten to take their business elsewhere. They never did. The next closest alley was fifteen miles away, and anyway, the grill and bar here stayed open. Diehard bowlers could still get a hot dog and tell lies about their scores.

Claudia walked into the bar and looked around, letting her eyes adjust to the dim lighting. An officer had run her from the salon to Earl's Rentals, where she chose a battered 1990 Imperial to ferry her around while the Cavalier was repaired—*if* it ever was. Remarkably, the Imperial's power windows operated flawlessly, though the air-conditioning didn't work and the interior smelled like something had died in it. Still, it had managed to get her to the bowling alley, which suggested it was better transportation than a backhoe or pogo stick, Earl's only other rentals at the moment.

Suggs sat with Moody, Carella, and Booey at a cluster of cocktail tables in the rear, where Sally had told her she would find them. The chief's back was to her, but Booey spotted her instantly and gave a spirited wave. He sprang up and shuffled chairs, making room for her. Suggs shared none of his nephew's enthusiasm. He didn't look at her until she sat down. She braced for his wrath, but all he said was that they'd already finished eating and if she was hungry, she should go ahead and order.

She looked at him, wary. His expression was unreadable, and his tone seemed artificially modulated. Was she imagining that, or was something up? Hungry as she was, she took a pass on ordering.

Suggs shrugged. "Suit yourself, but today's special is a meat loaf sandwich good enough to make the day worth rising for."

"Maybe later," said Claudia.

"All right. You're missin' out on a good deal, though. Fries come free with it."

Claudia glanced around the table, looking for a clue to the chief's uncharacteristic behavior. Booey lived in a world oblivious to nuance; he beamed at her. Carella and Moody kept their eyes down, studying their discarded napkins and empty plates.

"If you're not gonna eat, then you might as well get yourself some coffee," Suggs said next. "We're gonna be here a while."

Something was definitely up. Whatever it was, the chief clearly wouldn't be rushed. Claudia nodded and went to the snack bar. She got a cup of coffee and ordered the meat loaf sandwich. When she returned, it didn't look like anyone had so much as twitched.

Suggs fooled with the wedding band on his finger, then sighed. "Everybody's restless to compare notes on where we are with the Hemmer case. My original idea was to do that over lunch, and then catch you up if you surfaced before we were done. But just before I walked out the door to come over here, I got hung up on a phone call and it changes everything. I told the fellas to go on over and save me a seat. We've been doin' nothin' but chitchat since I joined them. That's because the call involves you and overrides everythin' else." He paused. "I need to tell you about it face to face, but I kept the others here because it impacts them, too."

Claudia took a sip of coffee, trying to steady herself.

"The call was from the mayor. I couldn't stay out of his line of fire anymore." Suggs looked up grimly. "There's no nice way to say this, so I'll put it to you straight. What Lane said . . . he ordered me to. . . ." The chief shook his head. "Aw, hell, I'm sorry, Claudia, but he told me to terminate you the minute you got back to your desk, and it's for serious."

Everybody gasped, but nobody moved. Claudia could feel them watching her, waiting for a reaction. She didn't know what to say, what to think, how to react. Her pulse thundered in her ears; she couldn't get past the idea that Suggs had called her by her first name. He *never* did that.

"He threatened all of this before—you know, right after you got in his face at his birthday party. I kissed ass and it passed, or I thought it did, but that's exactly the reason he gave me. Insubordination. He said it's all about a 'general attitude' you got. Called you unprofessional. Called you a loose cannon. Said you were burnt out, past your prime. And that was the nicest he got."

"That's bullshit," Carella hissed.

"I know, I know," Suggs said quietly. "Only now Lane says he's gettin' complaints from private citizens. Says he can't turn a blind eye to everybody else just to buff our egos."

Moody stroked his mustache. "What's the chance he'll rethink his position? He's clearly overreacting and—"

"Hell, yeah, he's overreacting!" Suggs said. "He's an excitable little prick with big ambitions. He takes anything negative about the town personally because he's petrified it'll tarnish his image and get in the way of his political goals. You think he's keen on growth here because he believes his own crap about bringing jobs and commerce to Indian Run? Uh-uh. That's just a convenient way to get attention so he can move on to something bigger—and never mind what he leaves behind."

The chief's eyes darkened. He was passionate about two things: fishing and "leaving Florida the hell alone." Lane didn't fish, and he didn't leave Florida alone. There was nothing in him for Suggs to like. There was much for him to hate.

"When you got a guy like Lane," he continued, "you don't need a crystal ball to see your future in gutted farms, crowded schools, congested roads—Bob's Barricades no matter where you turn. You know how many trees he knocked down to let Willow Whisper build here? A bedroom community like that is his biggest wet dream. You watch. There'll be more."

Booey fidgeted with his earlobe, as if seeking the earring he ordinarily wore. "Uncle Mac, there's *got* to be some way you can fix this."

"You think I didn't try?" Suggs's voice caught in his throat. "I said I was committed to seein' the Hemmer case through, and. . . ." He rubbed his forehead. "Truth is, I'm out of my element with this. Lane had a play I didn't see comin'. He said if I don't go along I'm out of a job, too. I could live with that—I told you all that I could—but when I put it direct to Lane, he one-upped me. He said, fine, go. But what gave him the trump card? He said with me and Hershey both gone, it would free him up entirely to gut the whole department and sign over services to the sheriff's office. He said they already do half our job anyway, and—"

"That's not true," said Moody.

"I know, I know, but Lane said he's got the support to totally disband us, and do it fast. I don't know if that's true, but I can't risk the entire department for two of us. I got people dependin' on me for their livelihoods. Hell, I got a whole *town* to watch out for." He paused when the grill cook slid a plate in front of Claudia.

"Here you go," said the cook. "On a scale of one to ten, our meat loaf is an eleven." His grin faded when no one responded. "What's with you guys? Somebody die?"

Suggs impatiently waved him off. When the cook was out of earshot the chief said, "I didn't think things would come to this, but it's where I have to draw the line. I'm out of options."

A gloomy silence descended. Except for an old man nursing a beer, and a middle-aged couple lingering over lunch, the bar had emptied. The only sound was the whir of machinery on the lanes.

Carella leaned back in his chair. He folded his arms across his chest. "I don't see how Lane can get away with this. It's outrageous."

"What he told me," said Suggs, "is that I serve at his pleasure, and he is not pleased. He said if I don't like it I can always run against him when his term expires next March."

And then they were all talking at once, making their owns threats, talking about mass resignation, looking for ways to get back. Suggs half-heartedly shushed them once—the middle-aged couple was turning to check out the commotion—but he didn't tell them to stop, nor could they. One of their own had been wounded.

Claudia sat back and half listened. The initial jolt had felt seismic, but when it passed she felt a calm settle in and, with it, a surge of appetite that surprised her. She loved that Suggs had used her first name. She loved that the mayor was as short on smarts as he was in stature. Together, those factors were inducement enough to pull on the thread Addison had given her, because in the end, getting canned was leverage. The meat loaf sandwich looked good, and the fries were hot and crispy. She asked Suggs to pass the ketchup.

Everyone had just about forgotten she was there, but they shut up now.

"Claudia?" the chief said, "you all right?"

Again! He'd used her first name again!

"I'm fine, but I want to eat before this gets cold."

He handed her the bottle.

"Thanks." She shook some ketchup onto her plate and dipped a fry. "Not exactly a power lunch, but it'll do."

"Did you hear anything I said?"

She swallowed. "Of course I did, and my answer is no."

"Your answer is 'no'? What do you mean?"

"I'm saying, no, I won't be fired."

Suggs pushed a hand through his hair. "Look, I know this is tough, but it's real. I'm up against a wall, and—"

"Nor will I resign, voluntarily or otherwise." She bit into the sandwich. "The cook's right. This is good. I'd give it a twelve, easy."

"You're in shock."

Claudia held up a finger until she finished chewing, then dabbed her mouth with a napkin. "Number one—and this is a technicality—but number one, I haven't been back to my desk yet."

"Which means Uncle Mac hasn't officially seen you yet!" said Booey. "He can't—"

"Number two, a question, Chief. How many officers have you fired since I've been here?"

"Say what?"

"Humor me."

"I . . . well, let's see. I fired Lester Fry when he started poundin' on a suspect right under my nose. That was—"

"You backed me up, but you didn't fire him. I did."

"Oh, right."

"Who else?"

"Well, this was a couple years before your time here, but I once let a fella go when I caught him foolin' with a woman who wasn't his wife. He was puttin' it to her right there in his patrol car. I caught him myself."

"Anyone else?"

"I'd have to look way back into my records. I'm not big on lettin' people go. Mostly I try to . . . where's this headed, Hershey?"

Claudia smiled. He was back to *Hershey*. "So you've never fired a female officer before?"

"Hell, up until you, I never *had* a female officer to fire."

"So I'd be the first."

"Yeah, but—"

"And the only one."

Moody laughed out loud. "It's beautiful."

"The only one to be fired," Claudia continued, "*and* in front of other people. That can't be policy."

Suggs sat upright. "Are you takin' this where I think you're takin' it?"

"I don't know all the governing bodies, but—"

"I do," Moody said swiftly. "It's been a while since law school, but a few of them stick with me, like the Equal Opportunity Commission, the U.S. Department of Labor, the National Labor Relations Board, the—"

"I get it, Moody, I get it," said Suggs.

"And that's just sex discrimination." Moody ticked off possibilities on a finger. "Firing her in front of us—and look, you got Booey here; he's just a private citizen—well, that raises the whole ugly specter of pain and suffering."

"Damage to reputation," Carella added. "There's another."

Claudia took another bite of her sandwich. Damn, but Moody was good.

Suggs abruptly stood. He stretched his neck a few times, then began pacing. "Oh, shit, oh shit, oh shit," he muttered. The middle-aged couple had left, but the beer drinker watched openly. Suggs scowled at him. "What're you lookin' at?" he demanded. The man wrapped a soggy napkin around his glass and hurried away. Suggs turned to Claudia. "You'd do this? You'd file some kinda action?"

She popped the last of the French fries into her mouth. "It'll never get that far. The threat will give the mayor pause. While he's brooding over the impact on his career that a public dogfight would bring, we'll be peeling back another layer on the Hemmer case."

Suggs regarded her doubtfully. "I don't know, Hershey. There's a lot to risk. How can you be so sure?"

Her coffee was cold. She swallowed the rest of it, anyway. "Because I realized today that we've been asking the wrong questions. This whole thing isn't about what anyone wanted. It's about what someone *didn't* want."

Suggs grunted. "Someone's blowin' smoke at us?"

"It's starting to look that way to me."

"I don't suppose you'd care to share your theory with us?"

"Only if I'm not fired."

The chief took his seat again. A half smile creased his lips. "You think I'd do that to my only female officer? In front of people? Especially when I can't even find her at her desk?"

Claudia returned the half smile. They weren't out of business yet.

CHAPTER · 17

FOR ANOTHER HOUR AND A HALF, they hammered at the Hemmer case. They wanted what detectives always want—irrefutable, in-your-face evidence that prosecutors could turn into a slam-dunk conviction impossible to overturn on appeal. Barring that, motive would be nice. On a good day, with a brilliant prosecutor and the right jury, motive could make for a circumstantial case when all else failed.

Suggs furiously chewed on ice from his beverage glass while they took turns laying out what they'd learned. Booey went first, too eager to wait; and anyway, no one wanted him to. He wasn't a police officer. He was a civilian, and not yet even 19. The less he knew of the case, the better.

"Mr. Hemmer's computers?" he said. "Documents were deleted from two out of three of them late Sunday."

"Damn," said Suggs. "Two days after Hemmer was killed."

Claudia nodded, unsurprised.

"The third, the laptop, nothing was on it. Mr. Hemmer bought it through one of those online auctions. He just got it a week ago. It didn't look like he'd loaded anything on it yet. But the desktop computers— one of them had his life on it. His work records. Databases. Spreadsheets. E-mail, including records of the laptop purchase. From what I can tell, he was using the other desktop computer strictly to fine-tune the coding on a software program he apparently developed himself. Based on some of the work records on his first PC, I'm pretty sure he was implementing the program on a freelance basis at some local businesses."

"Wait a minute," said Moody. "How do you know all this if the files were deleted?"

Booey lit up, thrilled at the opportunity for geek speak. His knee thrummed against the table while he described the password protection

Hemmer had on both PCs, then the process of ferreting out deleted files.

"I lost almost an hour breaking his log-in password," Booey said. He gave a small shake of his head, apparently peeved with himself for taking so long. "Mr. Hemmer used the last four digits of his phone number, his daughter's initials, and then transposed the first two digits of his home address. That's not as sophisticated as he'd have on a network computer in a big corporation, but for home use it's impressive."

"So whoever broke into his computers must've known the password or risked a lot of time to figure it out," said Suggs.

"Maybe, but more likely is that Mr. Hemmer's computers were in a sleep mode when they were accessed. The monitor screens would look like they were off and the computers would be so powered down that you might not even hear their fans. Touch a key, though, and they'd wake right up. Does anyone know if Mr. Hemmer shut down before he, you know . . . took hostages?"

No one could say with certainty. Police officers made a cursory check of the upstairs after the house had been secured, but there would have been little reason to dwell there. The horror had been confined to Hemmer's family room.

"Well, then, see? You almost *have* to conclude that the computers were in sleep," Booey said confidently. He tapped the table with a narrow finger. "I say that because whoever it was? The person obviously wasn't computer savvy enough to do more than delete files directly to the trash bin—which doesn't make them truly deleted—and that's even though Mr. Hemmer had a good scouring program right on his machines, and in plain sight!"

Booey looked around the table to see if anyone else had shared his epiphany. Rewarded with blank expressions, he sighed. "Maybe I didn't explain it well. But look, the person didn't recognize the scouring program for what it was! *The person didn't understand how to kill files!* Someone too inexperienced to grasp that probably wouldn't be knowledgeable enough to pick apart a fairly sophisticated password. Whoever it was? He got in without having to break a password, dumped files, and then shut down."

Carella didn't have Booey's computer expertise, but he was no slacker. He grinned. "Hard to argue the logic, and if Booey's thinking is on target, then it's good news for us. We're dealing with someone more desperate than smart."

"Yeah, but not altogether stupid, either," said Moody. "Presumably he knew enough to take any Zip disks or floppies Hemmer had. None turned up in his office, right, Lieutenant?"

"Not a one," said Claudia, "and I can't believe a meticulous man like Hemmer wouldn't have backed up at least some of his files."

"Oh, he did," said Booey.

He told them Hemmer had a backup program installed on both desktop computers. With more time, he could check the program log and see when it last ran, which would indicate whether Hemmer had shut down his machines prior to taking hostages, or had simply let them idle into sleep.

Suggs tapped the last of his ice into his mouth. "That's nice, son, but what we really want to know is *what* Hemmer had on his computers that someone was so damned keen to get rid of." He crunched and swallowed. "Did you get back what got dumped?"

Booey glowed. He did. He got it all. The files, hundreds of them, had been discarded, but not overwritten. He could queue them in a printer back at the police station and make hard copies of everything. Most of the file names suggested that the bulk of Hemmer's documents had nothing to do with Willow Whisper. But there was one, said Booey, one that might interest the lieutenant. He paused dramatically.

Claudia raised an eyebrow. "So? What leaped out?"

"Ready?"

"Don't wait for a drum roll."

"Sorry." He took a breath. "Crinkum-crankum! Mr. Hemmer had a file with that name on it."

They all leaned forward, so close they could feel each other's breath.

"Fat document?" asked Claudia. "Skinny document? What?"

"Um, neither, actually." Booey shrugged apologetically. "I mean, the document's there—he generated it a week before the hostage thing—but there wasn't a single word on it. He must've started writing something, did a save, but then erased the text before he quit the program. It could be he wasn't satisfied with what he'd written, but planned to come back to it later. Haven't you ever done that?" Booey paused. "No? I've done it. Sometimes you get stuck with your prose. Openings are especially tricky, and—"

Suggs cut him off with a look, then said, "So we got Hemmer's work files and a blank document he named 'crinkum-crankum.' That about right, Boo?"

"Yes, sir."

"And you can't tell what Hemmer mighta written before he erased the crinkum-crankum file?"

"No, sir. He erased his own text before he stored the file, so when the file was deleted after his death, it only showed what he had saved—which was nothing. See, it's different than if you have—"

"Never mind, Booey. You're making my brain hurt." The chief glanced at Claudia. "It'd be nice if *you'd* call me 'sir' every now and then," he muttered.

She ignored him. "So we're nowhere with that. Mitch, what about Kitner? He was going to drop off a written statement. Did he come by when I was out?"

Moody shook his head. "No, but it's possible he's been to the station while we've been here." He checked his watch. "The day's not over."

Claudia wished the day *were* over; her eyes watered from suppressing yawns. She nodded, though, and tried to stay on track when Booey offered a few more observations that reinforced his earlier conclusions. When he lapsed into techno-speak again, she looked pleadingly at Suggs, and a moment later he cut his nephew off. He told him to return to the station, back up Hemmer's documents, and leave the machines on when he left. Booey had made his contribution. He didn't need to know anything more about the investigation than he already did.

"Carella here can take a gander at the documents and figure which ones need to be printed out," Suggs said. "But you did good here, Boo. I'm proud you're kin."

Booey blushed and nearly knocked over the table as he stood. He waved and said his good-byes, then headed off, bobbing with every step. From the back, his ponytail looked like a spent firecracker.

"So much for crinkum-crankum," Suggs said. Then he stood. "Come on. Let's take a break. I need to stretch my legs and check in with Sergeant Peters, make sure that fart of a mayor hasn't already bulldozed the police station."

When they reassembled—Claudia with a tall iced tea and a candy bar from the vending machine—Moody and Carella pulled out notebooks and laid out what they'd learned in background checks on Bonolo and Addison. The process of gathering information could be numbing, and their recitation was delivered in monotones that reflected hours of plowing through official databases and trying to make nice with surly records clerks. Neither Bonolo nor Addison had police records or fingerprints on file. Good guys usually didn't. But no one believed Bonolo or Addison were good guys, which meant they'd either been incredibly lucky in not getting nailed for something, or the right databases simply hadn't been found yet.

"We're hitting a stone wall, especially with Bonolo," said Carella. He'd thrown water on his face during their break, and the hair around his ears was still damp. "We've been everywhere federal—AFIS, NCIC, ATF, Customs—you name it, we've been there. We're still wading through state and local agencies, but that could take a lifetime. We don't know where to isolate our searches, and anyway, half the places we're checking don't have but the last five years of information on computer databases. Imagine how thrilled clerks are to dig through archived paper files. I ran into one who didn't even know where they were stored."

"Not to mention that we don't have probable cause on anything," said Moody. "I don't even want to think about what could come back on us if we raise red flags with the wrong person."

Claudia understood. Most people assumed police could get information from any government office anywhere, at any time, merely by placing a phone call. But some records couldn't be accessed without a court order, which required justification that no one could provide—at least not yet.

"Bonolo's social security number was issued in New York," Moody said. "We're still working it, but it looks valid."

"Tread lightly," Suggs growled. "All we need next is some kinda privacy do-gooder to get riled. Bonolo would love it, and so would the mayor."

With the lunch hour long gone and the dinner hour not yet started, the bowling alley had been all but abandoned. Even the resurfacing machinery on the lanes sat silent now.

"What about interviews at Willow Whisper?" Claudia asked. "How'd Bonolo manage to get himself on the homeowners board, anyway? And why would he want to be on it?"

"Glad you asked." Carella grinned. "The same thing bugged me, so I talked to the treasurer and the secretary of the homeowners association. Then I read through the Florida law until my eyes watered. You want the long or the short of it?"

"The short."

"Okay. Bonolo's on the board because the developer of Willow Whisper put him there."

"Say again?"

"Basically, a developer can elect at least one member of the board as long as he still holds a minimum of five percent of the parcels for sale in the community." Carella consulted his notes. "In other words, the developer doesn't have to turn over the whole association to the homeowners until he's pretty much out of it. That's how Florida law reads, and guess what? Willow Whisper is only seventy percent complete."

Suggs groaned. "Tell me that's not true."

But it was. Carella explained that the builder, Hercules Homes, began Willow Whisper as a three-phase community. The first two phases, both complete, held two hundred forty homes. Ground had yet to be broken for the third phase, which would include seventy-two more houses and a community park.

"That wooded area behind Hemmer's house? It fronts onto eighteen houses in the phase-two section of Willow Whisper. It creeps back quite a ways behind the houses, then sort of parallels Old Moogen Road."

Claudia tried to picture it. Old Moogen Road was a long and lightly traveled two-lane road with woods on both sides. It fed a network of dirt roads that led to farms and ranches. She couldn't recall the last time she'd driven it, but she did remember the ruts in it were deep enough to rattle her teeth.

"Apparently," Carella continued, "the delay in moving forward had to do with laying in more infrastructure—plumbing, electricity, that sort of thing—and for a while there was a flap over whether access from Old Moogen into Willow Whisper would be private or public. That's all been straightened out. Hercules should break ground before the year is up."

"More trees comin' down and more people comin' in," Suggs muttered. "Just what we need."

"Anything sleazy about Hercules?" Claudia asked.

"That'd make it convenient, but no," said Carella. "The state shows Hercules as a privately held subsidiary of LH Builders in Coral Gables. LH does commercial buildings. Hercules is its residential arm. They're not publicly traded, so there isn't a hell of a lot of information to be had."

"All right. Who's on site for Hercules?"

"Guy by the name of Boyd Manning," said Carella. "He's been the prince of construction here since day one."

Claudia fingered her candy bar wrapper, disappointed to see there was nothing left. Manning's name rang a bell, but she couldn't place it. "Anybody know what the connection is between Bonolo and this Manning?" she asked.

"Uh-uh," said Carella. "And nobody much cares. The homeowners association vice-president is on vacation in Europe, and all I got from the secretary and treasurer was a lot of whining about how no one participates in the HOA. The secretary said they're lucky if fifteen people show up for meetings, which are held monthly."

"All right," she said. "One more angle for us to check. What's the story on Addison?"

"We got a little luckier with her," said Moody.

Carella nodded. "She's been more visible, mostly because once upon a time she obviously had no clue how to handle money."

He told her that Addison's house, one of Willow Whisper's original model homes complete with decorator upgrades, had been bought outright in cash. So, too, had the Alfa Romeo Spider. But before she'd ever surfaced in Indian Run, her only known earnings came from office jobs provided through temp agencies in the Miami area. Twice she had maxed out on credit cards, and once she got evicted from an apartment for being three months behind on rent. Somehow, though, she paid off her debts in full shortly before moving to Indian Run.

"We're talking about someone born and raised in Davie who barely graduated from high school," Carella said. "Davie's in Broward County, maybe an hour north of Miami. Miami's not very far as the crow flies, but compared to Davie it probably seemed downright exotic. She moved to Miami when she was 19 and started with the temp agencies right off. The last agency she worked for is going to fax me a list of the jobs they put her on. Maybe it'll hint at who gave her the glass slipper that turned her life into a Cinderella story. It sure wasn't a husband; our gal Gloria is 25 and she's never been married."

Our gal Gloria. Claudia pursed her lips, thinking. Lean muscles aside, Addison hadn't worn her years all that well. She looked like she was in her mid-thirties.

"Hershey," said Suggs, "I been waitin' a good chunk of time to hear about how you got your feet made nice, 'cause I suspect it has to do with whatever theory you're about to lay out. I imagine—"

"You *know* about the pedicure?"

"I know you hitched a ride with an officer from that salon to Earl's Rentals. The officer has a pretty big mouth, and Earl has an even bigger mouth. You really think it takes anything more'n that for word to travel in Indian Run?"

She shook her head. She supposed not.

"Anyway," said Suggs, "I'm thinkin' I'll like the feet story best and the theory not at all, but either way, don't keep me in suspense anymore. Spell it out for all of us."

"You have color on your toes?" said Carella. Moody chuckled.

Claudia shut them up with a look, then described Addison's unexpected arrival at the police station and their subsequent conversation at the salon.

"So this was like interrogation by pedicure?" Carella said. He hooted at his own joke. Suggs and Moody laughed with him.

"All right, all right," said Claudia, but she smiled slightly. "Look, a couple interesting things came out of it. For instance, Addison swore she wasn't being manipulated by Bonolo. And she got really hot at the suggestion that she was having a relationship with him, but for all her protests she sure knew he wore a concealed knife at his ankle. My thinking? If they weren't lovers, then they were teammates. And if they were teammates, then they had a coach."

She sat back, watching them take in the idea. Suggs picked at a scab on his arm, then looked up. "*Conspiracy* is an ugly word, Hershey, but it sounds like that's where you're headed."

"Try this out for size," she said. "Addison registered an unmistakable jolt when I said that if the two of them weren't manipulating each other, then maybe a third party was controlling both of them. I was only being facetious, but she shut up instantly. In fact, she bolted from the salon so fast, it was like watching someone being shot out of a cannon."

"Oh, man, Hershey. We don't need this."

"But it might be what we've got."

Carella held up a straw wrapper that he'd tied into knots. "Crinkum-crankum. 'Full of twists and turns.'"

They left it at that.

CHAPTER · 18

THANKFULLY, Sydney was out when Claudia finally dragged home at four o'clock. She'd been awake for thirty-three hours straight, and though she couldn't afford to sleep, she couldn't afford not to. The mayor's claim that she was too worn out to operate effectively wasn't true when he made it. It was now. She knew it. She knew he dared not find out.

Sydney had left a note: "You make lousy coffee. I drank it anyway. See you tonight." Claudia crumpled it and threw it away, then checked her answering machine for messages. Nothing. She set the air-conditioner to a lower temperature, fed Robin's cat, took a fast shower, then systematically closed any curtains her sister had opened. With luck, she could simulate nighttime well enough to sleep. But her yearning for bed paled beside her longing to connect with her daughter. She dialed Robin's camp and waited endlessly for a counselor to fetch her. Finally the phone clattered on the other end.

"Hey, Mom, what's up?" Robin asked, her voice breathless. "We're just about to line up for dinner. I'm supposed to stay with my group."

"Nothing's up, honey. I just wanted to say hi."

"Mom, nobody's parents check in." Robin's sigh filtered across the phone lines. "We're practically adults, you know."

Practically adults? No. Not even close. Claudia resisted saying anything, though. Everything was negotiation with a 14-year-old, and words were triggers.

"I'm not checking in," she said. "I miss you, that's all. Are you having a good time?" She waited. "Robin? You still there?"

"It's . . . okay. They keep us busy here."

Claudia sensed the unspoken words. "You know, it's all right to enjoy yourself, hon. It's not a betrayal. I got to know Sandi a little. I'm pretty sure she would want you to have fun."

"I guess. She more or less said the same thing."

"She called?"

"Last night. She wanted to thank me for the Pooh bear. I guess her grandparents are getting ready to take her back to Maine."

"Oh. I was under the impression they'd be around a little longer."

"Sandi thought so, too. But someone's already offered to buy the house, so that's like this big relief."

Claudia assumed Robin had misunderstood her friend. Once tainted with violence, even the best houses in the best neighborhoods sat on the market forever. But she was glad to hear that Sandi got in touch. Maybe the girl was trying to find a way to reconnect with a gentler world.

"We didn't talk long," Robin continued, "but she told me about the boots her dad got made for her. I probably ought to get some too, Mom. I'm the only person here wearing sneakers on a horse."

Claudia tried not to think about the balance in her checkbook. "So you like riding, huh?"

"It's better than great, and the riding instructor here said I'm a natural. When I get back, maybe we can go riding together. I know a place where we can rent horses and go out on a trail."

We? Not "me and a friend." Not "you drive me there and I ride." We! Together!

They talked for a few minutes more, then said their good-byes and hung up. Claudia savored their conversation over a half glass of wine, then crawled into bed and was asleep instantly.

She didn't see him coming. In the convoluted world of her dream, he was twice her height and weight, and in the half second it took to understand that he would kill her, he was on her, throwing her down with no more effort than he might have used to flip a playing card. She felt the breath knocked out of her and lay paralyzed, watching his knife move toward her face. He laughed and teased her with the blade, waving it back and forth in front of her eyes. But he took too long, played too casually; and in the moment before she expected to die, she felt a whisper of strength return. The next time he moved in with the knife, her arm shot out and connected. She heard him howl; his weight moved off her.

"Hey! Get a grip! Claudia!"

She flailed again, her heart thudding.

"Ow! Stop! It's me, it's *me*. Wake up."

Claudia blinked, coming awake. Sydney stood a foot away, massaging the side of her face. "You startled me," Claudia said.

"No shit." Sydney winced. "All I did was nudge your shoulder. You *slugged* me. I'm going to have a freaking black eye."

"Sydney, I . . . put some ice on it."

"Gee. Thanks for your concern. What kind of demons prowl your subconscious, anyway?"

Claudia swung her legs off the bed and stood. She rubbed crust from her eyes. "You really should put some ice on that." She slipped her glasses on. "What time is it?"

"Nine o'clock. You've been asleep forever."

Claudia did a groggy calculation. "Five hours isn't forever."

"Nine o'clock in the *morning.*"

She glanced at the clock on her night stand. "Great. I can't believe I forgot to set my alarm. I need to get going."

"No, you don't. Your boss said he didn't want to see you in the office until noon."

"You talked to Suggs?"

"He called about an hour ago. At first he thought I was you."

"And of course you let him."

Sydney smiled. "He was off and running before I got past 'hello.' Colorful kind of guy. He was surprised to hear you were still asleep, but pleased, I think. He was even more surprised to realize you have a sister."

Claudia pushed past her and into the bathroom. Sydney called through the door that Suggs also relayed not much had developed—nothing of urgency, anyway. Then she said she'd make fresh coffee.

Claudia sat on the toilet and glared at her feet. They looked ridiculous, the nails on one foot polished, the nails on the other plain. But she'd run out of time at the salon to get both completed and owned no polish remover, so she was stuck with them for the time being. She put them out of her mind, brushed her teeth, took a long shower, then washed her hair and spent a few quality minutes with a blow dryer.

When she made her way into the kitchen twenty minutes later, her sister was at the counter, perched on a stool. Sydney held a bag of ice against her face while reading the paper. Claudia's irritation slid into guilt.

"How's your eye?" she asked quietly.

Sydney turned her face so Claudia could see. A bruise was forming to the side of her left eye. "If you were trying to kick my ass, you missed."

"I really am sorry, Syd."

"Forget it." She smiled and faked a tough-guy voice. "And anyway, you should see the other guy."

Claudia poured coffee and sat. She thought about calling Suggs back, but if he'd really wanted to talk to her he would've hauled her out of bed himself if necessary. And anyway, he would ask about Sydney. She wasn't up to that conversation yet—not with Suggs, not with Sydney herself.

The cat leaped onto the countertop, jolting Claudia from her thoughts. Boo had taken to doing that lately, and she'd taken to letting him, or at least not actively discouraging him unless there was company in the house. Sydney felt more like company than kin; Claudia pushed the cat off. He looked at her balefully, just enough to stir her from her stool and dump food in his bowl. With a cat, it was easy to make peace.

"So when does Robin get home from camp?" Sydney asked. "It's been a long time since I've seen her."

"She's got a little over a week to go. You'll be long gone."

"What makes you so sure?"

"Indian Run's not all that big, Sydney. If you're here to shoot small-town life, you can catch the highlights in an afternoon."

"Maybe I'm here for more than that," she said softly.

The cat ate steadily from his bowl. Claudia reached down and scratched his back. His hind end rose automatically, and he purred. She watched silently for a moment, then straightened and looked at her twin.

"I've got a lot of work to do, Sydney. Let's just leave things alone for now."

Sydney cocked her head. "Coming from you, 'for now' sounds like a concession. So fine. We'll keep it simple. In fact, I've got two things for you that have nothing to do with what's between us." She slid off the stool. "They're in one of my bags. Give me a second."

Claudia sat back down and sipped at her coffee. She could have asked Sydney to leave. She'd had an opening and knew she didn't want her to stay. But maybe she didn't want her to leave, either. It was an unsettling thought, but her sister was back before there was time to pursue it.

"Here." Sidney tossed a manila package on the counter and, on top of that, two tickets paper clipped together. She reclaimed her stool. "Take a look."

Claudia picked up the tickets. "Dog Day Summer Bluegrass Festival?"

"Yep. Saturday afternoon, right here in town. It's an annual—"

"Yeah, I know what it is, Sydney."

Every year Indian Run flaunted the satanic summer heat by embracing it with a festival. Those who attended could expect guitar and banjo music, clogging, barbecued ribs, corn on a stick, sunburn, and heatstroke. The grass, of course, was not blue, nor was it even green. The August sun scorched everything in its path, and not even the most advanced sprinkler systems could compete. No one cared. The whole town turned out for the event.

"Don't automatically say no," said Sydney. "I'll be there anyway because it's a perfect opportunity for some great shots. I hope you'll come. You might enjoy it."

"I'm working a case."

"Twenty-four hours a day? Come on. Just think about it."

Claudia set the tickets aside and opened the package. There were three eight-by-ten black-and-white photos inside. The first she pulled out showed a man stepping off an elevator. His tie was loosened, and he appeared to be looking at his watch. He clutched a briefcase in his hand. The picture wasn't Sydney's best work. The image showed camera shake, and the top of the man's head was cut off. But despite the blur, Claudia could see that the man had a lean build, even though his salt-and-pepper hair suggested he was on the far side of middle-aged. She studied the picture more closely, then finally looked up.

"Am I supposed to know him?" she asked.

Sydney gestured at the other picture. "He goes with that."

The second photo was of a document. It showed a list of some sort, with handwritten dates, times, and names on lined rows. It, too, was grainy. Claudia was about to ask what she was examining, when one name leaped out: Bonolo. She put the photo down as if she'd been burned.

"It's the visitor log from the condo in Miami Beach, the one where Bonolo went when you lost him Tuesday night—or if you want to be picky, Wednesday morning." Sydney traced Bonolo's name to the date and time, and a name beside it. "Lyle Hendricks, suite 204. That's who your Bonolo signed in to visit." She tapped the first picture. "Presumably this guy is Hendricks, anyway, because when he got off the elevator, he entered the suite like he owned it."

Claudia said nothing for the longest time. The photos could be gold. They could likewise be trouble. But what she mostly grappled with were her feelings, for not only had Sydney invaded her personal life, she'd infiltrated her professional life as well.

"How did you get these?" she asked.

"What do you mean? I went back yesterday. It's a hell of a long drive, but—"

"Obviously you went back, Sydney. That's not what I'm asking. What I want to know is what did you *do* when you got there?"

"I get it. You're worried. Well, don't be. I can be a damned good schmoozer when circumstances dictate. It's a necessary skill I've acquired for sensitive photo shoots, and it helps me get things you can't, because I'm not bogged down with a badge. Do you really want to know more than that?"

Claudia swore softly.

"No one knew me as a photographer. No one saw a camera. No one got my name. You want to look at the last photo, or no?"

She did. She slid it out of the envelope and set it beside the first two. It showed a late-model BMW in a parking garage. Unlike the first two photos, the picture was crystal clear, revealing the car's license tag in back and, stenciled on the concrete wall in front, the number 204.

"Just a wild guess," said Sydney, "but given that the Beamer is parked in the spot designated for Hendricks's condo, I'd say the car is his. If I had to play detective—"

"Please don't."

"—I'd conclude that your man Bonolo and this man Hendricks are pals or business associates. If they're pals, they're not very good pals. Bonolo drove a long distance in the middle of the week to see this guy, and he didn't even stay long enough for a decent dinner." Sydney tapped the photo of the visitor log again. "See there? He signed out forty-five minutes after he signed in. He was back on the road before we were. Aren't you glad not everything is computerized yet? Getting a picture of the log would've been way harder."

"Yeah, good for you, Sydney."

"Nothing's going to pierce your armor, is it?"

"What do you want from me? Reimbursement for your gas? I'll write out a check."

"Oh, come on."

"Maybe you just want flattery. Fine. You're creative. You're magnificently energetic. You're devious. You're—"

Sydney abruptly stood. "So which is it *most*, Claudia? You're pissed because I got something useful before you could get it? You're pissed because I dared not to consult you? Or are you just pissed because I'm here at all?"

Claudia shot to her own feet so swiftly, her stool clattered to the ground. "No one invited you. No one asked for your help."

"Oh, that's right. The great and independent Claudia Hershey needs no one. Not now. Not ever. You—"

"I needed *them*, you bitch!"

Sydney's jaw dropped. "I didn't make their plane go down. I'm haunted every night by what happened—"

"Yeah? You weren't so damned haunted that you didn't capitalize on their death. You turned their tragedy into a farce with that book. Tell me, Sydney, how much money did you make on it? How many fat assignments did you get from it?"

"Did you even *look* at it? Read it?"

"I saw enough of it." Claudia closed her eyes against the image of the book, but it only appeared more starkly, with its black-and-white cover, its black-and-white photographs, its black-and-white text. She laughed bitterly. "*Swan Song: Embracing Life in Death.* Tell me, Sydney, how long did it take you to come up with that?" Her voice fell to a whisper. "You put the *crash* pictures in it! What kind of ghoul *are* you?"

Sydney flinched. "The book has been out for eight years, Claudia. Mom and Dad aren't the only subjects. The crash pictures aren't the only photos. They're the smallest part of what the book's about." She turned to go, then paused. "I made one book that touched death. And really? It's more about celebrating life. If you'd read it, you'd know that. But you? You've made a career dealing in death. So if I'm a ghoul for my one book, what does that make you?"

She didn't wait for an answer. She turned and left the kitchen. Claudia could hear her rummaging in another room. A few minutes later, Sydney was back, hefting camera gear and her satchel. Without a word, she tossed the house key Claudia had given her onto the counter, and then she was gone.

CHAPTER · 19

AT ELEVEN O'CLOCK the firearms range saw little business, and Claudia had the place to herself. Other cops would show up at shift change, but by then she'd be at her desk. Naturally, the range belonged to the sheriff's office, though it accommodated officers from smaller departments as well. Over the years, the range had steadily expanded along with the sheriff's budget. The handgun range boasted sixteen twenty-five-yard lanes surrounded by twenty-foot berms. It also offered a rifle range, a live-fire shoot-house, and an air-conditioned range house with vending machines, lockers, a classroom, and an honor board to announce the top precision shooters. Claudia's name regularly appeared on the honor board, but for her it was a hollow distinction. Marksmanship on a range bore little reality to marksmanship in a live situation when snap decisions and adrenaline could combust faster than a lit match on gasoline.

She stationed herself at Lane Seven, then prepped and loaded her service weapon, a .38-caliber Colt Special. Most officers had abandoned revolvers in favor of 9-millimeter semiautomatics, but Claudia thought them less precise and an invitation for recklessness. She'd stick with the .38. When she was ready, she donned ear protection and signaled the range master. He acknowledged her by calling out "lanes are hot," then settled a distance away to watch. Claudia nodded, took her stance, and sighted across the revolver's barrel at a metal, knockdown silhouette.

For a moment, she hesitated. She didn't need to be here. Suggs required that sworn officers qualify with their service weapons twice a year, but she was current. And, although she practiced at least monthly during open-range hours, she'd been at the range less than two weeks earlier. So why come?

Because you're a cop and you need to be ready.

Boom!

Because you're a cop and you deal in death.

Boom!

Because you're a cop and you need to be ready to deal in death in order to preserve life.

Boom! Boom!

To preserve life. To preserve life. To preserve life.

She fired some forty rounds, pausing only to reload. The air was sharp with the scent of cordite, and when she was finished, the afterimage of blue flame from the revolver's muzzle floated in her vision. Not all of her shots had hit dead-center, but none had strayed far from it.

When she checked out, the range master complimented her on her shooting. She almost shrugged it off to luck—no wind, no pressure, no rush—but she thanked him instead. She was a cop. She handled her firearm well. It's what she did, and neither required an explanation or apology.

"I don't care where you put it, Carella, but these bags are *not* stayin' here. They already smell like road kill—and that's before you've even opened 'em up."

The voice belonged to Chief Suggs, and Claudia could hear it rising above the drone of everything else before she'd even stepped fully through the back entrance. She paused, trying to get a handle on what she was walking into.

"Well, we can't open them in the multipurpose room," she heard Carella say. "We'd clear the whole place out."

Moody, then: "Problem is, we can't take them outside, either. If we've got evidence here, the heat might turn it sour before we could bag it for the lab. The lieutenant would have a heart attack."

"Fine!" Suggs boomed. "Then put the damned things in her office. She's the one who came up with this bright idea, anyway."

The voices sounded from a cramped side room that held little more than supplies, a refrigerator, and a small table where officers could eat lunch, though no one ever did. Claudia's heart sank. They could only be talking about Bonolo's garbage. The notion of taking his curbside trash had seemed reasonable when she proposed it at the bowling alley. Now that the garbage was here, she was less sure. She poked her head around the corner and got a whiff.

"Uh-uh," she said. "Not my office. *Definitely* not in my office."

Suggs gave her a once-over. "So what's the big deal, Hershey?" He elbowed Carella. "If you get a little stink under your nails, you and your buddy Gloria Addison can always get one of those fancy manicures."

Carella and Moody chuckled, and Claudia smiled back. "Sure," she said, "as long as you expense it this time." There were two bags, each loosely knotted at the top. She wrinkled her nose. "Let's get these outside. We'll be all right if we work fast."

She reached for one but Suggs stopped her. "I need a minute with you, Hershey." He told Carella and Moody to haul the bags away. "Smell's gonna linger in here all day," he groused. "Come on. Let's set a minute in my office where the air's fresher."

When they were seated he told her she looked better and thank goodness, because although the mayor had backed down from firing her, he'd seize any opportunity he could to retaliate. "I took my 'concern' about litigation right to his office," he said. "Never knew a man could turn so many shades of red. But he was smart enough to recognize we had him for now. Just watch your back. He'll be eyeing you like a snake ready to strike, and he'll be eyeing me the same way." Suggs looked at her reflectively. "You know what, Hershey? I don't know what this says about me, but I *enjoyed* watchin' that moron squirm. If we go down, I'll always have that moment."

"We won't go down."

"You know that for a fact, or you just feelin' lucky?"

"What I feel is rested. That'll bring me everything else."

He grunted and stood. "Let's see if you still feel that way when you're done muckin' around in the garbage at high noon."

Oh, yeah. That.

They stood on the asphalt beside the Dumpster in what little shade they could claim from an oak tree ten feet distant. Now and then a hot breeze stirred the air, but it did little to pierce the blanket of humidity. In minutes their shirts were soaked through with sweat.

"We got lucky with the timing," said Moody. He wiped his forehead with his arm. "Willow Whisper gets trash pickup every Monday and Thursday. Another day and all these treasures would've been gone."

"Some treasure," Carella murmured.

They'd split Bonolo's bloated garbage bags with scissors. The contents revealed a miniature mountain of decay and stench. For the first few minutes while they worked, no one had much to say. But after a while, it was hard to resist commentary on Bonolo's lifestyle.

Moody gingerly held up a soggy hot dog wrapper from the 7-Eleven. Coffee grounds clung to it. "Bonolo obviously isn't on a health kick. There's almost no food stuff in here that didn't come from a fast-food joint." He added the wrapper to a fresh trash can liner they'd flattened to accommodate each piece of trash as it was moved. "He's a cardiac waiting to happen."

Claudia stood. Her knees popped audibly. Moody and Carella had been at Bonolo's residence before dawn. Moody had photographed his trash can so that it clearly showed Bonolo's house number behind it. When Carella lifted two bags of garbage out of it, he'd photographed that, too. Claudia had told them she wanted it all documented, everything, including each item they removed. She had the Supreme Court to back up their right to lift trash from a curb, but she didn't need Suggs to tell her how loud the mayor would howl anyway. She snapped a picture of the wrapper, cursing the latex gloves that would probably leave her hands mottled with a rash.

They were taking turns with the camera. Claudia handed it off to Moody, then crouched beside the garbage again. They'd already plucked a few items from Bonolo's trash for potential evidence, each piece carefully bagged and tagged. Bonolo drank a lot of beer. Prints on the cans might show him to be someone other than who he claimed. But after another twenty minutes of pawing through his garbage, the only thing they learned with certainty was that he didn't recycle. Newspapers still in plastic sleeves took up almost half of one bag. No shredded or whole files from Hemmer's house, though. No pornographic tapes or magazines. And no hint of a female presence. If Bonolo was fooling around with Addison or anyone else, it didn't show from his trash.

"He sure doesn't spend a lot of time at home," said Moody.

"Not at work lately, either," Carella added. He stomped on a small candy wrapper that threatened to flutter off. "I talked to his boss again this morning. Bonolo hasn't shown his face all week, not even to brag about his role in the hostage situation. His boss is out of patience and Bonolo's out of a job. Won't he be surprised."

Claudia doubted he'd be surprised at all. "Was he home when you grabbed his trash?"

"No way to know for sure," said Moody. "He hadn't picked up his paper yet, and there weren't any lights on, but of course it was early. His vehicle wasn't parked outside, but it might've been in the garage."

She cranked her neck to work out a few kinks. "Okay. We got a couple things. We'll see where they take us."

Besides the beer cans, they'd bagged a handful of gummed-up store receipts and other odd bits of paper that she would examine more carefully later. But credit card invoices or ATM receipts—anything to suggest that Bonolo was more than a phantom—nothing.

"Mitch, can you run the evidence bags to the lab?"

"I'm on it as soon as I wipe the scum off my face and change my shirt," he said.

"Good. Hang out while someone runs prints, okay?"

"Done."

She gave him a few more leads to run down, then turned to Carella. "Emory, I got a couple of things for you, too."

"Imagine my surprise," he quipped.

She grinned. "All right. Let's clean this up and get back into the A/C."

Five minutes later, they'd finished. Claudia stayed behind long enough to smoke half a cigarette and watch a trail of ants scour the ground where they'd just lost their picnic. Life was tough all over.

CHAPTER · 20

CLAUDIA WENT HOME to shower and change. The only evidence that Sydney had been there at all was the key she'd thrown onto the kitchen counter and the festival tickets that lay beside it. Claudia fingered the tickets for a moment, then shook her head and tossed them in the trash. It was what it was. She showered briskly, picked at some leftover tuna salad, and was back in her car twenty minutes later, already thinking ahead to her next stop.

From the computer files recovered by Booey, Carella had been able to isolate Hemmer's businesses accounts. There were only six, all of them small independents in Indian Run or just outside the town's limits. Carella said it looked like Hemmer had been testing his software with them. Carella would visit three of the businesses. Claudia would take the other three. As much as it didn't seem likely that Hemmer's skirmish with the homeowners association had anything to do with his business activities, they couldn't eliminate the possibility without checking.

Claudia's first stop was Diller's Shoe Shack, not far from her house. She took Robin there now and then, and occasionally dashed in when she needed new knee-high hose. The owner was one of the few town residents who apparently didn't know her as a cop, and she always called her "Mrs. Hershey." Claudia cringed every time she heard the "missus"; she'd kept her married name only for Robin's sake. Still, asking the woman to call her "miz" would've been more complicated than it was worth, so she never bothered.

But the owner must have spotted her on the TV news, because this time she greeted her as "detective," a concerned look on her face.

"Good afternoon, Mrs. Diller," Claudia said. "How are you?"

"I'm fine, just fine." She lowered her voice and said somberly, "But how are you? You've been through such a terrible ordeal."

Claudia and Carella had rehearsed their approach, banking on the ever-popular mantra of "paperwork to finish, loose ends to wrap up" as an opening to elicit information. If they needed to go further, they would intimate that estate issues for Hemmer's daughter might be delayed if they didn't "touch all bases." Whether Hemmer was regarded as a crazed villain or not, no one would want a child to suffer.

Claudia told Diller she was fine, stepped her through the mantra, then quickly asked about Hemmer's work before the woman could probe any more. Diller called out to a part-timer to keep an eye on the shop, then led Claudia to her computer in a back office. She poked a key combination, and a splash screen opened with the name "HemmerWare" displayed on a gradient background.

"Steve—Mr. Hemmer, that is—didn't have an official name for his software yet," Diller explained. "He said it was too rough to bother with at this point. But he was being modest. The software is already wonderful, and Mr. Hemmer was brilliant. I still can't get over what happened. It seemed so unlike him. In here, he was always so—"

"I've heard many nice things about him," Claudia interrupted. "But the software . . . what does it actually do?"

"It's an all-in-one package with online distribution and sales capabilities, an accounting component, a customer database . . . well, just everything. And it's all customized. There are similar programs out there, but most are expensive and geared toward big businesses. They offer less customization and require frequent updates."

She gushed for a while more, poking keys and demonstrating the program components. Claudia interrupted again, this time to ask about Diller's business arrangement with Hemmer.

The woman lifted her hands from the keyboard. "I don't know that I'd call it an 'arrangement' at all. He loaded the software for free and refused to take any kind of payment until he was satisfied that every possible kink had been worked out."

"You're joking."

"He said his HemmerWare was in beta and he was testing it with me and a few other small businesses. He carried on about how major software companies thrust flawed programs on consumers, then abandon them when problems come up. He'd worked for some of those companies in the past, you know."

Claudia nodded. Files Booey recovered included documents pertaining to a software package Hemmer previously sold to another company. The software involved emulation, which she refused to let Booey explain, and initially there'd been friction over the deal. Hemmer apparently didn't realize he was handing over all of the rights when he signed the contract. But the issue was resolved without litigation. Hemmer got more money and a ten-year royalty provision. Shortly afterward he moved to Indian Run with enough of a bankroll to finance his house and fund his HemmerWare.

"His bad experience with big software companies was impetus enough for him to go solo," Diller said. "He didn't like their tactics, their culture, their shortsightedness. But I think the biggest reason he went out on his own was his daughter. He wanted a lifestyle that would keep him at home with her." Diller grew pensive. "He was a *good* man," she said softly. "I'll never understand what happened."

Claudia thanked the woman, bought half a dozen pairs of hose for herself and some socks for Robin, then moved on to an optometry shop in Flagg. The owner, showing marginally more restraint in his assessment of Hemmer's software, provided no new insights. He did, however, persuade Claudia that she should schedule an eye exam, and when she left an hour later, it was with an appointment card and a brochure describing laser vision correction. She immediately chucked the brochure. The day someone speared her eyes with a hot beam of light was the day that person would die.

The Indian Run Liquor Store bisected the short side of a small, L-shaped strip shopping center on the edge of town. The plaza begged for a facelift, but it thrummed with shoppers who apparently didn't mind its shabby appearance. Claudia maneuvered the Imperial between two vans so poorly parked that she could barely squeeze out the door. She stood on the hot asphalt for a moment to get her bearings.

The plaza was a conglomerate of old and older. Claudia shaded her eyes and spotted a thrift shop, a dry cleaner, a florist, a used books store, a diner, a dollar movie theater, a bakery, a real estate office, a children's clothing store, a barber, and a grocer. The stores showed their age in faded yellow paint, which Claudia imagined had once been gaudy enough to hurt your eyes. She had never been to the plaza. Robin, she knew, would never set foot in it.

The liquor store was surprisingly free of customers, though Claudia supposed it did most of its business after working hours. She found a sales clerk thumbing through a *People* magazine at the register, and asked if the owner was available. The clerk—Dale, according to a name tag crookedly affixed to his shirt—barely looked up long enough to mumble "not in." Claudia slid her badge under his nose, and Dale came to. His eyes gradually widened in recognition. He grinned.

"You!" he said. "You're that cop from TV! Man, that whole hostage thing—"

"The owner?"

Dale's smile dropped off. "Oh, sure. The owner, that'd be Gil—Gil Larch. Ordinarily he'd be right here, except for he had to go up north for a funeral and so I'm in charge. Mostly I run the register."

Dale had a narrow pink face, wispy blond hair, and scruffy stubble on his cheeks that had probably taken him three or four days to grow. He fidgeted with the pages of his magazine when Claudia didn't immediately respond.

"I know I don't look my age, but I'm 22, so I'm legal here." He cleared his throat. "You want to see some ID?"

"No, I—"

"Oh, man, is it *Gil* who's in trouble? That'd be like practically impossible, because he's this total straight arrow, goes to church and everything."

Claudia told the clerk to calm down, that no one was in trouble. She handed him a business card and told him to have Larch call when he returned.

Dale brightened, relieved. "Sure. I can do that. No problem." He caressed the business card as if it were some kind of souvenir. "This is so wild, man. We've had just about the whole cast of characters in here, and now you. If Hollywood makes a movie, think maybe they'd give me a walk-on gig?"

"What are you talking about?"

"They use a lot of extras. I could play my own part, me behind the register." He smoothed back his hair. "I've been told I have presence. You think?"

"I think I want to know what you mean about the cast of characters in here."

He told her. There'd been Hemmer, of course, with his computer program. But Gloria Addison stopped by with regularity, as did Bill Bonolo. And now the detective.

Claudia waited impatiently while Dale rang up a customer. When the customer moved on, she nodded for Dale to pick up where he'd left off.

His face took on a dreamy expression. "Gloria Addison . . . I could see she kind of liked me, if you know what I mean. She's got an eye for quality. Top-end gin. Top-end vodka. Top-end wine. . . ." He sighed and added, "She's one fine lady. If Hollywood *did* make a movie, maybe they'd cast me as the lover."

Claudia caught herself before she laughed out loud. "You *do* have charisma," she said, "but don't you think Bill Bonolo might have a problem with you playing his role?"

He gaped at her. "You're joking, right? Gloria and a cretin like Bonolo?" He furiously shook his head. "It'd *never* happen."

"Huh. I thought they were an item."

Dale snorted. "Yeah, like a fish and a kangaroo."

Claudia puzzled over that but chose not to pursue it. "Guess I had bad information."

"I saw them in here together a total of *once*. She was an ice queen with him. Believe me, they're no kind of . . . *pair*." Dale waved a hand, dismissing the whole silly notion. "Bonolo only comes in to buy low-life beer and drop off this funky fruit-flavored water."

"Ah. So you're on his distribution route."

"Was," Dale corrected. "We sell a so-so amount of water, so Gil likes to keep it on hand. I don't know *what* he was thinking with that flavored water, though." He made a face. "Probably doesn't matter. Bonolo hasn't been in at all since he killed Mr. Hemmer, so I doubt we'll be buying more."

"Everybody thinks it was self-defense."

He shrugged. "All's I know is they weren't fans of each other."

"Dale, are you writing a script now, or are you stating what you think is fact?"

The clerk looked offended. "It's a fact that they almost got into it once just outside." He gestured at the window. "See the bookstore?"

Claudia looked. It sat just on the other side of the plaza, giving Dale an unobstructed view.

"Bonolo's a regular there, too," he continued. "He was coming out of it once when Mr. Hemmer was leaving here. Bonolo dropped something. Mr. Hemmer picked it up for him, but before he was even straight on his feet again, Bonolo snatched it out of his hand and started waving his arms like a loon. They had words, and I thought I might have to call 911; you could see Bonolo was itching for Mr. Hemmer to make a move so he could flatten him."

Bonolo a reader? Claudia shook her head. She asked Dale if Hemmer frequented the bookstore, too.

"I don't think so. Only time I ever saw him go in there was that same day—*after* Bonolo peeled rubber out of the parking lot. It was a few days before the hostage thing. I remember that because when I caught the news on TV later, I thought, 'Oh, man, I just saw him.' Very unreal, you know?"

Claudia thanked Dale for his time, but when he asked for her auto-graph she told him not to push his luck, then left him to his magazine and daydreams. She felt a kick of optimism. Dale was no actor, but he told a good story. Her watch showed 4:50. There might be just enough time left to do something with it.

CHAPTER · 21

LIKE MOST OTHER EQUIPMENT in the Indian Run Police Department, the portable radios used in the field were relics that operated with a miserly output of four watts. There were six of them, but most of the time two were out for repair. The one Claudia carried had been dropped so often that its base was wrapped with tape to hold it together. She hated it. The tape had gone gummy over time and inevitably left sticky nubbies on her palms. Worse, she often couldn't make out what anyone was saying, no matter how much she fiddled with the squelch button. She did her best to accidentally forget it when she left the station but she had it with her now, and when it suddenly crackled with a burst of static just outside the liquor store she felt her heart lurch.

Sally's voice came on, spewing code. Claudia could distinguish only a few words, so she moved to the parking lot, hoping for a clearer signal, but the air waves weren't giving up anything. She shut it off and called the dispatcher with her cell phone, only to learn the call hadn't been sent to her at all.

"That was a dispatch for Charlie-12," Sally said, referring to a young officer who patrolled the north quadrant of town. "Unless you feel like picking up a trespass complaint, you're off the hook."

"So why'd it come over on my radio?"

"Who knows," Sally snapped, irritable because her replacement had called in sick. "If someone would upgrade us to 800 megahertz, we wouldn't have these problems. Gee. We could be just like a grown-up police department."

"All right, all right," Claudia said. "Anything going on?"

"No. The place is like a tomb."

"Give me thirty, thirty-five minutes. I'll be back in."

"Hey, do me a favor? Swing by Starbucks on your way and get me a nice, cool latte?"

Right. Like Indian Run had one of those.

They both laughed, the mood lightened. Claudia hung up, pushed damp hair off her forehead, and walked back to the shops. But the bookstore was closed. A hand-lettered sign announced its hours as 10 A.M. to 5 P.M. Mondays through Thursdays. Her watch showed the time at 4:56, but no one responded to her knock. She was miffed, but not surprised. Mom and Pop shops danced to their own drummers. The sign said the store was closed on Sundays but open Fridays and Saturdays until eight o'clock. Claudia headed to her car. If she wanted to know what Bonolo read when he couldn't even be bothered to unwrap his newspapers, she'd apparently have to wait.

The lab was unimpressed with Bonolo's beer cans. Moody had been treated to the same litany about low-priority cases that Claudia had heard when she tried to interest anyone in Hemmer's computers. The prints wouldn't be processed until the next day, which meant one more thing that had to wait in a case that had too much already on hold.

Claudia leaned against the outside of her office door and sipped stale coffee. She stared vacantly into the multipurpose room. It was 6:40 and she'd sent Moody and Carella home. No point in making them stick around; there was nothing more they could do right now. Carella's visits to the remaining businesses on Hemmer's client list had been even more unproductive than her own. He'd visited a pet store, a small accounting office, and a women's plus-size clothing shop. Claudia related her own interviews, stopping short of telling them about the hose she'd bought. No one was quite sure what to make of the bookstore angle, if there was one. Of course, that was the problem with the entire case, Claudia thought. They had a collection of suspicious facts, but nothing to tie them together.

Moody had verified that the BMW in the garage at the Miami Beach condo was registered to Lyle Hendricks, a wealthy investor and businessman who also maintained residences in Boulder, Los Angeles, New York, and the Cayman Islands. Under the generous umbrella of a Delaware corporation named AfLUX he owned in full or part more businesses than Medusa had snakes, and most of them catered to people who had as much money as he did and spent it freely on the exclusive cars, yachts, estates, and planes that Hendricks's companies manufactured. AfLUX, Moody told her, stood for "Affordable Luxury," which made for a good oxymoron but didn't bring them any closer to understanding why a man like Hendricks would entertain a man like Bonolo. Nothing did. If anything, Hendricks seemed to be retiring from his business concerns and, in fact, had handed over most daily operations to his three sons.

Moody had recited most of his information from newspaper articles and magazine profiles, and was trying to learn more about Hendricks without raising questions. But that could take time and it might be time spent pointlessly. More disappointing, Kurt Kitner had finally stopped by the station as he'd said he would, but only to leave word that nothing new had occurred to him. He was driving north to Illinois to visit a cousin. He didn't leave a written statement, nor did he leave a number where he could be reached.

Claudia gazed at a plant wilting on a desktop. The plant was a philodendron, and it took a lot to kill them. Someone was killing this one, though. She swallowed the rest of her coffee, then rinsed her cup in her office sink and filled it with water. She poured it into the planter. Some of it slopped over the side. She plucked a few dead leaves from the plant and stepped back to examine it. With luck, it would survive.

"So, Hershey, how come you never told me you have a sister?"

Claudia jumped at the chief's voice. She turned and said, "I thought you'd gone home."

"Headin' there now. So what's the story on your sister?"

"There's no story. I don't see her often."

"So I gathered. How come? Family's important."

"Sydney and I aren't particularly close."

Suggs grunted. "I got a brother like that. But at least his name comes up in conversation now and then. You've never even mentioned your sister."

"She travels a lot."

"All the more reason to stay in touch." He gave her an appraising look. "You oughta go home, too, Hershey. You got a life outside the job, don't you?"

"Of course I do."

"Well, then, if there's not a lot to keep you chained to your desk right now—and the way I hear it, there isn't—go on, get out of here."

Claudia nodded and said she would. When the chief was gone she sopped up the water on the desk, then went back to her office to make one more call.

* * *

Sandi Hemmer didn't sound overjoyed to hear from Claudia, but at least her voice registered inflection. Still, the girl asked for no updates on the intrusion into her father's office, and after a few strained pleasantries, she passed the phone on to her grandmother.

"Hello, Mrs. Bayless," Claudia said. "I was calling to see how Sandi's doing, to see how all of you are holding up. I know these have been some tough days."

"A week tomorrow," Mrs. Bayless said.

Claudia didn't hear an accusation in her tone, but the reminder of how much time had passed since Steven Hemmer took hostages and lost his life made her wince. She toyed with the phone cord and murmured a regret.

"Well," said Mrs. Bayless, "if there's anything good at all to be said right now, I suppose it's that we'll be out of this motel sooner than we thought. With luck, we'll be able to leave Wednesday morning. Sandi can start to put this all behind her."

"You've decided to come back later to clear out the house? I thought—"

"As it turns out, we won't have to. We've got a buyer for it."

So Robin had it right, Claudia thought. She started doodling on a phone message Peters had left on her desk. The Cavalier couldn't be repaired. She rounded out the "C" in Cavalier, turning it into a circle. Then she colored it in and asked Mrs. Bayless if she wasn't rushing things. "I'm sorry if this sounds morbid," she said, "but it's unusual for someone to buy a house that experienced violence so recently. I hope your buyer isn't trying to take advantage of you."

"I don't think so, not in this case. The builder at Willow Whisper stepped up with the offer. He said he feels bad for what happened. He's buying it at full market value."

"The *builder* is buying it back?"

"I know, and I'm not kidding myself. I'm sure he's also trying to deflect some of the stigma from the whole community. He mentioned that Hercules has more land to develop at Willow Whisper. He's a businessman, and what happened at Steven's house won't help him sell it."

"Mrs. Bayless, we're not finished with our investigation there, and—"

"I know, but I'm sure Mr. Manning will cooperate with you."

Mr. Manning. Claudia tried to flush the name from an earlier memory. Carella had brought it up during a briefing, but that wasn't it. Something else, some*where* else. She drew a box around "Cavalier" on the phone message, and almost in the same moment it hit her. Manning. *Boyd*

Manning. The name first surfaced during her confrontation with Arthur Lane outside the mayor's house. The mayor's wife used it in passing when she interrupted them. Manning was running late because he had a flat tire. Manning wasn't just the mayor's supporter. He was a personal friend.

"Mrs. Bayless," she said, fumbling to think of a way to delay the transaction, "our investigation aside, what about your son-in-law's property? You're still going to have to go through everything, aren't you?"

"My *ex*-son-in-law," Mrs. Bayless said firmly. "And no. Mr. Manning said he'd box the property up as carefully as if it were his own and have it trucked to us in Maine at his own expense. He's setting up a closing date for Tuesday."

"That's . . . generous."

Mrs. Bayless lowered her voice. "My husband and I aren't young, Detective Hershey. We've got a traumatized granddaughter to think about. As for the builder, he's got a business to think about. His sincerity doesn't matter to me. Helping us put this behind us does."

C H A P ╁ E R · 2 2

THE BOOK ITSELF WAS OVERSIZED, too tall and too wide to sit upright on an ordinary bookshelf, and the pages within the book were glossy, or most of them, anyway. Each chapter was separated from the next by a heavy sheet of parchment, light gray in color and overlaid with a faint watermark of a swan. The swan, the gray . . . they lent the book a quiet sophistication that somehow made death elegant in a way that it never was or ever could be.

This was Sydney's version of dealing in death, thought Claudia, though she recognized that her twin probably had nothing to do with the book's slick design or size. But the substance of the book—those black-and-white photos—it was Sydney all the way, her style of photography as much a signature as the name she had penned with a personalized dedication on the title page.

She read it once more: *To Claudia, who carries on the celebration of life with me when those who gave us life no longer can. Love, Sydney.*

The cat leaped onto the couch beside Claudia, nearly upsetting the glass of cabernet she held in her hand. It was her second glass. She'd needed the first just to get the book out of the closet and remove it from its wrapping. Boo turned a few times on the couch, then settled down and began doing the milk tread on Claudia's thigh. He purred lightly when she stroked his fur.

Claudia's intent was to view the book objectively, to put some distance between the images on its pages and the feelings that roiled within her. To the degree that she could manage that, she conceded that Sydney was right about a few things. The book wasn't just about their parents. In fact, each chapter was devoted to other people, people Claudia didn't know and whose deaths had come about in a variety of unexpected ways.

Some of those strangers had also plummeted from the sky: hot-air-balloon riders, sky-divers, a hang glider. Others had departed life from closer to the ground in professional racing competitions, mountain-climbing adventures, or white-water rafting mishaps. They'd all died doing something they passionately embraced. Claudia supposed that meant, in Sydney's words, that they had been "embracing life."

"Who would buy this book?" she asked aloud. "Who in their right mind would want this on a coffee table?" Boo stretched indifferently, then curled up in an impossible position and closed his eyes. "Yeah," Claudia said softly. "Not me, either."

She turned more pages. Obviously, as resourceful as Sydney was, she hadn't caught on film the moment life stopped being life for all of the people in her book. Indeed, it seemed that she'd actually been on hand for just three of them, including her parents. But somehow she'd been near enough to the others to capture the aftermath—the torn canopy of the hot-air balloon fluttering listlessly on the ground, a cleat from the mountain climber barely affixed to rock. . . .

The photos were grim, but not gruesome, and to Claudia's surprise most of the pictures depicted Sydney's subjects and their families in much happier times. Family members had supplied a few. In others, they posed with a photo of their doomed husband or son or wife or daughter. Claudia couldn't imagine how Sydney had talked them into it. Then again, maybe she didn't have to. Maybe they'd cherished an opportunity to etch their loved ones into some sort of permanency that the world could see. Markers on a grave.

When she first thumbed through the book eight years earlier, Claudia had focused only on the airplane shots. There were others of her parents, though. A wedding picture. Her mother on a hospital bed, looking bedraggled but proudly showing off two identical babies. Her mother and her father washing down the plane. Her father hoisting Claudia as a toddler, so that she could touch the wing of the plane. They must have been shot with color film, but on the pages they were black and white. Claudia thought artistic license had no business in a book like this, but she was suddenly riveted to another shot, and her objection fell aside. The picture showed her days after the wreckage had been cleared from beside their house. She stood where the plane had crashed, gazing at the earth still torn. Her face was barely visible, but grief showed in the slump of her shoulders. She remembered standing there, but didn't realize Sydney had taken the picture.

Claudia took a shaky sip of wine. Her nasal passages felt clogged and her breath seemed loud and ragged. She was not a crier, and even when she fumbled with her jeans pocket to pull out a rumpled Kleenex, she vowed that she wouldn't cry now. But a few of her tears stained the page. She blotted at them, and she blotted at her eyes, cursing Sydney, damning Sydney, and working furiously to not think about how they'd both been abandoned. Then it was over. She disturbed the cat long enough to get a fresh tissue and blow her nose properly.

A while later, she finished—not looking at the pictures or reading the brief accompanying text; she'd been done with that for some time. But she was finished dwelling on the book, and though she didn't like it any better and didn't believe she genuinely understood it any better, she thought that perhaps, finally, she could persuade herself that Sydney had created the book because, for some reason, she had to. Maybe it was all right to leave it at that.

Claudia's legs tingled when she finally moved her feet from the coffee table and stood. Boo hissed at being bothered for a second time, then immediately took the warm spot she'd vacated. It was nine-thirty. She strolled with a cigarette and half glass of wine into the backyard. Whole weeks could pass without her going back there to do more than mow the infernal lawn.

The property was fairly large. When she and Robin first moved to the house, she'd laid a patchwork of flat walking stones in alternating colors of Cleveland gray and Florida pink. Her back ached for days afterward—it hadn't occurred to her that she'd first need to dig out the sod—but the stonework made a decent patio. It held a small round table and two chairs. That was it, though. The rest of the yard was all about trees and hedges that grew two feet the minute she turned her back.

Claudia took a sip of her wine and a drag on her cigarette. She listened to the night noises. You could always count on frogs and katydids to lend their raspy song to a Florida night. She wondered where the birds went after dark, but before she could complete the thought, a rustling in shrubbery caught her attention. There was just enough moonlight to see movement, but not enough to determine the animal making its nocturnal rounds. Probably a raccoon or opossum, she thought. Nature was great; she loved nature. But nature sometimes foraged in dismaying ways, overturning trash cans or clawing holes that later needed to be filled. Claudia's mind flashed back to the trespassing call Sally had dispatched an officer to in the morning.

The officer—"Charlie 12" on the road, Ryan Richardson otherwise—had concluded in his report that some "varmint" had been "working the ground" on private property. But the officer was a rookie, and he'd written the same thing on another trespassing report from a day or two earlier. Claudia hardly knew Richardson. She made a mental note to read his reports again, this time more carefully. He was probably right, but his job was to record details, not draw conclusions.

For now, though, she put it all out of her mind and concentrated on her wine and her cigarette and the beauty of the dark world around her. When she'd had her fill of it and the bugs had started to bite, she went back inside. It wasn't quite ten o'clock, ordinarily too soon for bed. But she still felt weary from her all-nighter earlier in the week, so that's where she headed, hesitating only long enough to rummage through her kitchen trash and retrieve the festival tickets she'd thrown away that morning.

C H A P T E R · 2 3

A BELL ON THE BOOKSTORE DOOR jangled when Claudia walked in shortly after eleven o'clock Friday morning. A sales desk slapped together with unfinished wood stood near the entrance. The desk was unstaffed, although a smoldering cigarette rested in an ashtray on top. She called out a hello. A man's voice replied from somewhere in back that he'd be with her in a minute and she should go ahead and browse, take her time. Claudia looked around. The store was small and shaped like a boxcar. Used paperbacks with yellowed pages and cracked spines nested on six-foot-high metal racks, which were so tightly aligned they appeared locked together. Hand-lettered cardboard signs taped to the racks announced the categories. Romance dominated.

Claudia glanced impatiently at her watch. She moved toward the back of the store to seek out the source of the voice. A blue curtain so filthy it almost looked black blocked entry to what she supposed was the owner's office or stockroom. It hung limply from a shower-curtain rod. She reached to pull it open, when it abruptly parted and an old guy emerged.

He yanked the curtain closed and clutched his chest in a signal of surprise. "Jeez, lady, you almost gave me a heart attack."

"You almost gave me one right back," said Claudia. And she meant it. He'd blown through the curtain like a leaf caught in an unexpected gust of wind. She pointed toward the front of the store. "Your cigarette's about to go out."

"Oh, yeah, right. Thanks. I figured I could sneak one in before the store gets jammed with customers."

Sure.

He walked her to the front, then eked one last puff from the filter, coughed, and stubbed it out. "Dell Martinlow," he said. "Most people call me 'Boxer.' I used to be fierce in the ring. Being a gal, you probably aren't much into that." He reached to shake hands. "Welcome."

Claudia reluctantly took his hand. Dry and leathery, it sported a pricey ring studded with diamonds. She said it was nice to meet him, but she didn't introduce herself. Since he didn't seem to recognize her, she might get better mileage acting the part of a shopper rather than a cop.

Martinlow apparently didn't notice the breach of etiquette. "Not too many women go for boxers, but the ones who do. . . ." He wriggled an eyebrow suggestively, then shrugged when she didn't react. "I never went big-time, truth be told. Could've, but the whole system's rigged."

"So I've heard."

"Anyway, you looking for anything special?" he asked. "I'm the owner and I know most of my customers, but you. . . ." He wagged a finger at her. "I *know* you've never been here because I'd never forget a foxy gal like you." He winked. "I may be old, but I'm not dead." He winked again and cackled.

The guy never gave up, thought Claudia. She watched his laugh sputter into a cough that left him breathless.

"Whew," he said, pounding on his chest. "That was a seven on my personal scale of one to ten."

"I bet it was," Claudia said wryly. When he recovered enough air to carry on a conversation, she asked whether he took trades or simply sold his books outright. He did both, and while he described his collection of used books and system for trades, she took the opportunity to catalog his physical characteristics for future reference. His face was weatherworn and lined, but he had astonishingly thick hair that men much younger would envy, if not for its white color and some unpleasant streaks of yellow. Her eyes strayed to an expensive watch on his wrist and stopped. He had what looked like candy wrappers tucked beneath the band.

"What's that?" she asked, pointing. "Some kind of bookstore abacus?"

Martinlow threw back his head and roared. "Good one!" He held out his arm so she could get a better look. "These here are from butterscotch candies. I suck on 'em when I'm desperate for a cigarette but can't light up because of a customer in the store."

"Why don't you just put the wrappers in your pocket?'"

"Used to. Problem is, I'd forget about them and they'd mess up the laundry. This is just easier. You want a butterscotch?"

Claudia almost declined but then thought better of it and said yes. Martinlow reached below the sales counter and brought out two. He popped one into his mouth and crammed the wrapper under his watch-band with the others.

"So, what'll it be? Romance? Mystery?" He steered her through the aisles, pointing out books that other customers swore were wonderful. When she didn't linger, he led her farther back. "Got some nice nonfiction here, too. Gardening books. History. Biography. True crime." He coughed for a while, then sneezed viciously. "Damn candy went down the wrong pipe."

The door jangled up front. Martinlow peered around a rack. "Give me a second, hon," he said to Claudia. "Might be a live one up there."

As soon as he was out of sight, she tried to peek through a gap in the blue-almost-black curtain to find out what was in the back room. It was too dark to see squat. She heard the rumble of Martinlow's voice up front, but it seemed intentionally muted. She repositioned herself so she could watch undetected, then slowly moved closer so that she could hear, too.

She didn't catch much. Martinlow sounded agitated, though, and she heard him say "not now" and "later, when . . . store's empty." The customer was tall, stooped and so thin his shirt billowed from him like a sail. But his back was to her and she couldn't make out anything he said. She edged closer and saw him pass cash to Martinlow. The store owner whisked a trio of plastic containers from beneath the counter and handed them over. They vanished beneath the customer's shirt. A second later he was gone.

Claudia smiled. She headed to the front, randomly plucking a paperback from a shelf on her way.

"Ah, good. You found something," Martinlow said. He took the book from her and glanced at the title. "Romance, after all. Two bucks plus tax."

Claudia handed him a ten. He opened a scarred metal cash box and made change. She asked for a receipt and a bag. Martinlow chuckled indulgently but wrote the title, price, and date on a blank sheet of paper. He stamped it with the store name and handed it over. Then he slid the book into a used paper bag and gave it to her.

"I don't know how you manage to make a living from this," Claudia said conversationally.

Martinlow shrugged. "I'm retired. Bought the place about a year ago to keep me busy and youthful enough to catch a nice lady every now and then." He showed her a full set of dentures with his smile. "Any time you're lookin' for more than a good read, you just let me know."

Claudia smiled back. "Matter of fact, I *am* looking for more than a good read, Mr. Martinlow."

"Boxer," he corrected, his smile broadening. "Just call me Boxer."

"I don't think so." She held up her ID.

"Whoa." Martinlow stepped back.

"Whoa is right." Claudia leaned forward. "Now let's talk about what's behind the blue curtain, shall we?"

He popped another candy into his mouth, buying time to think. Then he crossed his arms. "Uh-uh. No can do." He gave her a smug look. "That part's private, so unless you got a warrant we're done doing business. Them's the rules."

"Well, now, that's a disappointing attitude," said Claudia. "But wait." She snapped her fingers as if she'd just had her own flash of insight. "I believe I have something almost as good as a warrant." She held up the bag with the romance inside. "I've got your fingerprints. I bet when I run them they're going to tell me a story better than anything on your shelves. Cooperate with me now and I might be inclined to accept an abridged version. Don't cooperate and . . . well, I'm sure you know how 'them' rules work, too." She spread newspaper photos of Bonolo and Hemmer on the counter. "Let's start with these guys."

Martinlow's response was delayed by a coughing fit. Probably closer to a nine than a seven on his personal scale. But when he caught his breath again, he nodded. Yeah. He knew all about the rules. And maybe he knew a thing or two about the pictures on his counter.

Carella was unwrapping a homemade sandwich in the multipurpose room when Claudia got back to the station. "Brown-bagging it today?" she said.

"Yep. I figured I'd mostly be strapped to my desk with phone calls and records checks," he said brightly, never happier than when he could do his policing from an air-conditioned room. He held up half his sandwich. "Want half?"

"Thanks, but that's not enough to feed a rabbit, Emory. If I were you, I'd chew slow. Make it last."

"It'd be hard *not* to chew slow. We're talking peanut butter and jelly here. I wasn't awake when I packed the girls' lunches for day camp this morning. One of them'll be horrified to find a fat roast beef on rye in her lunch box, and I'll be hearing about it tonight." Carella faked a little girl voice. "'Oooow, Daddy, dead animal on bread.'" He shook his head fondly. "It's some kind of phase they're going through. Last month it was toxins in housecleaning supplies."

A wave of loneliness flooded Claudia. Robin would be gone for another week. There were no men in her life, no close friends in her life, and she'd slammed Sydney out of it. She wondered how much smaller her universe could shrink before she'd be invisible. Suddenly the sandwich looked good. She picked up the second half and mumbled through a mouthful of peanut butter that she'd order a pizza later.

Carella told her that the chief was at a Rotary luncheon. Moody was on a funeral detail.

"Tell me you're joking," Claudia said. "The chief could've sent anyone to coordinate traffic."

"I know, I know, but he's in a pissy mood and Mitch happened to be drumming his fingers on his desk when the chief walked through. We have one guy out on personal time, another on vacation, and Peters was jammed up." Carella licked a spot of jelly from the corner of his mouth. "I'm just lucky he didn't spot me first. Mitch had to listen to the chief's lecture on limited resources."

Claudia thought guiltily of her own neglected work. Nothing but the Hemmer matter cried for attention, but that didn't mean it was her only case. She was also the loosely defined training officer for the department, which mostly meant making sure rookies didn't screw up. Carella tore his napkin in two and gave her half. She wiped her mouth and sighed. If nothing else, she needed to review Richardson's trespassing reports before the day was done.

"I take it there's not much new to report," she said.

"Uh-uh. I finally got a fax from the Miami temp agency where Addison last worked, but nothing interesting leaps off the page." He shuffled through some papers and handed it over. "It's just a listing of company names and dates. I'll try to find out more about them."

Claudia scanned the fax. The agency had sent Addison on twelve clerical jobs in an eighteen-month period. Some of them lasted no more than a week. She'd worked for an ad agency, three real estate offices, a holding company, a parts supplier, a bank, a law firm, an import company, and three doctors' offices. None of the names sounded familiar.

She handed the fax back. "All right. Let's talk fingerprints. Anything yet?"

He shook his head. "That's why Mitch looked like he was lost in space when the chief walked through. He'd just hung up from the lab. They told him to check back after two. Think they're sandbagging us?"

"I'm not quite that paranoid yet," she answered. She fumed at the delay, but Bonolo's beer cans weren't a smoking gun. She filled Carella in on her visit with Dell Martinlow. The bookstore owner didn't need much of a push to talk. He'd seen the inside of a cell before, and he'd serve up his own brother to prevent a repeat stay. He'd given Bonolo's name within five minutes, verifying the hunch that had brought Claudia back to the shopping plaza.

"Bonolo's his *brother?*" said Carella.

"No, no," Claudia said impatiently. "I was being figurative. Stay with me here, Emory."

Bonolo had been running porn videos through Martinlow's store for nine months. To hear the bookstore owner tell it, the porn distribution was a small operation, and he swore he didn't know Bonolo by that name until after the Hemmer situation. Previously, he knew him simply as "Fred," and Fred regularly came by to drop off a small collection. Martinlow sold them at outrageous prices to people on a "select customer list." He got a cut of the action, enough to buy himself expensive jewelry and feed his lottery habit. What Bonolo got—or Fred or whoever—Martinlow didn't know, and didn't much care.

"So you believe Martinlow's story about not knowing who Bonolo was?"

"Nah. They probably have a history together. But Martinlow's an ex-con. His instincts are to hold out on whatever he thinks he can get away with."

Claudia told Carella that according to Martinlow, Bonolo made drop-offs nearly every Friday. Normally he came by around noon, conveniently timing his visits to coincide with legitimate deliveries to the liquor store.

"So he should've been in earlier today?" said Carella.

"Yeah, that's what Martinlow told me," she said. "But last evening Bonolo called him and switched gears. He told him that he wouldn't be by until eleven-thirty *tonight*. That's long after the bookstore closes and an easy hour after the dollar theater's last show lets out."

"So the plaza will be dark and vacant," said Carella.

"You got it. In fact, this is all about concealment," she said. "Bonolo told Martinlow he'll park around back. He told Martinlow to park there, too. There's a narrow alley there for truck deliveries to the stores. It doesn't show from the front. Naturally, we'll be there, too."

"Changing his timing like that—someone's *gotta* be tipping Bonolo there's some real heat on this thing," said Carella. "Martinlow might warn him off about tonight. He might do a disappearing act himself."

"Maybe. But he's an old guy. He's not lying about wanting to stay out of jail. He says he's done two stints, one for dealing in stolen property and another for selling porn." She smiled. "There's a shocker, huh? Anyway, he claims he's been straight for the last six years and would've stayed that way until Bonolo made it too easy for him not to give it another whirl."

"What'd you deal him?"

"If Bonolo shows, we bust them both, but I soft-pedal Martinlow to the state attorney's office and he'll probably walk without hard time. Meanwhile it'll look to Bonolo like they were both taken by surprise, like Martinlow had nothing to do with it."

"The chief won't like this."

"Probably not," Claudia agreed. "But we've got Bonolo tied to the porn. We're a hair from showing that he planted the video in Hemmer's home office. We still don't know why, but we're on our way to finding out."

Carella worked his tongue to prod peanut butter from the roof of his mouth. He chuckled. "I love the idea of the blue curtain. Blue movies. Blue curtain."

"You ready for this? Martinlow never kept the videos back there. He kept them under his sales counter, not even locked up. There's nothing behind the curtain but a tiny desk, boxes, roach turds, and a crapper you wouldn't use even if you were desperate." She arched an eyebrow. "What he said? He doesn't even carry *Playboy* or *Hustler*. Afraid they'd offend his 'lady customers.'"

Carella hooted.

"Dig into Martinlow's past. Let's see what his jacket really shows. I'm going to grab an hour to catch up on some other work. We'll get with Mitch and the chief when they return."

She was halfway to her office when she heard Carella call her name, telling her not to forget about the pizza. She pretended not to hear, but deftly pivoted in time to catch the balled-up sandwich paper he lobbed at her. She threw it in the air and batted it into a trash can ten feet away. Carella whistled appreciatively. Then he looked at her. She looked at him. They took turns making baskets until she had him six out of ten. When they were done, she felt like her universe had expanded just enough to carry her through the day.

CHAPTER · 24

OFFICER RYAN RICHARDSON was 22 years old and had finished academy training a whopping two weeks before he joined the Indian Run Police Department. His idea of law enforcement came from one-hour police dramas on TV, which always included exciting chases and excluded the tedium that made up the bulk of most officers' days. He was a city boy from Pittsburgh and never would have left if not unexpectedly smitten by a Florida girl visiting a cousin there. She had lush dark hair and Julia Roberts lips that rewarded him in his dreams before he'd ever touched them in real life.

The girl, Marietta, likewise had fallen hard for Ryan. But she didn't fall hard enough to want to abandon her immediate family, all of whom resided on the outskirts of Indian Run. Richardson caved. He moved south, married Marietta, and eked through the required testing and training that would allow him to drive a patrol car with flashing lights.

Suggs hired him because the chief favored local folks—and although Richardson wasn't local, Marietta was. Good enough.

The first time Claudia read Richardson's two trespassing reports, she'd paid scant attention except to be annoyed at his poor grammar and spelling, fuzzy description, and wild conclusions. Now, as she zeroed in first on his Monday report, her irritation only mounted. The location he'd noted in his narrative was so vague she would need a compass to find it:

> *Property where trespass allegedly occurred is an abandoned Parcel with overgrown weeds and some trees on a chunk of Land in northmost reach of town (zone 8) which cannot be acksessed redily. Officer discovered dirt entryway off of unmarked Road where it curves a mile or so north of farmers market and drove through. No trespass-*

ing perpetrators were found. There was some signs of digging on Prop-
erty, which officer believes to be of animal nature due to how ani-
mals seek pray for food.

Claudia stopped. Florida law required sworn police officers to hold at
least a high school diploma or its equivalency. How had Richardson managed it? She shook her head and read on:

Complainant (Mrs. Evans) is a woman who lives behind chunk of
Land and who believed she saw from her upstairs bedroom window
some lights where normally it is only dark at night. She concluded
the lights were flashlights and that is why she called, but officer saw no
flashlights or evidence of flashlights, just the signs of digging which has
already been explained as of an animal nature. Officer will advise
complainant of same.

A cigarette to stem her annoyance would be nice, but Claudia shoved
the thought aside along with Richardson's first report. She began to read
the second, recognizing it as the trespassing call mistakenly routed to her
portable radio the day before. Richardson mostly worked nights, so he'd
apparently pulled a day shift to catch the call—no doubt covering for the
absence of Moody and Carella. The report droned on in a fashion jarringly
similar to the first, though Claudia sat up straighter almost immediately.

She glanced back at the first report, then swore out loud. In less than
a three-day period, the idiot had responded to the same general complaint
from the same woman—a detail that begged to be noted. In fact, the
report form specifically included a box for officers to check if they
believed the call they took might signal a trend. Richardson hadn't
checked the box. He hadn't flagged his second report in any way.

While Claudia fumed, she read the rest of Richardson's report. The
only difference on the second call was the time and the woman's claim
that she saw two men acting suspiciously. Richardson didn't indicate why
the woman thought they appeared suspicious; but worse, incredibly, was
his conclusion that the Evans woman might have "mistooken" large dogs
for men.

Claudia shot out of her chair. She wasn't sure with whom she was most
furious—Richardson for his sloppy work, or Peters and herself for not
paying enough attention to it. Granted, the trespass calls sounded like
snoozers. And two did not automatically spell a trend. *Probably* didn't. But

that wasn't the point. Carelessness was. Cultivate carelessness on the small stuff, and you could find yourself dead when something big came along.

Claudia told Carella he could reach her on her cell phone, then asked Sally to raise Richardson and get his location. The Hemmer case was at a standstill and she could use a diversion. Richardson had just handed it to her.

The rookie didn't look happy to meet Claudia, perhaps because of the way she was leaning against the Imperial with her arms stiffly folded when he pulled up in his patrol car. She was waiting for him at a tire shop in Richardson's patrol zone because she had no idea where his "unmarked road" was. She'd been biding her time for ten minutes, and while she watched him get out of his patrol car she vowed that if he learned nothing else today, he would learn how to render a location that a blind man could follow.

He approached her slowly, a wary smile on his face. "Hi, Lieutenant," he said. "Hot one, no?"

"Get your hands out of your pockets," she snapped.

He complied instantly, blushing. "I didn't even realize they were there," he said.

"There're a lot of things you apparently don't realize, Officer Richardson." Claudia slapped his reports on the hood of her car. "Explain these to me."

Richardson bent over the reports. He studied them as if he'd never seen them before. Then he shook his head. "They're 51s?" he said, giving her the code number for a trespass call.

"I know *what* they are, Officer. I asked you to explain them. Tell me why the second wasn't flagged. Tell me why I can't determine the location of these trespasses by reading your reports. Tell me what makes you an expert on animal digging behavior."

Richardson's hands retreated toward his pockets. He caught himself and jammed them under his armpits. Then he rocked back and forth slightly. His bit his upper lip, where a mustache was beginning to take shape.

"I'm not sure what you're getting at," he finally said.

"Are you sure you knew what Mrs. Evans was getting at when she talked to you?"

"I'm, uh, *pretty* sure," he said. His left eyelid began to twitch. "At least I *was*."

An 18-wheeler blew by them, kicking up bits of gravel and hot wind.

"Right." Claudia sighed. She decided to ease up before Richardson hyperventilated. "Think you can find the location again?"

"Oh, yes, ma'am. It's simple, really. I just couldn't think of how to write it better."

"Uh-huh. Well, let's go out there, Officer Richardson. We'll try a little show-and-tell. You show. I tell. Think you can handle that?"

He nodded glumly and led her to his vehicle. His hands were back in his pockets.

For reasons she couldn't isolate, Claudia began to get a bad feeling before they were even halfway through the junglelike growth that flanked the highway where Richardson had eventually pulled over. The highway had a name, of course. It was called Clowe, and though its street sign was bent and partially obscured by palmetto scrub, it wasn't invisible. It wasn't even a mystery. Clowe bisected Old Moogen Road, and the dirt entryway that Richardson described in his report was less than a tenth of a mile north of the intersection.

For a moment Claudia wondered if her unease stemmed from Old Moogen Road itself, merely because Carella had mentioned that it buffered the far end of Willow Whisper's undeveloped land. Then again, Old Moogen was a feeder road that provided access to dozens of farms and ranches. It ran for miles, and Richardson hadn't brought her anywhere near to the gated community. In fact, it didn't look like he'd brought her anywhere near to civilization at all.

Claudia batted at a cloud of gnats. More likely, her unease flowed from the idea of snakes. Legions of them probably lived in the prickly foliage Richardson was leading her through, and every spur that snagged at her ankles reminded her of how poorly dressed she was to be playing in a field. She squinted into the sun, regretting that she'd instructed Richardson to take them directly to the location of the trespass site, rather than the complainant's house. But she hadn't wanted to embarrass the young officer in front of a civilian. Still, where the hell did this Mrs. Evans live? Claudia couldn't see past the trees to get her bearings, and the woman had a numbered street address, which in Indian Run meant that it defied geographic logic. You could turn a corner on Northwest 40th Avenue and find yourself on Southeast 38th Street. It's just the way it worked.

She asked Richardson how much farther.

"Not much," he said. "Three minutes, maybe?"

She kept her eyes down, alert for unfriendly wildlife, and trudged behind him. Neither of them had much to say, and in the silence Richardson's three minutes blossomed into ten by the time they finally reached the land he identified as "the right place." Claudia shaded her eyes and took stock of where they stood. It took a minute, but when that minute had passed, so did her sense of foreboding, because now there was something to replace it: an unmistakable feeling of dread.

"See those holes, Lieutenant?" said Richardson. "They're like scuff marks, like how an animal might—"

"Richardson?"

"Yes, ma'am?"

"Don't talk."

"Yes, ma'am."

"Don't move, either."

He nodded.

Claudia dug through her purse for her cell phone. She called Carella, gave their location, and told him to send two uniformed officers and a crime-scene unit. The only animals who had recently been where she and the rookie stood were human.

C H A P T E R · 2 5

THE SHERIFF'S OFFICE sent one two-man crime-scene unit. Within thirty minutes of their arrival, the senior technician called for more help and requested night lights. They might be at the scene long enough to need them. Within an hour, six technicians swarmed an area of woods and field some one hundred by eighty feet, hoping like hell they wouldn't need to expand it. They hadn't called for a medical examiner yet, but no one doubted that they would. It was only a matter of time before someone unearthed a body, parts of a body, or evidence that a body had been there.

The region had been secured and marked off by two Indian Run officers. It showed more than a dozen dig marks, most of them superficial but others deeper than one foot. The dig marks were concentrated near an oak tree crippled by lightning. A thick, grizzled limb lay along the ground, its charred end slightly raised and butt-up against the trunk. The rest of the tree stood listlessly, blackened where its limb had been dismembered. Dig marks fanned out from the tree in an ever-widening circle that looked increasingly random.

Claudia stood beside Suggs and watched the technicians work, setting markers, measuring, taking photographs. The chief had arrived just before the second crime-scene crew. For once he said nothing about turning to the sheriff's office for help.

"Whoever was out here wasn't exactly subtle," he remarked. "Crime scene gonna bring in infrared to pinpoint location on a grave? There's a lot of ground here."

"If their preliminary work doesn't pan out, they'll go the distance, but that's expensive and it might not be necessary. The way it looks is someone was trying to dig up an old body, not bury a new one." She gestured vaguely at the dig marks. "We're guessing they had an idea where to look but couldn't pinpoint it, maybe because of a lot of growth over time. The landscape would look different. They had an idea, though, so we're banking on their dig marks as a general guide."

"So the body's old."

"Hard to think otherwise."

Suggs licked perspiration from his upper lip. "You got any theories?"

"Not yet," she said, although that wasn't entirely true. An idea was forming in the back of her mind, but it was like a mild itch too vague to find. "I don't like the location, though."

Richardson's "chunk of land" stood on Willow Whisper's undeveloped plot, some forty feet behind Hemmer's house. Trees blocked the view. It was, however, perfectly visible from Mrs. Evans's house, an old structure that stood perpendicular to Willow Whisper but wasn't part of the gated community. All that separated her house from the undeveloped land was a six-foot berm, giving her an unobstructed view from her upstairs bedroom window. Richardson could've walked from the woman's back door onto the land in less than a minute. He'd taken the long way "so as not to tromp through her flower beds."

"We talk to the Evans woman yet?" said Suggs.

"I sent Carella out. He called just before you got here." Claudia waved her hand in an arc. "All this property used to be hers and her husband's. They were small-time vegetable growers. But she couldn't keep it going after her husband died some seven years ago. She had it cleared, planted some trees, and 'gave it back to nature,' was how she explained it to Carella. What she didn't think through, though, were property taxes. They were killing her. When the developer made an offer, she took it."

"Hercules."

"Right. The builder wanted to raze her house and take that smidgen of land, too, but she wouldn't go along. Eventually he plugged some mature trees onto her property to separate it from the corner lot Hemmer wound up buying."

Suggs wiped his face with his sleeve. "It's hotter'n hell out here, Hershey. Your nose is burning."

Claudia shrugged.

"What'd you do with Richardson?"

"I sent him back on patrol."

"You gonna let him live?"

"I told him I've taken a personal interest in him and that we're going to work closely together in the coming weeks."

Suggs smiled. "That's brutal."

She was about to comment, but then her eyes darted left. "Heads up, Chief," she whispered. "We've got company."

Mayor Arthur Lane and a lean man in tight jeans and a polo shirt were striding toward them. Claudia didn't need an introduction to know that the man in jeans was Boyd Manning. He'd been notified about a "situation" on his property; his presence was requested. Lane's presence had not been requested, but she wasn't surprised to see him.

Manning stood about six-two. He had dark wavy hair, cobalt eyes, and skin made ruddy from long hours in the sun. Women would notice him, and he carried himself with the confidence of someone who knew it. He smiled thinly when he introduced himself with a handshake, first to Suggs and then to Claudia.

"Chief," he said. "We've met before, haven't we?"

"Back at a town council meeting, back before you first broke ground."

"Right. I remember. You weren't keen on growth in Indian Run."

"I'm still not."

Manning shrugged indifferently. "Can't keep people from wanting to move to Florida, and there's not a whole lot of room left on the coast."

Lane began to sputter about "an invasion of privacy" on Manning's land, but the builder stopped him with a casual lift of his hand.

"It's all right, Art," he said. "Let's just hear what Detective Hershey has to say before we get all worked up." He turned to Claudia. "So what's going on here? You people prospecting for gold? Someone found sacred Indian burial grounds?"

When she didn't react. Manning looked at Lane, and the mayor laughed obligingly.

"We didn't dig those holes, Mr. Manning," said Claudia. "We found them when we followed up on a trespassing complaint."

Manning tucked a piece of gum into his mouth and surveyed the crime technicians at work for a moment. "Okay, so someone was out here digging," he said. "Vacant land, lots of trees . . . kids playing, probably, looking for arrowheads or something. It wouldn't be the first time."

"I'm sure it wouldn't," said Claudia. "But that digging pattern isn't the work of kids, Mr. Manning. Amateurs, yes. Kids, no."

Manning frowned. "Well, whatever it is, I hope you're not planning on being here long. I'll be clearing this land soon and starting the final phase of Willow Whisper."

"His permits are all in place," said Lane. He glared at Suggs. "If this show of yours is some kind of asinine way to block—"

Before Lane could continue, a cell phone on Manning's belt rang. He held up a finger to his audience, then stepped away a few feet and turned his back. The mayor gestured for Suggs to follow him for what he called "a private chat." Claudia didn't need to guess at what the mayor might have to say, but her interest was solely on Manning and what little she could overhear from his phone conversation.

He talked for a few minutes. When he finished, he clamped his phone back on his belt. He looked agitated.

"Something's come up in the office," he said. "When you're done drilling for oil on my property, let me know." He pulled a business card from his shirt pocket. He held it between two fingers but pulled it back slightly when Claudia reached for it.

"Something you want to say?" she asked.

"I'm not sure what kind of game plan you have—"

"There's no game plan."

"—but whatever it is, you ought to rethink it. You're riling people needlessly. It could backfire on you."

"How nice that you're concerned for me, Mr. Manning."

"I'm not. But I'm concerned for the community."

"Ah."

He looked at her. Then he handed over the card, his jaw set. "It's easiest to get me on my cell."

"Thank you."

He opened his mouth as if to say more, but instead he gave a slight shake to his head, then put his thumb and forefinger to his lips and whistled sharply. The mayor whirled from Suggs and trotted toward him like a puppy. They walked away without a backward glance.

By four o'clock Claudia felt as withered as the field grass that grew thick in erratic patches across the property. The chief had left an hour earlier, leaving her to shepherd the crime scene and percolate in the heat. But she didn't complain. The men and women actually working the area had it far worse. For fear of destroying evidence, they could only move inches at a time as they brushed aside decaying vegetation and probed at dig marks, widening them with flat-bladed spades and hand trowels. They had established a side bet on who would turn up something first.

Claudia watched from beneath the shade of a tree. She had no idea what it was, could only identify a handful of Florida's trees, which in her estimation always bore scrawny leaves compared to the trees she'd grown up with in Cleveland. But it occurred to her that she no longer missed Ohio, not really, and she wondered when that had happened. A second later it didn't matter. Her cell phone rang and it was Moody on the other end—Moody with real news, news that mattered, news that would alter the way they proceeded with the investigation.

"Here's one that'll make your day," he said. "The crime scene finally got around to running the prints on the beer can from Bonolo's garbage. Guess what?"

"Bonolo's not Bonolo."

"What you thought all along, right?"

"Not all along, but for a while. The only thing that surprises me is how he's managed to fly below the radar so long. So give me the details."

Moody did. Bonolo's real name was Robert "Big Bob" Farina. He'd done serious time on three occasions, once for assault and twice for distribution of pornography. The Mafia was known for its marketing edge in the porn trade, but there was no evidence that Farina was connected. Moody had managed to track down his parole officer, who had seen Farina exactly once before vanishing four years earlier. A warrant was issued, of course, but except for a rare and unverified sighting, Farina seemed to have become invisible. He'd apparently survived by hiding in the open and assuming the identity of someone who really was named Bill Bonolo. The genuine Bill Bonolo, however, was in a Georgia nursing home, where he'd been stashed by the state after a traffic accident left him a quadriplegic. He had no known relatives. He had no money—nothing that would leave bread crumbs for investigators to follow.

According to the parole officer, Farina worked porn as a distributor for small studios that usually survived only long enough for starry-eyed actors to cut their teeth in the industry and move on to bigger pornography enterprises that *were* mob-connected. Farina stayed away from those, and to supplement his modest income from blue movies, he worked as a bouncer in seedy nightclubs or as a bodyguard to businessmen who cared less about his history than his size. He'd buddied up to Dell Martinlow in prison, their dealings in porn an obvious bond.

"Farina's no ace in the deck, but he pulled off a good racket with this," said Moody. "He picked the right guy to clone as himself, he picked a nondescript job to make things look good and give him access to distribution points, and apparently he uses cash for everything—just some of the ways he's managed to stay hidden so long."

"Try not to admire him, Mitch."

Moody laughed. "Not to worry, Lieutenant."

They batted the Bonolo-Farina deceit around for a while. Although it made sense for Farina to hide in a little-noticed town like Indian Run, it wasn't a perfect fit. Even before the Hemmer situation, he'd attracted attention by participating on the Willow Whisper homeowners association. Moody attributed it to the arrogance of a criminal mentality, but Claudia thought it went beyond that.

"The question, Mitch, is who's giving Farina enough cash to live the lifestyle he's been enjoying? And what's he doing for it? His goodies didn't all come from the porn gig he's got going now. That can't be more than a little side action."

Claudia heard Moody pop the top on a soft drink. She tamped down envy by reminding herself that if she had a soda in her hands right now she'd only attract bees. She asked what he was drinking.

"Mountain Dew," he said. "You'd think someone would create 'Flat Dew' for Florida."

"You'd think. Meanwhile, when you're done enjoying that, put some uniforms in plain clothes and see if you can pick up Farina on the outstanding warrant. Try for quiet. Let's see if he's stupid enough to be available."

"If he's not?"

"We'll see if he's stupid enough to show at the bookstore tonight."

A crime-scene tech named Levine won the bet at six-thirty when he unearthed a skull less than a foot from one of the original holes he'd expanded with a spade. Its burial place lay beneath the dead tree limb, and Levine let out a whoop when he found it. The rest of the technicians would have to pony up ten bucks each.

Suggs had already left, but Claudia hurried over. Richardson's "trespassers" had been close. If not for the downed tree limb, they probably would've found it. She crouched for a closer look. The skull lay in a cavity about two feet deep, maybe less. Levine had immediately stopped probing when his spade encountered it, so the skull was only partially uncovered. But it appeared intact, and with luck, the rest of the remains would be as well. Claudia stood and backhanded a beetle from her pant leg. Hours of work lay ahead. After they moved the tree limb, technicians would need to stake the site and lay a grid of string over it. They'd have to photograph and measure it, and then sift every inch of dirt as it was removed. The remains wouldn't be handed off to the medical examiner until all of that had been completed.

Claudia stared at the skull. Someone had buried a body here. And then someone wanted to retrieve it. Surely, though, someone else must have missed the victim. She thought about that, then put in a call to Carella and told him to start checking missing persons reports for the last five years, beginning with locals. The body could have been buried earlier, but five years seemed a plausible starting point. For one thing, the Evans woman hadn't instantly turned the farm into wilderness upon her husband's death; more than likely the body had been shoveled underground a few years later, after field had taken over. On a more practical level, though, only the last five years of Indian Run's missing persons records had so far been computerized.

She talked with Carella for a few minutes, disconnected, and looked from the grave toward the trees that hid Willow Whisper from the undeveloped land. The she turned back to the dark hollow in the ground where a body lay forgotten; she bowed her head and whispered a clumsy prayer.

CHAPTER · 26

PHILBY'S GROCERY STORE closed at nine o'clock. Claudia made it there with fifteen minutes to spare. Other than half of Carella's peanut butter and jelly sandwich, her only meal had been a handful of pretzel sticks at the crime scene. By now she craved something substantial and maybe even nutritious. She trolled the store aisles, eventually settling on a salmon fillet, a broccoli crown, and a small red potato. All of them could be nuked, leaving her with time to relax before getting in place for the Bonolo takedown at eleven-thirty. Claudia shook her head. *Farina.* Not Bonolo. Farina.

She paid for her groceries and made perfunctory chitchat with the checkout clerk, her mind on the crime scene that had defined her day and the bookstore that would define her night. Technicians were still at the plot of undeveloped land, along with the medical examiner. He would work through the night, not because the skeletal remains screamed for sudden urgency, but because the media had found out.

Claudia fired up the Imperial and chugged toward home. For now she was playing it quiet, and so far luck was with her. Word hadn't leaked that Bonolo was an alias for Farina, nor had neighbors paid any attention when Moody and two cops in plain clothes knocked on the big man's door, dressed more like Jehovah's Witnesses than police officers. To no one's surprise, Farina hadn't answered and Moody said the place appeared deserted. They could toss his house later, though Claudia suspected Farina already would've cleared it of any incriminating evidence about his past, his porn, or anything relating to Hemmer. He was a man on the run.

Claudia parked and carried her groceries in. She moved methodically through the kitchen, pulling out plastic containers for the microwave. This business with the body behind Willow Whisper . . . something was squirrelly there. She smiled dryly, thinking of a brief conversation she'd had with Suggs. It was shortly after crime scene uncovered enough of the skeleton to know they had the whole thing. She'd called him with the update.

"Hershey," he'd said, "I don't know what stirs my ulcer most, the idea that maybe the body behind Willow Whisper is somehow tied to the Hemmer thing, or that we now got two equally ball-breaking cases on our hands."

They'd traded their impressions on Manning—his feigned disinterest in what crime scene was doing on his property, his rush to buy Hemmer's house back from Sandi's grandparents, his buddying up with the mayor, his bringing in "Bonolo" on the homeowners association. Claudia told Suggs she'd overheard Manning say "Gloria" when he was on his cell phone at the crime scene. She couldn't tell whether he was talking *to* a Gloria or *about* a Gloria, and no way could she know whether the reference was to Addison.

"Yeah," Suggs had said gloomily, "but if somethin' looks like a skunk and smells like a skunk—"

"Then it probably is a skunk," Claudia had finished on cue.

The salmon came out overcooked and the broccoli undercooked, but to Claudia they tasted like something from a five-star restaurant. The meal also surprised her with an energy kick she applied to overdue floor exercises and a half-assed session with her oboe. Her spirits were buoyed; real food could do that. She played with Boo for a few minutes, cleaned his litter box, took a fast shower in cold water, and then headed back out into the night. Whatever came her way, she was ready.

They were in place by eleven o'clock, their vehicles hidden from view. Claudia positioned herself inside the bookstore with a grim-faced Dell Martinlow. Moody huddled behind a concrete post outside the entrance; Suggs had the alley where Farina was expected to park. The chief was no night owl, but Carella was off celebrating his wife's birthday with a posh dinner out and Suggs refused to bring in a patrol officer from his already depleted staff. They had portable radios that actually worked in close proximity, and twenty-ounce cups of coffee. All they needed was Farina.

The interior of the store was dim, lit only with a small security light that cast purplish shadows. Claudia could read the apprehension in Martinlow's face well enough, though. And he *should* be apprehensive, she thought. He'd lied to her about not knowing that Bonolo was really Farina. She wasn't surprised at his deceit, but she warned him that if he spun another lie or didn't give an Oscar-winning performance tonight, she'd toss him in jail for the rest of his natural days—and not just any jail.

"I've got friends in the state department," she said. "Cross me and I'll figure out a way to send your ass to a Turkish prison. Inmates there dig their own toilet holes on a daily basis. You up for that?"

"Talk about lies," Martinlow mumbled. "But you made your point."

"Good," she said. "Now tell me again what you're going to do if Farina shows."

"I bitch about the late hour. I remind him I'm an old man and ask what's the deal with that." Martinlow unwrapped a piece of candy and popped it into his mouth. He tucked the wrapper under his watchband. "I tell him he better not be bringing heat onto me."

Claudia nodded. She hoped that before they surprised Farina, the bookstore owner would get him to say something interesting. He certainly wouldn't talk after the fact.

"Then what?" she said.

Martinlow sighed. "Then we do our business. I bring him to the front counter. He gives me new tapes. I give him cash for the last batch. You pop out of hiding, and I act as shocked as Farina, like I had no idea you'd be lurking in my store. Fat chance he'll buy it."

"You don't like your odds, I can take you in right now."

He waved a hand. "We'll go your way."

There wasn't much to say after that, and they waited silently for the clock to wind down to eleven-thirty. Even though Claudia didn't think Farina would show, she felt herself tense with each passing minute. Martinlow's anxiety showed visibly. He'd chewed so many candies, the store smelled like butterscotch air freshener.

Eleven-thirty came and went. Then eleven-thirty-five . . . forty . . . forty-five . . . fifty.

"You better not have called him," Claudia said to Martinlow.

"I didn't. I swear. He calls me. I don't even know how to reach him."

Claudia's radio crackled and the chief's voice came on. "How much longer you wanna give this, Hershey? Bugs are bitin' me in places I didn't even know I had. My wife gets a look and— Wait a minute, wait a minute." The radio hissed. "Here come some headlights on low beam." He paused, then his voice dropped to a whisper. "I don't recognize the vehicle. It's some kind of sports car, looks like."

A sports car?

"Hang on, hang on . . . the driver's parkin'. I'm talkin' ten feet from me now. Driver door's opening. Hang on, hang on . . . whoa. It's a broad gettin' out."

Moody's radio sputtered. "Addison?" he asked.

"Everybody stay in position," Claudia snapped. "It's her. Got to be her. Go to silence. Let's play it like it was Farina." She wheeled and faced the bookseller. "You know who Gloria Addison is?"

"Who?"

"Addison, Addison. Gloria Addison."

"Uh-uh, no."

"Well, whether you're lying or not, you'd better be ready to show me how flexible you can be. Play this like you'd play it if I weren't here. Got it?"

He nodded and started for the rear door. Claudia threaded her way through the book stands and into Martinlow's cramped office. She sidled into a corner, concealed by the blue curtain. A second later she heard a rap on the door. Martinlow took a breath, then cracked the door open.

"What the . . . who the hell are you?" he growled.

"Bill sent me."

Addison's voice all right.

"I don't know nothin' about a Bill," Martinlow said. "And I sure as hell don't know nothin' about a lady. If you're lookin' for a book, come back during business hours and use the front door." He made like he was shutting the door.

"Hey! You do *too* know about a Bill, and if you want what he sent, you'll open the damned door."

Claudia risked peeking from behind the curtain. She could just make out Addison holding up a fat package wrapped in plain brown paper.

Martinlow grunted. "I don't like this."

"Let me *in*," Addison said petulantly. "It's creepy in this alley."

Still Martinlow hesitated. "Bill *who*?"

"Bonolo, you ass. Now come on, already. I've got places to be."

The bookseller opened the door wider, made a show of peeking left and right past Addison, then let her in. "See? All I needed was the magic word. A fella can't be too careful." He started toward the front.

Addison muttered something unintelligible. Claudia caught a whiff of her perfume when she passed, then silently followed, barely breathing for fear of jostling the book racks. Earlier, they'd arranged one book stand so that it ran perpendicular to Martinlow's makeshift sales counter. She peered through a gap between science fiction novels on its top shelf. Martinlow stood on the seller's side. Addison stood on the customer side, impatiently shifting from one foot to the other. She'd placed the package on the counter. Even in the dim light, Claudia could see all she needed to.

Addison thumped a knuckle on the counter and said, "Come on, sugar. What're you waiting for? Let's get the show on the road. You're supposed to have something for me, too."

"I got all kinds of things a pretty gal like you might want," Martinlow crooned. He wriggled his eyebrows. "All *kinds* of things."

"Sweetie, whatever you could give me would probably level half this hick town in less than an hour and keep the health department busy for the rest of the decade. Let's get Bill's business done and over with."

"You're just playing hard to get," Martinlow said. He tapped the top of the package. "I got to see the goods first. Open it up."

"Bill didn't say anything about that."

"So call him."

"What? I won't be able to reach him now. This was supposed to be in and out. I don't even know what's in the package."

"So what do you want to do? I told him last time I wouldn't accept new product without him first showing me. Are these things even rewound?"

"How the hell would I know?" said Addison. "You think I'd watch this crap?"

Claudia could've kissed her for that statement alone, but she waited to see what would happen next.

Martinlow reached below the counter and brought up a thick wad of cash held together with a rubber band. He flipped through the money and told Addison it was her call. She swore. But she fumbled with the string around the wrapping until it was off and the paper fell away. Claudia squinted. Eight videos.

"There. You happy?" Addison said. But she didn't wait for Martinlow to examine the tapes. She grabbed the money from his hand. "This better come out right," she said, counting it swiftly. When she was finished she smiled triumphantly. "Pleasure doing business with you, you filthy pervert."

Good enough. Claudia stepped out. "You're not the lady I thought you were, Gloria."

Addison wheeled toward the voice, but before she could respond, Martinlow gasped. "Jeez, lady, who the hell are you?"

Claudia stepped out of the shadows and held up her shield. "Both of you—hands on your heads, and don't misbehave." She waited until they complied, then spoke into the radio. "Got 'em." The words were barely

out of her mouth, when Addison made a clumsy lurch toward the front
door. Claudia half anticipated the move and was on her before the woman
managed two steps. She yanked Addison back in the same second that
Moody, gun drawn, burst through the door, which probably would've
knocked the younger woman senseless.

"Holster your weapon, Mitch. We're good here." She faced Addison
to the wall and nodded for Moody to cuff her. When he was done, she
spun Addison around. "That was so remarkably stupid, Gloria. Resisting
arrest gives us one more charge we can throw at you." She heard Suggs
coming through the back door. "We're secure," she called out.

The chief made his way to the front. He wiped sweat from his forehead
and glared from Addison to Martinlow. "What a piece of work you two
are." He watched Moody handcuff Martinlow and read him his rights.
Then he told him to call two patrol cars for transport. He nodded for
Claudia to step off with him a distance.

When they were out of hearing range, he said, "I can't figure whether
this is a good thing or a bad thing, getting Addison instead of Farina."

Claudia smiled. "Oh, I think it's a good thing. We weren't even expecting Farina to show. At least with Miss Ditz I have something to work with."

"You need me anymore?"

"No. It was comforting to have muscle at the front and back. But it's all
talk and paperwork from here on out."

"Good, 'cause I got a cramp in my leg from crouchin' by that stinkin'
Dumpster. I'm gonna head home, see if I can work it out. Call me later."

"Yes, sir."

Suggs stopped halfway to the back door. He turned to her. "You just
call me 'sir'?"

"You know, I might've. I just might've."

"Damn. Nobody was even within earshot to hear it."

Claudia shrugged. "I'll see if I can work it in again, sometime when
we're in a crowded room. Sir."

He gave her a backhanded wave, then headed out.

Addison leaned sullenly against the wall and refused to make eye contact when Claudia returned to the front. Martinlow reacted just the opposite, pleading with his eyes for her to honor their deal. She was still
irritated with him, but she gave him a slight nod. He'd done his bit.

"Mitch," she said, "when the units get here have them take Mr. Martinlow to county lock-up. Get him processed. Tell them to bring Miss
Addison to the station for questioning. I'll get her through the system

later." She pretended not to notice when Addison glanced up, startled.

"Got it," said Moody. "Anything else?"

"No, I think—"

"Wait a minute," Addison said, a thin note of hope in her voice. "I'm not under arrest?"

"I'm still making up my mind. Mitch? I'm out of here. As soon as you're done with Mr. Martinlow, go home and get some sleep."

"What about you? It's after midnight. You must be beat."

"Nah. I'm wide awake." She looked at Addison for a very long minute. "In fact, I feel downright energized."

CHAPTER · 27

THE VIDEO CAMERA WAS OLD, a relic taken as evidence in a low-ball burglary case that predated Claudia's arrival to Indian Run. According to Suggs, the case went south when the suspect jumped bail. No one ever claimed the camera, so Claudia occasionally put it to use for suspect interviews. Right now the camera was positioned on a tall metal file cabinet in her office. It beamed down at a chair beside her desk. She had also arranged the tapes confiscated from Martinlow's bookstore beside a heap of file folders on the corner of her desk. The top file had Addison's name on it, and Claudia had stuffed it with enough paper to make it bulge significantly. Finally, she had turned on the faucet in the utility sink just enough so that it would drip annoyingly, and she'd aimed a small fan toward the chair Addison would take, then set it on high. When she was satisfied that she'd made her office environment as uncomfortable as possible, she stepped into the multipurpose room, where an officer was babysitting the young woman. Addison looked up, her expression a blend of apprehension and defiance.

"Thanks for hanging around, Officer," Claudia said. She removed her jacket so Addison could get a look at the .38 holstered at her waist. "I'll take it from here."

"Okay, Lieutenant. Give a holler if you need me to come back."

"Will do." She turned toward Addison. "Come on. Let's talk in my office. It's not as hot in there."

Addison followed wordlessly and sat in the chair beside the desk. Claudia closed the door, then leaned against the file cabinet and for a moment just stared at her. The fan immediately began agitating the young woman. Each time it rotated past her, Addison fumbled at her hair, trying to keep it in place.

"We've got a situation here, Gloria," Claudia said at length. "Actually, you've got more of a situation than I do, because when I leave I'm going home to a warm bed. But you might be headed for a hard mattress in a cold jail cell."

Claudia pointed at the video camera and explained that she would be taping their conversation for the record.

"I thought I wasn't under arrest."

"At this very moment you're not. But if that's what winds up happening, then it's to your advantage to have a record of our conversation, don't you think?"

At first Addison said nothing, and Claudia worried that she might start howling for a lawyer or simply walk out. But she only shrugged unhappily. Claudia quickly flipped the video camera to RECORD, and a red light came on. She established the date, the time, their identities, and the circumstances. Then she leaned back against the cabinet and crossed her arms.

"There is some good news here, Gloria. A first offense on a porn charge isn't even a felony. It's a first-degree misdemeanor. You might get off with a stiff fine and probation. On the other hand, the courts take a dim view of porn these days, what with the hubbub over porn and kids, so it's possible you could wind up doing as much as a year. Really, how you come out of this depends on how lucky you get with a judge. But then, I'm sure you knew all that before you decided to drop off eight videos at Mr. Martinlow's bookstore." She gestured at the stack on her desk.

"That's not how it was."

"Then how exactly *was* it?"

Addison fought with her hair and frowned at the utility sink.

Ping. Ping. Ping.

Claudia rapped lightly on the file cabinet. "Hey. Gloria. Try to stay focused. I'm probably the only one who can help you out of the jam your good friend 'Bill' put you into."

"He's *not* my good friend."

"You said that once before, but if he's not your lover and he's not your friend, then why would you go out close to midnight to break the law on his behalf? I mean, you *do* understand that he set you up, don't you?"

Addison squirmed in her chair, trying to angle herself away from the fan. Claudia moved close to her, then crouched down to her eye level. "Look at me, Gloria, and listen. He had a date with the bookseller, and if he'd kept the date instead of sending you, he'd be in this chair right now, not you." The fan kicked their hair into a cloud. Addison tried to sit farther back, but Claudia didn't budge. "Obviously he wasn't sure if going would be safe. And by now he knows it wasn't, of course, because you'd have already delivered the cash to him, or at least given him a call. Talk to me, Gloria. Tell me where Farina is. Tell me how you met him. Take me through everything."

"I don't . . . look, can't you turn that faucet off?"

"Forget the faucet, Gloria. It needs a new washer. Now what about Farina?"

"I don't know anyone named Farina."

"Fine. If it helps we'll call him Bonolo. Either way, he's the one who gave you up."

"I . . . you're crowding me," Addison mumbled.

"No, I'm not, Gloria." Claudia leaned in almost nose to nose. "*This* is crowding you." She held the pose for a moment, then backed off and stood. "Get used to it. It's what a jail cell feels like all the time. Bonolo, Farina . . . he knows that. It's why he didn't risk going to the bookstore himself. Are you really so naïve that you don't get that yet?"

Addison pushed furiously at her hair, trying to tuck it behind her ears. Her eyes flitted to the sink, then to the video camera. She was fighting tears, and her mascara had begun to run.

"You're in over your head, Gloria. Talk to me."

"I can't."

"You can. You need to."

"No! I'm not even supposed to be here! Nothing was supposed to be like this!"

"Like what?"

"Like people dying!"

"Hemmer."

"He wouldn't quit about his house! His paint! His precious patio! But now, everything's gone bad. Bill told me if I didn't drop off his package, he'd make sure I went down if the Hemmer thing got worse. I swear I didn't know what was in it. He told me books. I *guessed* it might be something else, but—"

"You weren't guessing, you knew. But never mind that. Back up. How could 'the Hemmer thing' get any worse? The man's dead."

"I . . . I don't know. They kept me out of that."

"Who's 'they'? And kept you out of what?"

But Addison had stopped feigning confidence long ago. She began to cry seriously, the sultry woman morphing into a scared girl. Claudia watched the transformation, and when Addison rooted through her purse for a Kleenex, she handed her a box of tissues, content to watch the young woman's face grow blotchy with emotion and failing makeup. She felt a twitch of sympathy for Addison, not because of her tears but because she'd learned how to be provocative without understanding that it wasn't a survival skill.

Finally Addison tapered off, and when she did, Claudia handed her a cup of tap water from the sink. Then she quietly asked what frightened her more—jail or "they." Addison's eyes welled up all over again, but she bit down on her lip and took a deep breath. Claudia turned the fan off, then asked again. Addison looked at her gratefully, and this time, in a shaky voice stripped of hope, she started talking.

CHAPTER · 28

FOR A MAN who professed not to be a night owl, Chief Suggs sounded wide awake when Claudia called him from her office at one-thirty in the morning. She heard a TV on in the background and supposed he'd been injecting himself with reruns to keep his eyes from slamming shut.

"It's about damn time you called, Hershey," he said by way of greeting.

"How's the Charley horse?" she asked.

"Better. What've we got from our little she-devil?"

Claudia gazed at the chair Addison had vacated a short time earlier. "More than we had. Not as much as we wanted."

Suggs groaned.

"What Addison told me sort of fleshes out some of our speculation, but—"

"But no smoking gun."

"You took the words right out of my mouth."

While the chief nattered on, Claudia stretched the telephone cord to her office door and peeked into the multipurpose room. A lone patrolman labored over a report at a far desk. She closed her door, then turned her back to it and lit a cigarette. The office was small enough to stretch the phone cord to the utility sink. It made for a good ashtray when the risk factor was minimal.

"So what exactly *did* Addison give us that we speculated but that still amounts to zip?" Suggs asked.

"Well, for one thing, she's sleeping with Boyd Manning."

"Well, you said you overheard him use the name 'Gloria' on his cell phone. I guess I shouldn't be surprised."

"Manning's the one who paid for her house, which she spends almost no time in because mostly she lives with him in his Feather Ridge home."

"Bigger. More plush."

"Uh-huh. The Willow Whisper house is actually an investment. Manning's thinking is that three or four years after the development is built out, the house can be turned around for a much higher price."

"Manning pay for Farina's house, too?"

"Addison says she doubts it. She claims Manning hates Farina. He didn't bring him in by choice."

"So who *did* bring Farina in?"

"Our princess claims she doesn't know." Claudia heard Suggs scoff, and she said, "Yeah, I'm not convinced, either. She's protecting Manning. Every time I asked her about him, she'd dummy up. She says they're lovers and that's all."

Claudia frowned at smudge spots on the faucet. She wiped at them with a Kleenex. Addison said she'd originally met Manning at a club in Miami, but she didn't recall which club or the circumstances, just that their encounter turned into "head over heels love" for both of them. She drove up to Indian Run to see him twice afterward. On the third visit she moved in, happy to put her temping jobs aside forever.

"Hershey! You still there?"

"I'm here." Claudia tossed the Kleenex into her trash can. The smudges hadn't come off. "Just thinking."

"Well, try and think out loud every now and then. You got any idea what Addison might be protectin' Manning about?"

"I wish." Claudia tapped an ash into the sink. "What she said is that Farina told her Hemmer might've known 'some stuff' that he wasn't supposed to."

"Like what?"

"Addison claims ignorance. Farina supposedly told her it was about business and insisted that if Hemmer didn't go, Manning could wind up with more than just a black mark in the community."

"Yeah, and if he got bounced from Indian Run there'd go her meal ticket," said Suggs. "Still, you'd think she'd ask him *something* about all this—use a little pillow talk, get him to open up."

"Addison's sense of curiosity is about as advanced as her intelligence," said Claudia. She took a satisfying pull on her cigarette, then waved at the smoke in the air. "She never liked Farina, but harassing Hemmer didn't seem that big of a deal if it would make life easier for Manning. So she went along."

For a minute the chief said nothing. Claudia listened to the muted tones of his TV while he absorbed the information. It was too late for Leno. She cranked her neck a few times to work out kinks, wondering what he was watching.

"Everything goes back to Hemmer," he said at length, "so what is it he knew that was so threatening he had to go? What the *hell* did that man know?"

"That's still the million-dollar question," said Claudia.

"What about Addison?"

"I let her go for now with the impression that I have a soft heart." Claudia ignored Suggs's snort and said, "She'll run straight to Manning, and maybe he'll make some kind of play we can capitalize on."

They kicked it around a little longer, then Suggs asked whether the medical examiner had been in touch yet on the skeletal remains. He hadn't, nor did he seem to appreciate Claudia's call for an update.

"He told me I'd get it when I get it," she said. "Should be a preliminary tomorrow, though. I left my home number with him."

"Sounds to me like you're actually thinking of getting some sleep."

Claudia looked at her watch. It was 1:45. "Might as well. There's not much else I can do here tonight."

"Except maybe clear the cigarette smoke from your office," Suggs growled.

Claudia whirled, as if she expected to see the chief standing behind her. She took a hasty last puff, then ran the tap and doused her cigarette. She thought she heard him chuckling, but that might've been his TV.

"Good night, Hershey," he said evenly.

"Good night, Chief."

CHAPTER · 29

MOST SATURDAY MORNINGS were leisurely defined in the Hershey household. Robin was old enough so that Claudia didn't need to bound out of bed to put breakfast on the table, nor did she really have to cut the grass or wash her car or run six loads of laundry before her coffee and the morning paper. She could do those things later in the day, or on Sunday, or not at all.

On this particular Saturday Claudia had grudgingly set her alarm for eight o'clock because there was much to do on the Hemmer case and the John or Jane Doe case that practically sprang from Hemmer's backyard. But it wasn't the alarm that woke her. It was the slow realization that she had more or less been awake for at least a half hour, bathed in sweat and tangled in bedding. For a while, she lay as she was and listened hopefully for the sound she knew in her gut would not be forthcoming. The air-conditioner's steady drone had ceased.

Claudia swore and disengaged from the sheets. Even if it was possible to get a repairman out on a Saturday, it wouldn't be possible without paying a premium. She fumbled into a robe and went to investigate, recalling the last time she'd had a problem with the A/C, remembering that she'd told Hemmer about it.

She stared at the thermostat, flipping it on and off a few times. She explored the air handler tucked away in a hall closet, then went outside and studied the condenser. It was nothing but a giant metal box with a fan inside. A lizard on top eyed her warily but didn't move, and why should it? She had no idea how to bring the ugly box to life again and therefore scant reason to do more than look at it, which would not get it fixed.

Claudia retreated to the kitchen and put on coffee. While it brewed she fed Boo, then thumbed through a phone book in pursuit of A/C repair shops that advertised weekend emergency service. The first two she called answered with a recording. She was about to dial a third when the phone rang in her hand. She jerked with surprise, then barked "Hershey residence, what?"

After a pause, a voice said, "The 'what' is a John Doe, Detective."

Claudia recognized the caller as Paul Morrison, chief medical examiner for Flagg County. He was respected for his expertise, but almost no one cozied up to him socially because he was curt with peers and treated those who weren't peers as idiots. Personally, Claudia liked Morrison well enough, but she recognized the futility of trying to smooth her gruff greeting. She shot ahead with questions.

"So we're talking a male?"

"It's all in the pelvic bones."

"Right." She scanned the kitchen counter for scratch paper, then settled on the margins of a page from the phone book to scribble notes. "What about age?"

"Ossification indicates late teens, early twenties."

"Race?"

"Preliminary indications suggest Caucasian. Without advanced tests I can't be more specific."

"Height? Weight?"

"Five-seven to five-eight. Thin to average weight."

"Any identifying characteristics?"

"His right arm measured dominant, predictive of a right-handed individual. His left leg was slightly shorter than the right. That might suggest a mild limp. I also noted a fracture of the left tibia, but it was indicative of an injury that would have predated his death. His teeth, though intact, showed signs of decay and other neglect consistent with someone who rarely saw a dentist."

"So I shouldn't count on dental records to help with an ID."

"No, but all is not lost. We can extract mitochondrial DNA from the bones, which would verify or discount identification if you were able to suggest a preliminary ID from some exemplar source. Are you with me?"

Oh, yeah. She was with him. He was telling her to figure out who the victim was, then bring him the victim's comb, toothbrush, bedding—something still likely to have a trace of the person's DNA. He'd compare it to the DNA isolated from the bones, then award her a gold star if there was a match. That could be useful later. It didn't help now.

"Any idea how long the victim had been buried, Dr. Morrison?"

"As little as one year. As many as three. There were no hair remnants, but the deceased's clothing was remarkably well preserved, which along with other factors would—"

"So crime scene got clothes! That's something."

"I wish you wouldn't interrupt."

"My apologies."

"As I was saying, the clothing was surprisingly intact, and given other variables, I believe the body was probably concealed beneath the ground closer to a year or two, rather than three. Greater precision obviously calls for additional tests."

"Obviously."

"As for the clothing itself, your victim wore nondescript, lightweight blue jeans, a cheap, short-sleeved cotton shirt, tattered socks, a vinyl belt, threadbare jockey shorts, and brown loafers so worn he could probably feel pebbles through the soles. He had no watch, no rings, no wallet."

Claudia had filled the margins of one phone book page. She flipped to another, pen poised, mind racing. "What about cause of death? Can you give me that?"

"Not with any medical certainty. But I *can* narrow down the *manner* of death to blunt-force trauma. John Doe had two severe skull fractures, the most significant one depressed on the outer layer of the cranial vault."

"In other words, he was bashed on the head with something."

"Very good, and if that bit of information makes your pulse quicken, then you'll be ecstatic to learn that *what* he was bashed with was recovered beneath the remains."

"You're joking."

"I don't joke. The victim was struck twice on the head with a piece of rebar that measured two feet and four inches in length and one-half inch in diameter. Crime scene pulled it up after the remains were removed."

What Claudia knew about rebar could be measured in a thimble. Morrison must have suspected as much, because he lectured her about its properties as if she were just joining the construction trades. She filled margin after margin in the phone book while the medical examiner informed her that rebar described steel reinforcing rods used in concrete construction. It was manufactured in a variety of standard diameters and typically sold in lengths of twenty to sixty feet.

It occurred to Claudia that Morrison was really just Booey in a different package. She ached to hurry the medical examiner along, but she'd already offended him once and she needed him on her side.

"Builders cut rebar all the time to suit their specific purposes," Morrison said. "After all, one wouldn't use the same size of rebar to reinforce concrete blocks in a house as one might use to shore up the concrete work in a bridge."

"No," said Claudia, "one wouldn't do that."

If Morrison detected her sarcasm, he didn't show it. "The rebar that crime scene found is in the lab undergoing further analysis. Rebar is often coated with epoxy or zinc to help prevent corrosion, and perhaps our piece can be traced to the original manufacturer and, from there, to buyers."

That would take forever. Claudia sighed, and Morrison must have heard her.

"Take heart, Detective. I don't need further analysis to tell you right now that the characteristics of the rebar found in the grave perfectly match the fractures in the victim's skull. Thus, manner of death is blunt-force trauma. Mode is homicide. You have the murder weapon. Really, all you need now is ID on the victim—"

"—and the killer," Claudia finished.

"Have a good day, Detective."

"And right back at you, Dr. Morrison."

They hung up and Claudia tore her scribbled pages from the phone book. She opened some windows and poured a cup of coffee, then checked in with the station to see if Farina had been spotted overnight. He hadn't, which came as no surprise. But a BOLO was out on him now. Maybe they'd get lucky and someone would recognize him.

Claudia dampened a paper towel and wiped perspiration from her face. The air rolled in still and heavy through her open windows, and the sky sat low with thick clouds. Showers had been forecast, although of course half the time that the weather gurus predicted rain, they were really only covering their asses in case some freak storm sneaked by their radar. She tossed the paper towel into the trash and roused Carella with her next call. She brought him up to date on Addison and the John Doe, and asked whether the description of the victim matched anything he'd turned up in missing persons reports.

"The reports are on my desk at the station," he said, "but there weren't that many cases still open, and none of those that are sound like our guy. I'll go in and give the files a closer look, but my memory is that from the last five years we've got four females and three males unaccounted for. We now know we'd only be looking at the four guys. Two were teenagers and believed to be runaways. One was an old guy. Other fella was middle-aged, but you said the M.E. has our guy in his late teens or early twenties."

"All right, Emory. Thanks."

"You don't sound surprised."

Claudia tapped her pen against the counter. "Our John Doe had bad teeth and cheap clothes. He could've been homeless or a drifter, someone no one cared enough about to call in missing."

"Maybe no one even noticed him missing."

"Maybe." She took a swallow of coffee and lit a cigarette. Her house. She could do what she wanted. "The crime scene's too old to tell the whole story."

"But the rebar. . . ."

"Yeah. That's interesting. Willow Whisper might've been under construction at the time our guy took a hit. Rebar could've been all over the place."

"So you're thinking he was killed right there?"

"It's got that feel to it, Emory." Claudia pushed hair from the back of her neck. "And the fact that the rebar was tossed in the grave with our guy makes me think it was an impulse kill. Someone panicked. Someone knocked our guy on the head and got rid of him and the evidence in one go."

"And . . . maybe that's what Hemmer knows? Could that be it?"

Claudia thought about the timeline. "I don't know," she said doubtfully. "Hemmer's house probably wasn't even finished. But check with the building department and see what kind of sign-off dates they have on the development."

"You mean Monday, right? Because this is Saturday. The building department is closed."

"So try to rouse somebody."

"I'm not sure I like this detective business as much as I thought," Carella muttered. "The hours are lousy, you have to make people hate you, the—"

"And here's a news flash: The pay's not all that much better than being on the road. By the time you calculate— What's all that banging in the background?"

"Sorry. I'm making breakfast for the kids. The wife's really milking her birthday. I told her she could sleep in and I'd do the morning shtick. Come on over and I'll fix you something, too."

Breakfast with the kids. Breakfast with anyone. It sounded good.

"Thanks," she said, "but I already ate."

"Caffeine isn't eating, Lieutenant. You ought to give that stuff the boot."

"Not on your life." She smiled. When had these guys gotten to know her so well? "I'll take a rain check, though."

They talked until Carella was ready to summon his girls to the table. Afterward, Claudia opened the refrigerator's freezer compartment and basked in the cool air for a minute. Then she poured fresh coffee and sat back down at the counter. Give up caffeine? Never. It was the elixir of life, the oil in her engine, the—

Wait.

The boot. He said, give that stuff the boot.

"God love you, Carella," Claudia murmured. She took a hasty swallow of her coffee, then made a fast call to the chief to coordinate other details that would leave his Saturday in rubble, too. Ten minutes later she was dressed and on the road, with a destination and an idea that was leading her to it.

CHAPTER · 30

CLAUDIA HAD NO IDEA how much she liked the earthy smell of leather until she entered Buddy's Boots and inhaled the scent on a welcoming tide of chilled air. She looked for the boot maker. As he had before, Buddy Dunn sat elephantine behind his wooden bench, his fingers shaping leather. They were thick as stogies, but they evidenced a dexterity that elevated mere craft into art.

Dunn caught her eye and smiled a greeting. "I guessed you'd be back," he said. By some trick of light his solitary ruby earring threw a sparkle when he raised his head. Or maybe it was just the contrast with his bald head that made it seem so. He wiped his hands on a stained towel. "You've decided you can't live without boots after all."

"I don't know about that. I'm pretty tough." She matched his smile. "But as a matter of fact, I do want some, for me and my daughter. Only not today. I'm here for another reason."

"Well, I'm happy to help if I can."

Claudia pointed at a pair of boots on a shelf behind Dunn. "Those," she said. "Aren't those the boots one of your customers never finished paying off?"

Dunn was too big to swivel around and look. He slowly dismounted from his stool, then angled to face them. "Yup. You've got a good memory." He regarded her quizzically. "This is your other reason for being here?"

"You said he'd been paying toward them weekly, right? And that he suddenly stopped paying a year ago or so?"

"Yes, to both, but I don't understand." Dunn began to reach for the boots. "Is there—"

"Please don't touch those," Claudia said so sharply that the boot maker flinched. "I'm sorry. It's possible they're evidence, though. Let's just talk for a minute."

"Talk's good." Dunn heaved himself back onto his stool. He took a moment to get settled, his breathing labored from the mild exertion. "What's this about?"

"Last night we recovered the skeletal remains of a man buried in an overgrown field. You might've heard something about it. The press was out."

Dunn nodded. "Caught a report on the radio this morning. They didn't have a lot to say."

"Well, we don't have much to tell yet. We don't know who the victim is, and frankly we don't have a lot to go on in identifying him. But the medical examiner's initial report . . . well, there are some physical characteristics that brought to mind what you told me about your customer."

"Aw, no," said Dunn. "I really liked this fella."

"Let's not jump to conclusions. Tell me what you know about him, what he looked like, what he talked about . . . that sort of thing."

The boot maker steepled his fingers and rested his chin against them. He focused on Claudia, though she knew he really wasn't seeing her now; he was calling up memories, scraps of recollections. Finally, he shook his head.

"Juan-Carlos Santiago is his name. Mexican, I believe. He had a small build, but he looked strong enough, probably from outdoor labor. I guess I'd put him at about twenty years old."

He spoke so softly, Claudia had to lean in to hear.

"He was just a little guy, just an everyday little guy tryin' to make his way in the world the same as the rest of us. I can't think of a soul who'd want to hurt him." He blinked. "Funny, I really did think he'd walk back in the shop one day and claim his boots. At least I wouldn't have been surprised. He wanted them *that* bad. He'd try them on every time he came in. I imagine there weren't too many people he didn't tell about those boots of his."

"When you say he was 'little,' can you be more specific?"

"Oh, maybe he stood five-six or five-seven—in that neighborhood. He had an ever-so-slight limp 'cause his left leg was a smidgen shorter than his right, just enough so I had to make an adjustment in the boots." Dunn smiled. "What he told me was that he'd never had footwear that would let him stand proper."

Claudia felt a knot of certainty seizing her belly. "Do you know if he was right-handed or left-handed?"

Dunn furrowed his brow. "Right-handed, I'd say."

"What else?" she said softly.

"Not a lot. I don't know how long he'd been here, but he told me he'd worked vegetable fields and citrus groves for a few years. He took what odd jobs he could between picking seasons. He sent most of his money home—at least it's what he said—and I believed him. What little he kept, he put toward the boots."

The boot maker had just described a migrant worker. Florida's cheapest labor. Florida's biggest shame. But no matter how feverishly the drumbeat rose to banish their exploitation, it persisted. There was too much to be made in undocumented labor. And there were too many migrants willing to do the backbreaking work that no one else would.

"Was he legal?"

"If you mean did he have a green card or whatever, I don't think so. But I never asked. It wasn't any of my business. Damn. He was such a likeable guy. Really, really likeable."

The boots Santiago longed for cast a shadow on the wall behind them, making them appear larger than they were. Claudia admired the cactus-and-thistle design again, and she wondered who had decided that Santiago should die, and she wondered why. She asked Dunn if he had a phone number or address on the migrant worker, knowing how remote the possibility.

"I doubt he had a phone," Dunn said. "If he did, I would've tried to reach him."

"Right."

"But I have an address." He smiled at Claudia's startled expression. "I guess I didn't look like a threat. Anyway, my grandmother keeps the records. She's always talking about purging the old ones, but I doubt she has." He pushed aside a piece of leather and retrieved a portable two-way radio from his bench. "Grams got a pair of these off eBay. If there's a gadget to be had, she wants it. Of course, these things are actually kind of useful. I can check to see if she's still breathing upstairs. She can check to see if I'm still breathing down here." He pressed the talk button and, after a burst of static, said into the unit, "Grams, you up yet?"

Claudia heard a crackle and then the old woman's voice: "Buddy! You're breaking up. How many times I have to tell you not to talk the instant you press the button? Why are you bothering me?"

Dunn told her Claudia was with him, then asked if she'd bring down the Juan-Carlos Santiago order sheet. The radio crackled back with her response.

"You talking about that tall woman who had the hots for Tom Dixon? The one who—"

Dunn fumbled to muffle the radio, too late to do much good. He shrugged apologetically. "Sorry about that. She's never been afraid to say the first thing that comes into her head."

"I remember that from the last time," Claudia said. "Don't worry about it." But she was mortified just the same and hoped Mae Dunn would fold the Santiago order sheet into a paper plane and sail it down the stairs instead of bringing it personally. Her hopes were dashed when she heard the woman descending a few minutes later.

"It's you, all right," she said to Claudia as she shuffled over in slippers. "I never forget a face, and yours makes an impression. I mean that in a nice way."

Mae wore a long flannel nightgown with a purple flower pattern. It was at least one size too large for her, making her appear even tinier than Claudia remembered.

"How do you do, Mrs. Dunn," she said, trying to modulate her tone into something neutral. "It's nice to see you again."

"Hah! You're only here 'cause you thought Dix might show up. You youngsters wear puppy love on your sleeves."

"Grams," said Dunn. "Come on, now. . . ."

"Here." She thrust a piece of paper at her grandson. "One day I'm going to get these things in a spreadsheet and do some number crunching."

"Is that before or after you purge the files?" the boot maker said.

The woman waggled a finger at him. "Don't get mouthy with me, young man. I'd be done with the files *and* a spreadsheet if I didn't have so damned much work to do on the World Wide Web." She looked at Claudia. "That's the Internet. I'm putting Buddy's store online."

"I remember."

"That's right." She nodded. "You're the one who put me in touch with that Booey." She shot Dunn a look. "Now *there's* a courteous young man." Back to Claudia. "You got a cell phone?"

"I . . . well, yes. I do."

"Can I see it? I've been thinkin' of getting one."

"Grams," Dunn said gently, "you already have one."

"I *know* that! Think I don't know what I do and don't have?" She shook her head. "Sometimes I think you spend too much time breathing leather and dye. So," she said to Claudia, "can I see it? I'm thinking of getting a *new* one."

If the cell phone would distract the woman long enough for Claudia to conclude her business and flee, she was happy to comply. She pulled it from her purse and handed it over. Mae murmured something unintelligible and wandered off, poking buttons and having a conversation with herself. Claudia hoped the old woman wouldn't drop it. When she bought the cell phone, she'd passed on the extended warranty.

The Santiago order sheet showed that payments had actually stopped nineteen months earlier—not the year that Dunn remembered. The boot maker was surprised it had been that long, but Claudia supposed that in the cloistered world of his shop, time lost meaning. She looked at the address Santiago had given, recognizing it as part of a neighborhood she'd visited months earlier. That time, a lead on a petty theft had brought her there, but the lead fizzled abruptly when she stepped out of her car. Most of the residents were Hispanic and had regarded her with undisguised suspicion. Surely some of them spoke English, but they played dumb, and she spoke no Spanish.

Claudia jotted down the address and silently vowed to crawl all over Suggs until he hired a Latino, an African-American, an Asian, a Native American, and more women, in no particular order. Meanwhile, she'd send Moody to see if he could ferret out any information on Santiago. Moody spoke Spanish reasonably well, and he had more patience than she did.

"It doesn't look good for Juan-Carlos, does it?" Dunn asked quietly.

Why lie? "We'll know more later, but . . . no. Look, I'm going to need to take those boots with me. Eventually you'll get them back."

He shrugged. "Take your time. It's not likely anyone else will want them." He clambered off his stool and shuffled beneath the counter to get her a box.

Claudia turned and scanned the shop. Dunn's grandmother stood in a shadowy corner as far from them as possible. She was cackling merrily, the cell phone to her ear.

"Grams!" Dunn called. "You're gonna have to part with that. The lady needs to get going."

Mae irritably waved a hand and took her time concluding her conversation. Finally she shuffled back and handed the phone to Claudia. "Yours works a lot like mine, but I like mine better," she said. "The buttons on yours are too damned tiny."

"Glad I could be part of your consumer test," Claudia murmured.

She was nearly to her car when she heard the boot maker's grand-mother calling something from the doorway. She nodded her head as if she'd understood, then eased herself behind the steering wheel of the car. A half mile later, Mae's parting words caught up to her brain:

Check your speed dial. I might've messed something up.

They tossed Farina's house in ninety minutes. Neighbors gawked from the sidewalk, reminding Claudia of the last time they'd watched the police come out. It had to hurt; the security they cherished had been violated twice in little more than a week—both times from inside. Their gates had not brought them trouble, but they hadn't stopped it, either.

Suggs had roused a judge for the warrant and arranged for the search himself, then happily informed the mayor that Bonolo was not Bonolo, but a convicted felon on the run. Lane insisted on attending the search, but he didn't interfere. Claudia imagined he was trying to figure out how to distance himself from the man he'd cast as a hero. She watched him tag along behind Suggs, his mouth pulled into a worried frown.

Farina's taste in furnishings ran to dark leathers and even darker woods. His family room had been converted to an entertainment center and boasted an enormous flat-screen television, a sophisticated stereo system, a wet bar, an overstuffed couch, and a reclining chair. His bedroom held a towering armoire, leather-trimmed water bed, another huge TV, and floor-to-ceiling mirrors that made Claudia dizzy. But the rest of his house contained so little furniture it looked like an afterthought.

They came up empty. Farina had been a step ahead of them, and there wasn't a trace of pornography or Hemmer to be found. The big man had cleaned out and cleared out, leaving little more than a messy kitchen and a pair of Speedo swimming trunks to talk about. The kitchen suggested a hasty departure. The Speedos suggested nothing, but provided a good minute of lively banter for Suggs and an officer posted at the front door. Lane glowered at them but said nothing. Claudia wondered if he had a pair himself. It was an image too ugly to dwell on, and she was grateful when the mayor bowed out a minute later.

Suggs watched him speed-walk past the neighbors and drive off. He turned to Claudia. "Want to put any bets on how long it'll take him to go whining back to Manning?"

"How long has he been gone?"

"About thirty seconds."

"Then he's probably already there."

Thunder rumbled in the distance. Claudia peered through a window at the neighbors outside. Their ranks had thinned with the mayor's departure, but a cluster remained, now looking anxiously toward the dark sky.

"Come on," said Suggs. "Let's get out of here. Those toads want to stay and get wet, fine by me. But I put freshly laundered pants on this morning, and I'm not of a mind to let rain soak the crease out of 'em."

Claudia thought of her own clothes. The humidity had taken the snap out of them hours earlier. But there was nothing more to do in Farina's house, and with luck she'd still have time to summon an air-conditioning repairman to her own.

"I'm on your heels, Chief," she said.

"Good to hear you know your place."

She glanced at his face to make sure he was joking, then groaned obligingly and followed him into the muggy outside. Adjusting to the chief's improved demeanor was a little like adjusting to the big-ass Imperial after the now-dead Cavalier. She knew it was better, but she wasn't sure how much to trust it.

Claudia stopped at the station on her way home to check for messages and call around for an air-conditioning repair service from the chilled comfort of her office. There were no messages that couldn't wait, and she was grateful for that, but any hope of getting her A/C unit promptly repaired vanished thirty seconds into a conversation with a harried service technician. He informed her that air-conditioners were dead or dying all over town, and unless her name was preceded by "Pope" or "President," her unit wouldn't get fixed until Monday afternoon. No, he couldn't say exactly when. He advised her to buy a table fan in the meantime. Claudia took the appointment and hung up.

She ached to be home but loathed the thought of sitting in the heat, so she reached for the Hemmer file. Again. Always again. But there had to be something they were missing, and she started reviewing her notes and reports from the beginning, trying to come at it from different angles. She was so absorbed that it took her a moment to realize the phone on her desk was ringing.

She picked up. "Hershey."

"I'm married, so you can't kiss me, but if I weren't you'd want to."

"What's up, Emory?"

"What's up is that it took a string of phone calls, but I found the building inspector at home and, through a combination of cunning and charm, persuaded him to meet me in his office. Edgar Wiles. Nice man."

"Did he have much to say?"

"Yeah, but Wiles is older than dirt, and first I had to listen to endless stories about how things used to be done. I tell you this so you'll appreciate my persistency in learning anything at all."

"Cut to the chase. What did the permit dates show on Hemmer's house? Anything useful?"

"Wish I could tell you. Wiles went to the file cabinet where the permits should be. They're gone, and so are any cross-references to them. I thought Wiles was gonna have a heart attack."

"If you're joking, Emory, now's a good time to say so."

But he wasn't, and for the next fifteen minutes Claudia took notes without lifting her pen from the page. After they hung up she stretched, threw water on her face, and then tried to make sense of what he'd told her.

Wiles was 73 years old, which hardly made him older than dirt but did put him past an age when most people held full-time jobs. Even so, not counting one gap in his work history with Indian Run, he'd served as the town's sole building inspector for an astonishing thirty-eight years— longer than most marriages, he'd boasted to Carella. If a new store went up in town, Wiles was there. New house? There again. He signed off on permits for foundations and framing, plumbing, insulation, heating, and more; and most importantly, he eventually signed off on permits for occupancy. He took his job seriously. Build your structure to code and you'd have no problem. But if at any point in the process, standards weren't met, you could kiss your project good-bye until you made things right— period, end of story.

Wiles's hard-line attitude didn't make him particularly popular with builders, because to save a buck here and there, they sometimes cut corners, and Wiles was a pain in the ass when it came to shortcuts. Even so, he mostly got along with the construction trades, and his stubborn adherence to standards never became an issue, which was why his face still flamed red when asked about that one gap in his work history.

Claudia understood. Wiles fully expected to live to a hundred and get a centenarian birthday card from the White House. He was healthier than men half his age and, he told Carella, still sharp enough to cut paper with his brain. But he was of a time when certification to be a building

inspector wasn't necessary, so he wasn't certified; and he was of a genera-
tion that pooh-poohed technology, so he balked at getting building
records onto computers. For those reasons he was asked to retire at the age
of 70 and, at the time, was so taken aback that he didn't resist. He went
gently into that good night and stayed there for two years.

A man named Frank Tinnerman took Wiles's place. Tinnerman was
certified, and he had a degree in computer science. For a town lockstep-
ping into growth, he seemed an ideal replacement, especially with Willow Whisper about to break ground. He wasn't much liked by the office
staff, but then, apparently they weren't much liked by Tinnerman, either.
Wiles kept up on office gossip and told Carella that Tinnerman was perceived as moody and secretive, and when one day he upped and quit, no
one felt anything but gratitude. It was Wiles's favorite part of the story,
because after Tinnerman's abrupt departure, the old man was asked—
begged, according to Wiles—to come out of retirement and take his job
back. He got a big party and more money, and he loved to tell anyone
who would listen that Tinnerman never did get any of the department's
records on computer. So there.

Claudia abruptly looked up from her notes, distracted from reading by
a small movement to her right. She squinted toward her coffee cup. Was
that a. . . ? It was. An ant. She flicked it off her desk and scanned the sur-
face for others. None waved a flag and said hello, but that meant nothing. Everyone knew the little bastards left invisible trails for their buddies
to follow, and she checked her bottom desk drawer just to make sure she
still had a can of Raid inside. There it was, beside an unopened package of
knee-high hose. Satisfied, she went back to her reading.

Tinnerman was a little like that ant, she thought. He'd come out of
nowhere, and if Wiles was right, he'd faded into nowhere, too. One late
afternoon he went out to a job site and simply never returned. He mailed
a thin package with reports to the office along with a kiss-my-ass letter of
resignation that said he'd had it with the hours, the heat, and an uncoop-
erative staff. A final check sent to the address he had on file was returned
as undeliverable. Gossips speculated that Tinnerman had girlfriend or
gambling troubles. They favored the latter explanation because no one
could imagine Tinnerman with a woman, and discarded lottery tickets
had been spotted in his office trash can more than once. And anyway, who
cared? No one liked him, and Wiles was back.

When Carella recounted Wiles's story, Claudia flashed to the body in
the field. Tinnerman? Not Santiago, but Tinnerman? The inspector had

quit right about the same time Santiago stopped paying off his boots, so the timing was good for both. But no. Before she could even ask, Carella told her that Tinnerman was middle aged and stood six feet tall, and he didn't show on their missing persons report. So that was that.

Except. . . .

The building department's permits on Hemmer's house were missing.

Except. . . .

The mayor hired and fired department heads. He was the one who booted Wiles out and brought Tinnerman in, then rehired Wiles when Tinnerman quit.

Except. . . .

The timeline for everything ran suspiciously close to the development of Willow Whisper. Claudia needed more specific dates to be sure, but it appeared that Tinnerman quit right after issuing a certificate of occupancy on Hemmer's house. It also looked like Tinnerman and Santiago both went missing at about the same time, perhaps within days of each other. The vexing reality, however, showed that their histories abruptly stopped nearly a month before Hemmer moved into his house. So where was the connection?

Still, there *was* one more exception. . . .

Hemmer had quietly visited the building department once, three weeks prior to his death. He'd come in to photocopy all records relating to the construction of his house. He'd signed for the records, copied them on the department's machine, paid a nickel for every page—more for over-sized pages—and then handed the records back and signed out again. That was procedure, and no one was more surprised than Wiles to discover that the original files had subsequently vanished. It just didn't happen, not on his watch, and by golly, heads were gonna roll when he figured out who misplaced those dern things.

Claudia distractedly brushed away another ant, then another. Ideas were coming at her fast now, so fast they were colliding before she could assemble them into one coherent whole. She reached for a fresh legal pad and started writing them down. By the time she looked up, it was four-thirty and ants were streaming across her desk as if they owned it. She could vanquish them with one blast of Raid, or she could walk away and salvage the rest of her day—and maybe something more. She closed her legal pad and chose more.

CHAPTER · 31

FOR A WHILE when Robin was little, her terror of thunder was so great that Claudia had to hold and rock her until the sound diminished to a barely discernable rumble in the distance. Claudia fumbled for simple explanations that would lessen her daughter's fear: angels bowling in heaven; skies with fierce belly aches; trains with heavy loads. Robin bought into none of them, and if anything, she showed keen disappointment that her mother would try to trick her with such lame invention.

Claudia smiled at the recollection and handed her ticket to a woman at the entrance to the bluegrass festival. Thunder boomed in the distance, and surely it was raining somewhere, but not here. Then again, that meant nothing. In Florida it could rain on one side of the street and not on the other.

The woman handed Claudia a red-and-white checked bandanna. She looked at it, puzzled.

"Your first time here?" the woman said.

Claudia could barely hear her over the thunder and the music thumping from the festival grounds. She pointed to her ear and then shrugged apologetically.

"It's part of the ticket price," the woman shouted. "The women's club does them up every year, just for the festival. Better souvenir than a hand stamp, don't you think?"

Claudia agreed that it was, then moved onto the festival grounds, which sprawled from the town's central park onto two streets blocked off for the occasion. She paused to get her bearings beneath a colorful banner proclaiming DOG DAY SUMMER BLUEGRASS FESTIVAL. Some of the festival-goers had wrapped the bandannas around their foreheads or necks. Others had tucked them through a belt loop. Claudia tried to knot hers around her head but couldn't make it work. She stuffed it into a jeans pocket, making sure the tail spilled out enough to show her community spirit, then began to amble.

People jostled good-naturedly in every direction—throngs of them, hordes of them, all of them slick with sweat and insect repellant. Claudia let herself be swept along, ignoring half a dozen alcohol violations as she moved past game booths, food vendors, and kiddy rides lining the circumference of the park. A young girl in clown makeup flapped her bandanna at Claudia. She smiled and flapped hers back, feeling the weight of the day begin to lift.

Indian Run did things its own way, and the bluegrass festival was more carnival than music event. Claudia lost two dollars on the ring toss, another five on a shell game that couldn't possibly be legal. Then she meandered toward a vendor selling funnel cakes. Her cholesterol level always ran high-normal, but never mind; Robin wasn't around to push her guilt buttons.

Later, after she had satisfied the craving and washed it down with a lemonade—the kind with chunks of real lemon floating at the top—she fell back in with the crowd. The optometrist she'd met from Hemmer's client list spotted her once and waved her down. He introduced her to his family—three round kids and a round wife, none of whom wore glasses. Claudia wondered if they'd had laser vision surgery, and shuddered to imagine it. But she held up her end of the conversation, and when the optometrist said he looked forward to their appointment, she smiled pleasantly and lied that she did, too.

If anyone besides herself was unaccompanied by friends or family at the festival, she didn't see them. But she wandered on, her eyes on the crowd, scanning faces, always scanning faces.

As the hour drew closer to night and still no rain fell, the crowd increased, blocking what little hot breeze might have wheedled through. Claudia stood at the side of the bandstand and watched a banjo player and guitarist duke out a version of "Dueling Banjos." She glanced at her watch. She'd made a circuit of the festival grounds three times and gorged on so much junk food that her stomach felt queasy. She'd run into Suggs and Carella, both of whom attended the festival every year. Carella had his wife and two daughters with him and didn't linger. Suggs didn't linger, either, but for a different reason. His mind was on crowd control, because with the inky night came boisterous drunks, pickpockets, and teenagers feeling each other up in dark corners. He told her to keep an eye out, and she said that she would.

Later, she'd bumped into Moody, too. He was with a date, which for some reason surprised her, but he politely excused himself long enough to tell Claudia that Santiago had to be their John Doe.

"Everything points to it," he'd said. "The people in his neighborhood weren't exactly eager to talk to me, but they opened up a little once they understood I wasn't from INS."

Claudia had nodded. The Immigration and Naturalization Service held far more sway over their lives than the local police, and little of it positive.

"Santiago evidently shared an apartment with a few other guys. Some were legal. Some weren't. They came and went, mostly working the fields and odd jobs."

"Just like Dunn figured it," said Claudia.

"Yeah, but get this. The last few months before he disappeared, Santiago got hooked up with a subcontractor who handles local jobs. The work wasn't steady, but it paid better than anything else he'd done. One day he went out on a job with them. He never came back."

"What kind of subcontractor? What kind of job?"

But Moody was already shaking his head. "I don't know, Lieutenant. Santiago had a girlfriend in the apartment complex. She doesn't live there anymore, but one guy said he knew another guy who might know where she went. The second guy wasn't around, but the thinking is that he will be tomorrow."

Claudia had told Moody to forget about it until then, and it annoyed her that even in the midst of the festival she couldn't manage to do that herself. She shifted her weight and tried to clear her head. Cloggers in impossibly heavy shoes were taking the stage. A ripple of applause went up. When they began pounding their feet to the zip of a guitar, the bandstand shook visibly. Taiko drummers made less noise.

"It's like tap-dancing in concrete slippers," a voice said into her ear.

Claudia turned slowly. "I wondered if you'd show," she said.

"I was wondering the same thing about you."

"Here." Claudia pulled a festival ticket from her rear pocket. "You left this on my counter."

"I know. I had to buy another one to get in." Sydney wore khaki shorts and a photographer's vest over a black T-shirt. A camera with a long lens hung from her shoulder. "You owe me twelve bucks."

"I hope you can wait. I'm tapped out from buying junk food."

"It's killer, isn't it?"

"Deadly. Especially the funnel cakes."

"You go with the powdered sugar and cinnamon?"

"Like there's any other way?"

"Right."

They turned their attention to the stage for a minute, letting the cloggers fill the awkward spots. Claudia idly wondered if their legs tingled for hours after a performance. She asked Sydney her opinion.

"My guess? Their legs will throb clear into next week. Look, are we gonna have to try this hard every time we see each other?" She waited. "Claudia?"

"I looked at your coffee table book."

"Oh, boy. Here we go. I should've—"

"No, no. No." She sought Sydney's eyes. "I'm all right with it. I don't get it, but I'm all right with not getting it, so let's just let it go."

"You're all right with it," Sydney repeated.

Claudia shrugged. "Fifty percent all right with it, okay? Maybe sixty. It's where I am."

"You came here to tell me that?"

"I've been sweating here for two and a half hours. I'm bloated from fried dough. What do you think?"

Sydney swung her camera to her other shoulder. "I think you should've worn shorts. You're the only one here in long pants."

"Robin tells me I have no fashion sense."

"This isn't about fashion sense. This is about common sense."

Claudia tentatively stepped closer and gave her a playful cuff on the head.

"Hey, hey! My black eye is just starting to fade." But Sydney laughed. "We used to wrestle, remember? We were both such tomboys."

"Don't worry. I'm too tired to wrestle now."

Sydney sobered. "Claudia, I should've told you about the book before I did it. At least before I mailed a copy to you." She smiled. "Well, I'm fifty percent sure I should've, anyway."

"We're not very good at this, are we?"

"So maybe we don't have to be, not all at once. What do you say we get out of here before someone realizes we're twins. I hate that fawning shit, don't you?"

"Can't stand it."

They walked out of range of the cloggers.

"I can almost hear again," said Sydney. "Got any cold beer at home?"

"I don't have cold anything at home, not even the house. The A/C went south this morning."

"Plan B, then. I'm in the Holiday Inn just outside town. It's got two double beds." Sydney pawed through a vest pocket and pulled out a key card for the door. "Here. Room 314. I've got maybe another half hour of shooting to do, and then I'm history. Go on ahead of me. You can turn the A/C to high, shower, and collapse."

"Syd, I don't have any clothes with me, never mind a toothbrush."

"So buy one on your way there. You can wrap yourself in a sheet, call your home machine for messages, talk to Robin . . . whatever you want. It's got to beat sweltering."

Claudia took the key card. She touched Sydney's hand for a second, then pulled back. "I . . . you know, I think the 7-Eleven's on the way to the Holiday Inn."

"Right. You might be right. Good. Now go. Let me work."

They parted, but like the mirror images that they were, they reflected each other when they turned simultaneously to sneak one look back.

Sydney rolled her eyes. "Film at eleven," she mouthed.

Claudia laughed out loud. She wiped her face with her bandanna and scouted for her car. As festivals went, Indian Run's was all right. Next year she'd bring Robin.

The shower—excellent. The air-conditioning—divine. Claudia reveled in both, running the hotel's A/C at maximum speed and leaving it there even when goose bumps stood out on her arms and legs. She took Sydney's advice and wrapped herself in a sheet, then snickered and rooted through her sister's clothes until she found a nightshirt instead. It was a nice one, too; one hundred percent cotton. She slipped it over her head, plumped pillows on the second bed, then climbed aboard with her cell phone. Bliss.

Out of habit she punched her speed dial for the station. No messages, and not much going on. Most of the guys were still working the festival, which wouldn't end until eleven o'clock. Claudia glanced at the hotel's clock radio. It was only nine-thirty, not exactly late-late, but nevertheless too late to call Robin. She drew her knees toward her chest and pulled the sheet over them. She thought through the sequence for accessing messages from her machine at home, then poked the speed dial for her house. The phone rang once, twice, and then a man answered.

"Whoops. I'm sorry," said Claudia. "I'm afraid I misdialed."

"No, you didn't. Not if you're Claudia Hershey."

"Excuse me?"

"This is Tom Dixon."

Claudia had once viewed a TV special on people who supposedly self-combusted. They might be sitting in a chair and then, for no scientific reason, *poof!* They just went up in flames. She wondered if she could achieve that. Her face felt hot as a lit match.

"Hello? Claudia?"

The boot maker's grandmother. Of course.

"You still there?"

"I'm here," said Claudia. "Well, this certainly is awkward as hell." But she felt another kind of sizzle now and hoped Sydney wouldn't trash it by walking in the door. "Mae Dunn played with my cell phone today."

"I know. She sort of told me while she was programming it. Anyway, I heard you were at the festival tonight and I would've warned you there, but obviously our paths didn't cross."

Claudia eased lower into the pillows. "Except for the portable toilets, I can't think of a place I didn't visit there. Hard to imagine I could've missed you."

"The pony rides. I was running the pony rides for kids up until nine o'clock. Then I bailed for the night."

"Ah. And all this time I thought you did cows."

"Horses, cows . . . I can see where you might get confused. But actually, if you're going to get to know me—and I hope you are—then you should probably think of cows as cattle. Not to split hairs, but in the business we mostly call them cattle."

"That's the lingo, huh?"

"There you go."

"You've got a wonderful voice," Claudia blurted. She clapped a hand over her mouth. "What I mean to say is, you've got a wonderful way of explaining things."

Dixon laughed, the sound a low, melodic rumble that stopped her breath.

"That being the case, maybe I should explain something else," he said. "Like for instance, I'm secretly glad I didn't get a chance to warn you what old Mae was up to. No telling if you'd ever call me on your own. Mae thought not."

"She's a frightening woman."

Dixon laughed again. "You don't know the half of it."

"Maybe one day you'll tell me."

"Sooner rather than later, I hope. Because I'd like to get to know you. Because I'd like to show you some . . . *cows.* Because, well, because you attract me in a pretty powerful way."

"I do?"

"You do."

Claudia realized she was gripping the sheet so hard, her knuckles had turned white. She relaxed them and watched the flesh tone flow back in.

"You still there?" Dixon asked.

"Mmm."

"Good. Because now would be an excellent time for you to flirt back with me. That's how this is supposed to work."

"Is that what Mae Dunn told you?"

"Nope. I thought of it all on my own."

"Okay, give me a minute. Let me think." She did, too. "How's this: I can no longer drive past big animals on four legs without thinking of you. It's like some alien life force has taken over my mind."

"That's not bad. You, uh . . . free to date?"

"Yes, but I'm not very good at it."

"Neither am I, so we have that in common right off."

They stopped short of phone sex—which apparently Mae heartily endorsed as foreplay for busy people—but managed to work in plenty more flirtation in the next twenty minutes. After they hung up and Claudia had time to reflect on the call, she realized that ineptitude in dating wasn't all they had in common. He was divorced. She was divorced. He had a boy. She had a girl. He had cows. She ate cows. It got a little dicey after that, but hey, you had to start somewhere.

CHAPTER · 32

SYDNEY SNORED. Claudia almost woke her just to tell her that, to lord it over her a little, but then she worried that perhaps she snored, too. She'd fallen asleep before her sister; no telling what nocturnal horrors she'd unknowingly revealed. And anyway, Sydney's snoring wasn't seismic, nor was it responsible for stubbing out her sleep. The rain did that, and one thought: Hemmer's house.

The evidence in the investigation might be vague. Connections between suspects might be loose. But Hemmer's house was an absolute. Everything started with the house—not with Hemmer the man, but *with his house*—and maybe it had more to yield yet.

She needed to go back. In only forty-eight hours, Sandi's grandparents would sign the house over to Manning. That quick, and he would own it. Hemmer was no longer a factor, but Manning wanted his house badly.

The house, the house, the house. It was all about the house.

Claudia showered and quickly threw on her clothes from the day before. She winced at every sound she made, but Sydney never budged. They'd shared wine late into the night, rolling out childhood stories, fast-forwarding through the last eight years, and giggling over banalities too stupid to recall now. One day, they'd get to the tough stuff. For now, it could wait.

The rain sheeted against the hotel window, driven by a wind that would render umbrellas useless. Claudia scribbled a note. Then she grabbed her red-and-white bandanna from the dresser top. It would come in handy to wipe off her hands before she touched the steering wheel. With one look back at Sydney, she eased out the door.

* * *

Moody caught her on the cell phone just after she parked the Imperial in Hemmer's driveway. He was calling from a phone booth a few miles from Santiago's former neighborhood. Rain hammered Claudia's car with such ferocity they had to shout to hear each other, but he had news. He'd found and roused the friend of a friend who might know Santiago's girlfriend. The friend didn't know where she lived now, but he knew what church she attended. Moody was there now, and he'd approached her coming out of an early Mass.

"You've done all this already?" Claudia shouted, checking her watch. She'd gone home only long enough to change clothes and feed the cat. "It's only nine-twenty, Mitch."

"You're disappointed we finally caught a break?"

"You're sure we did?"

"It's him. It's Santiago. The boots, the timing . . . everything fits. And his girl, Maria González, I think she can help us with a positive ID. She's got some of his personal items and . . . oh, Lieutenant, it'd break your heart to see her, to talk to her. She still lights candles for him at Mass. She still hoped he'd come back one day. She had to know he wouldn't, said she figured something bad must've happened, *had* to have happened, but even so. . . ."

Thunder boomed over Moody's next words, and Claudia didn't hear them. She caught an aggrieved waver in his voice, though, and through it could almost feel the anguish that gripped Maria González. Life went on when someone disappeared; but against all odds, against all reason, hope waited.

". . . and then, because Santiago was here illegally, no one ever filed a missing persons report."

"They didn't trust the police," said Claudia. "Big surprise."

"What? I can barely hear you, Lieutenant."

"I said, they didn't trust the police."

"Still can't make you out."

"We'll talk later, Mitch," she yelled. "Good work."

"What book?"

"No! Work! Good work! Never mind. We'll talk later!"

Claudia jammed the phone in her purse. The car windows were fogged over, and the interior of the vehicle was unbearably stifling. It would be muggy in Hemmer's house, too, but maybe less claustrophobic. She braced herself and flung open the door to the pelting rain.

* * *

If there were such a thing as ghosts, Hemmer wasn't one of them. His scent did not linger in the house. He cast no shadows on the wall. But Claudia felt his presence in the grim memories she'd stored from their encounter, and while rainwater puddled at her feet, she wished for clairvoyance long enough to stir a detail that might hint at what he'd known and what she didn't.

For a minute she stood motionless in the foyer, where Hemmer had greeted her with the name "Charles Gottu."

Got you.

She shook her head. Yeah. He'd got her, all right, and good; but for a man who talked about trust like he owned a patent on it, his stunt was more shameful than any of the carnival hustles she had seen at the bluegrass festival. Of course, he'd insisted on calling it a "ruse," as if the distinction would elevate his trick into something admirable. And maybe for him it did. For all his erratic ramblings, Claudia remembered being struck by how carefully he seemed to choose his words. She moved into Hemmer's family room, reminding herself to go slow and resist substituting her own words for his.

The crime-scene cleanup crew had done a masterful job removing all signs of violence. A prospective buyer would see nothing but gleaming tiles and unmarred walls—all of it so white, the room looked new. It hardly mattered; Manning had made sure real estate agents wouldn't be showing the house.

Claudia retreated from the family room just long enough to find the thermostat for the air-conditioning. Policy be damned, she needed the house cool to think. When she returned, she sat on the floor where Hemmer had instructed her to sit. She gazed around, struggling to reproduce in her mind's eye what now seemed more the stuff of a bad dream than a real event. But it had been real; the lump on her head from Hemmer's gun, though no longer painful, was reminder enough.

She gazed at the wall where Hemmer's aquarium had been. What did he call the fish? Platys? Tetras? The names didn't matter, but Claudia seized on them, anyway, in a mental exercise that might open her mind to details that did matter. The others came to her after a moment. Swordtails. Guppies. And she remembered that the water was cloudy.

Incredibly, it had been only nine days ago. Hemmer was dead. A migrant named Juan-Carlos Santiago was dead. Bonolo wasn't Bonolo, but Farina—and he was on the run. It all tied to Willow Whisper, and desperation marked every turn; but for all of that, what did Indian Run's finest have to show for it? A grizzled old guy in jail, and even he wouldn't stay there long.

Claudia shook off the failures and concentrated. Hemmer had talked about movies and he'd talked about games. He liked Twister, she remembered. They'd discussed her problem with an air-conditioning company, but no . . . that was nothing; she'd brought it up herself. He'd been all over the board—paint, bats and radar, drug abuse, trust. Intermittently, he'd ranted about security and community, the point of it all, the lack of a point.

Links? Any links at all? She gave it a few more minutes, then shook her head, frustrated, and moved upstairs to Hemmer's office.

Without the computers on his desk, the room looked twice as big as she remembered it. She flipped on a desk lamp and walked the room as she'd done before. Her certainty that the house had more to yield diminished with every drawer she opened and every file folder she turned. But the house gushed cool air, and she took her time, trying to imagine Hemmer bent over his desk, tapping on a computer, carefully filing papers away.

By nature he had been a cautious man. In the last few weeks he'd grown paranoid as well. But, if anything, paranoia would've made him more careful, not less. It simply didn't follow that a man so driven would allow whatever damning papers he'd compiled to be casually available. He might have come close once. Claudia recalled the "crinkum-crankum" computer document with nothing on it. Booey had suggested Hemmer probably started the document, then erased the text before he ever stored it.

That damned word.

It lived on his computer. It lived on his blotter pad. What was that about? Claudia glared at the red dictionary on top of Hemmer's bookcase. The damned word didn't even appear in a damned dictionary, not in her damned dictionary and not in any damned dictionary. She grabbed Hemmer's dictionary and shook it, as if the stupid word would flutter to the floor. Nothing did, of course, and she set it back down, struck again by the irony that she and the man who took her hostage used the same dictionary. His showed more wear; otherwise it looked practically identical to her own. But so what? They both had daughters, too. It didn't make them kin.

Irritated, she started to cross the room to the closet, then paused midway when her own word caught up to her. *Practically.* She murmured it aloud. Her dictionary and Hemmer's dictionary were not identical. They were only *practically* identical. His was more worn because it was older. She grabbed the book again and checked the copyright date. Look at that, 1980. Old, old, old. She thumbed to the "C" listing and flipped some pages, tracing the columns of words with her finger.

"Well, how about that," she whispered.

There it was. *Crinkum-crankum.* And check it out, the dictionary called it "archaic." The editors apparently struggled whether to include the word at all, because they'd given it a miserly one-sentence definition: "anything full of twists and turns." That much Claudia already knew. (Thank you, Booey.) But what made the entry interesting was the word *twists.* It was faintly underlined in pencil.

A paranoid man would do that, and Hemmer was paranoid. A paranoid man would ascribe meaning to it, and Hemmer ascribed meaning to virtually everything. Claudia looked at the underlined word. Six little letters. On their own, so what? But she knew where Hemmer was taking her now, had decoded enough of his thought process to see the only place he could be taking her. Sure. Drop the last *S* from *twists*, and add *er*. It gave you *twister.*

Twister. The game of Twister. A crinkum-crankum kind of game if ever there was one, and he'd given it to her outright, just like he'd given her the names of the fish, all of it sounding like just so much drivel. But "Twister" wasn't drivel. He'd asked if she knew it. She did. He'd said "good," then scoffed at the hostages and told her they probably wouldn't; *they* would probably never get the significance. He'd handed her a clue and, with what small measure of faith he still retained, trusted her to figure it out if need be.

Or maybe he was showing off, just a little.

Claudia rubbed her eyes. It didn't matter now. He died before he could explain his motives, and as she thought of him gasping in her clutch, she thought she understood the last word he'd breathed into her ear, the garbled word that sounded like "dishree.*"*

Dictionary.

No wordplay that time, just the last utterance he could manage.

She set the dictionary aside and went in search of Twister. Thirty minutes later she found it in the garage in a box marked "clothes for donation." It wasn't the first place she would've thought to check for files, and she wondered why Hemmer hadn't thrown out a hint to bring her there earlier. But maybe he had and she'd dismissed it with most of his other ramblings.

Claudia quickly flipped through the contents of the Twister box, then brought it inside and set it on Hemmer's dining room table. The rain had taken a time-out, so she headed for the patio to smoke a cigarette and call Suggs. He'd want to know she'd found what the intruder had missed. When she was done with both, she turned off Hemmer's air-conditioning, locked up, and hurried to the Imperial before the heavens burst again. With luck, the bookseller would have company in jail by day's end.

C H A P T E R · 3 3

FROM SOMEWHERE in her memory bank, Claudia recalled the seven deadly sins as pride, envy, gluttony, lust, anger, greed, and sloth. In context of the Hemmer case, she wasn't sure about gluttony, and she discounted sloth altogether; but she understood that one way or another, the remaining five sins drove the desperate acts that left two people dead—and maybe three. Condense the sins to their basic components, and you were left with money and sex, the trigger in most murders.

It wasn't a revelation. Even a rookie knew that money or sex—or both—trumped all other motives in crime; and the Hemmer case, stripped of its bizarre crinkum-crankum, revealed itself no differently. But money and sex had only been the genesis. Fear, thought Claudia, propelled them along.

For three tedious hours she'd been at her desk, eating junk food and squinting between files and her computer screen. The ants were gone, maybe discouraged by the rain that once again fell steadily. Claudia suspected they'd return with the sun—if it ever surfaced, which looked less likely as the day wore on. Already, flash flood warnings had been issued, and officers were working double shifts to cope with abandoned vehicles and motorists who mistook canals for roadway.

She frowned at her computer screen and queued a document to her printer from the Division of Corporations at Florida's Department of State. She would never gush over computers like Booey did, but on a Sunday when most government offices were closed, an Internet connection could still extract at least some information from them. She waited impatiently while her printer toiled over the document, the last she needed for now. When it finished, she correlated the details on it with her notes, grabbed her office camera, and brought her files into Suggs's office.

The chief had been working the roads along with his officers, and his hair lay patchy against his scalp from rain. She showed him what she had and told him where she was going. He didn't like it, and argued against it until she vowed to make her visit nothing more than a visual check.

"You've poked a nest of hornets, Hershey, and pretty soon one of them is gonna sting you," he said, his eyes boring into hers. "That's one thing, and I tell you so you get it into your head that I can't get backup out if you do something stupid enough to need it. The other thing is the rain. I got Carella on the road now, and if Moody ever makes it back from that neighborhood where you sent him, I'm gonna put his ass out there, too. So go make your check—and just a check—and make it fast. One more inch of this stuff comin' down and I'll need you wading through water with the rest of us."

Claudia nodded and turned to leave before he could change his mind.

"Hey, Hershey!"

She hung back.

"Don't forget your damned radio."

The rain showed its muscle everywhere, pushed by gusty winds that howled and bent palm trees nearly double. Debris clotted the roads. Traffic lights swayed at dangerous angles. Once, Claudia nearly swerved off the road to avoid a plastic patio chair that pitched across her lane like tumbleweed. She didn't have time to ponder where it came from; the storm consumed all her attention.

Above the roar of the wind and rain and thunder, her portable squawked incessantly with officers conveying information on malfunctioning traffic signals, washed-out intersections, and downed power lines. Paramedics fought for the airwaves with their own troubled reports— heart attack victims they couldn't get to, fire-rescue trucks breaking down, a broken communications link to the hospital. No one with a scintilla of sense would be outside now, but by the time Claudia considered a retreat, she was more than halfway to her destination, her progress measured by street signs she could barely see.

The Imperial's brakes felt mushy, but otherwise the car impressed her. It soldiered through flooded intersections like a Humvee, and twice she used it to nose stranded motorists in lesser vehicles onto safer ground. It wasn't a cocoon, however. Rain spilled through a back window that in the absence of air-conditioning had to remain cracked open to minimize condensation on the windshield. The car smelled like a locker room.

Claudia wrinkled her nose and peered past the shuddering wipers, cursing the meteorologists who had predicted light showers. But she was inching forward, always inching forward.

Lights glowed dimly from inside some of the estate homes in Feather Ridge, but most appeared uninhabited—and probably were. The houses in Indian Run's most exclusive community were typically winter retreats for those who could afford them, and few of its residents chose to hang around in the sticky summer. Claudia drove slowly, studying street signs and navigating around puddles that in some cases flowed curb to curb. Her last visit to Feather Ridge had ended in an arrest. This one wouldn't, not yet, but a reconnaissance on the location would reduce the likelihood of trouble when it did.

She pressed her lips together. The explanation sounded good to her ears, and she'd sold the chief on it, too. Time wasn't on their side. They needed to be ready to move on events soon. Logic dictated extraordinary caution. Blah, blah, blah—she almost bought it herself. But coming here was an idea that had seized her in Hemmer's house and gripped her with an intensity that only in the solitude of her car would she concede smacked dangerously of obsession. Point of fact, she was here because she wanted to see where the psycho son of a bitch behind the dead bodies lived.

The homes in Feather Ridge had little in common with those in Willow Whisper. Residents weren't required to choose from among model homes. They hired their own architects and were governed by their own unspoken assumption that rich people understood aesthetics in a way that less-moneyed people did not. If squabbles arose over colors or landscaping, they rose unobtrusively and were settled quietly. Homeowners association? No, thank you. Not here. Gates? Déclassé.

Far from the street, Boyd Manning's house erupted from the ground between pine trees and artificial hills that must have cost a fortune to build and sod. It stood three stories tall, a modernistic structure of glass and sharply angled balconies, apparently designed to simulate a mountain view. Around the hills wound a man-made stream, which may have been pleasant on pristine days but now overflowed and made passage treacherous.

Claudia took it painfully slow, giving the car just enough acceleration so that it wouldn't stall out. For a hundred yards from the street, Manning's driveway stretched straight and true but then abruptly began to angle up to follow the path of the stream. She held her breath and inched the Imperial through water that at times crested to her door. Once again she toyed with a retreat, but turning around would be next to impossible except from higher ground.

Neighboring structures weren't visible from Manning's property. Feather Ridge estates claimed two to four acres, but even if his house sat on a patch of earth only large enough to contain it, a barricade of ten-foot hedges concealed the property. The hills, the trees, the hedges—all of it cast shadow that contributed to the gloom of the day. It was five-fifteen but might just as well have been midnight.

Manning's driveway ended in the shape of an inverted Q, allowing for parking in front of the dwelling and discreet access to a garage at the side. By the time Claudia got there, her hands were cramped from clenching the steering wheel. She idled for a minute to get her bearings, then parked on soggy grass behind a cluster of trees at the edge of the driveway. She sat and flexed her fingers. The house was dark except for a dim glow from the first floor on the side farthest from her. Kitchen? Dining room?

Clearly it wasn't an optimal day for entertaining, but three cars were parked in the driveway. She immediately recognized Gloria Addison's Alfa Romeo. Another car looked vaguely familiar, but the rain obscured detail, and she could tell only that it was light in color. The third looked dark blue or black but brought no recall whatsoever.

Claudia picked up her camera. She fiddled with settings and focused at the vehicles through the Imperial's window. She snapped a few pictures, then put the camera down, careful not to set it on the damp bandanna still on her seat. As visuals went, she now had some. The house. Cars in the driveway. But she couldn't make out the license tags—and those she wanted badly. She sighed. A rain slicker was balled up in the trunk, but she'd be soaked by the time she retrieved it; and anyway, it was orange, with POLICE emblazoned on the back. If anyone peeked out Manning's windows, it would signal her presence as effectively as a knock on the door.

Wind whistled through the rear window in the Imperial. Claudia listened to it for a moment, muttering at her folly. Then she squirmed against the seat and awkwardly stuffed a small notebook and pen into her pants pocket, hoping they'd stay dry long enough to scribble the tag numbers. On the count of three, she thrust the door open and half ran, half skidded toward the vehicles, hunched to protect the notebook.

She squatted behind the dark car, worked the notebook and pen from her pocket, and wrote down the license number. Before she was done, the characters began to bleed on the page. Quickly, she duck walked to the lighter car. She started to scrawl the tag number, when she realized where she'd seen the car before.

Her heart banged so loudly in her chest she was surprised she couldn't hear it. But then, the rain impeded all sound but its own, including the swish of footsteps behind her and the thump of something hard against her head. She slipped noiselessly to the slick pavement, not hearing. Not feeling.

Nothing.

CHAPTER · 34

"YOU'RE AN UNINVITED GUEST, and an unwelcome one."

Claudia lay prone on a couch in clothes still wet. She didn't know the voice, but through eyes glazed with pain, she recognized the silver-haired man speaking. Lyle Hendricks.

"I didn't know who you were when I hit you, but I do now." He gestured toward Boyd Manning, who stood rigidly a few feet away. "My stepson isn't good for much, but he was able to tell me that."

Incredibly, she wasn't bound, but when Hendricks saw her struggle to sit, he said, "Careful, careful. Give it a minute. Your head's not bleeding anymore, but if you move too fast you'll feel a stab of pain that'll make you wish you were dead. I did a tour of duty in Vietnam with the Marines—early Vietnam, before the public understood the atrocities on both sides. I learned how to inflict pain. I learned how to receive it. Incidentally, my name is Lyle Hendricks, or is that already old news for you?"

Now, when it no longer mattered, every sound seemed magnified. She heard a clock ticking, classical music turned low, and, against the windows, the steady thrum of rain, always the rain. She didn't feel capable of words yet, but she slowly nodded a yes to Hendricks's question. He wouldn't have identified himself if he thought she didn't already know who he was. No point in lying. Not yet.

"I imagine you haven't fully absorbed how it is you've come to find yourself in surprisingly familiar circumstances. What was it? A week ago Hemmer had you hostage? Two?"

She didn't respond.

"There's a sensor built into the driveway. And cameras discreetly placed on the property as well. When someone drives over the sensor, an alert sounds in the house. The rain defeated the cameras, but not the sensor.

We knew someone was coming."

"The chief of police knows I'm here." Claudia didn't know if she actually spoke the words or just thought them, but Hendricks chuckled.

"No, actually he doesn't. He thinks you *tried* to come out, even sent an officer to check, but . . . well, look. You've been out for a while. We had time to conceal your car. Actually, all but Boyd's have been hidden away, and when—"

"They looked for me?" She struggled to push to an elbow. The pain nearly blinded her, and she fell back.

"Shh, shh, shh . . . you need more time," Hendricks said.

The effort to talk pushed the taste of vomit to her throat. She swallowed thickly. "They'll be back," she managed.

"Oh, I don't know that I would count on that. Phone lines are down all over. Drivers are stranded everywhere. And the officer who came—some kid named Richardson?—he told me your own radios are hit and miss, even in good weather." Hendricks paused. "Nice boy. He left with the impression you're stuck somewhere and can't get in touch. So there's some concern, but not alarm. And by the time they are alarmed? This'll all be over. Now close your eyes and sleep."

She did.

The second time she came to, she heard the same sounds as before, along with voices murmuring in the background. Despite their low tones, the voices carried urgency, and Claudia struggled to play possum against an impulse to open her eyes and shift her weight. She resisted, buying time to think and assess her injuries.

Déjà vu, her head throbbed. Hendricks had nailed her in nearly the same spot as Hemmer. Her right knee hurt as well, probably from the fall. Surprisingly, the nausea had subsided. She drew some comfort from that, though not enough to believe that when she stood—if she ever did again—the urge to vomit might not return.

What role Hendricks played in Willow Whisper's horrors remained an unknown. The state's Division of Corporations indirectly revealed him as the majority owner of Hercules, but it was a distinction so veiled by layers of AfLUX holdings that it would never leap out—not without tediously linking one business to another, reading through lists of filings, company officers, and agents of record. Claudia had Hemmer to thank for pushing her to the task. Notes in his Twister box showed that during his skirmish with the homeowners association he contemplated suing the builder. He never followed through, but one cryptic note he'd written to himself said, "Conspiracy? Corruption at top? Trace true ownership." In light of Hemmer's final actions, anyone else would see his note and others like it as the absurd ramblings of a sick mind. Claudia had learned better.

"I see you're awake." Hendricks's voice was smooth and unhurried. "Sit slowly." As if concerned for her well-being, he talked her up with "easy, easy—not too fast," and then after she complied, he said, "There you go. Already the color is returning to your face."

He seemed pleased, and Claudia sensed that her longevity might depend on her ability to downplay weakness. And she *did* feel stronger, more than she expected to, but less than she hoped.

She zeroed in on the gun in his hand, a .45 held casually at his side. She spotted her .38 second, parked beside him on a handsome wet bar made of cherry wood. He saw her looking.

"My stepson has good taste in furniture. He has lousy taste in women. If he had listened to me on the second, we wouldn't be in the mess we're in now. Or at least we'd be in less of a mess. Or do you know that, too?"

"Enlighten me," Claudia said.

Hendricks smiled. "Don't feel you need to hide your fear on my account. Nothing personal, but you're going to die in a tragic car accident today. If not for the rain, you'd already be dead."

No regret in his words. No anxiety. If anything, just a hitch of annoyance in his tone. She'd blundered onto something, and now he had to deal with it.

Tragic car accident.

Claudia felt her breathing go shallow, opening the door to a full-scale panic attack. She fought it, took deep breaths.

Think, think, think.

In a way, he'd delivered good news. The gun was for control, but he didn't want to use it; too much blood, too much forensics evidence. No. Better to wait out the storm and stage a car wreck when the roads had gone from flooded to merely dangerously slick. Sure. Wrap the Imperial around a tree, or ditch it in a canal—something like that. But it was good news, *good* news, because it bought more time. Time was advantage. She shuddered once more, then stopped.

Hendricks was frowning toward a window. "I control a lot of things. I'm accustomed to it. Unfortunately, no one can control Mother Nature." His eyes settled on her again. "Would you like something to drink, Detective Hershey? Scotch? Bourbon? Wine?"

Alcohol might ignite the nausea. But Hendricks wasn't a man you'd ask for milk.

"Wine would be nice," she said. "Red, if you have it."

Claudia watched him casually set his gun on the wet bar and pour two glasses of wine from a decanter. He hummed lightly to the classical music. To look at them—her on the couch, him at the bar—you'd think they were friends. But if she tried to spring at him he could retrieve the .45 with leisure and still shoot her before she was fully on her feet. It might be his last recourse, but he would use it.

Hendricks took his gun from the bar and crossed the short distance to the couch. He handed her one of the glasses, then offered her a cigarette. She accepted and he lit one for both of them, then stepped back, once again set his gun on the bar, and leaned against it. He watched while she inhaled. He ignored Manning completely, who stood as silently to the side as before. Claudia took a small sip of wine and blanked him out. She had one enemy in the room.

"The wine's excellent," she said. Smoke curled from her cigarette. She held it up. "I take it this is the proverbial last cigarette before execution?"

"Detective, you're getting way ahead of things. And who knows? Maybe I'll find some reason not to kill you." He smiled. "Maybe you'll kill me first, eh?"

Claudia pointed at their guns on the bar. "You have all the toys."

"True. I have something else, too." He turned to Manning. "Get them."

"Lyle, we don't have to—"

"I said get them!" he roared.

Manning froze momentarily, then murmured, "All right, all right."

"And, Boyd," said Hendricks, just as his stepson moved to leave, "don't challenge me again, understand?" His voice had dropped back to a conversational tone, but his eyes stayed cold with anger as he watched Manning stalk into a hallway.

"Kids," said Claudia. "They can twist the screws better than anyone."

"You don't know the half of it," Hendricks replied. "This one," he said, glaring toward the hall, "he's a real piece of work."

Claudia nodded encouragingly. There they were, just two soccer moms at a match, discussing their obstinate children. "You've got other sons, right?"

"Three *real* sons, all of them carrying my blood, all of them in my businesses now. Boyd's mother—my second wife, dead now—she spoiled him. It's why he's like he is."

"Mmm."

She waited for Hendricks to continue. When he didn't, she dropped the topic and asked for an ashtray. Now was not the time to push. Later, though? Maybe. Hendricks treasured control, but he'd lost it for a second, hinting at a vulnerability. She thanked him when he gave her an ashtray. Then she settled back into the couch and waited for whatever came next.

That Manning returned with Gloria Addison was less a revelation than an expectation. Claudia had seen her car outside. But she didn't expect to see Addison with a gag in her mouth and her hands tied behind her back. It stunned her, though not with the impact of seeing the mayor beside her, likewise tied and gagged. She felt fear percolate into something close to terror. On her own, she had a chance. But the last time she had the responsibility of victims. . . .

Don't go there.

Hendricks instructed Manning to seat Addison and Lane in opposing arm chairs beside a fireplace. He regarded them dispassionately, then took a swallow of wine and turned to Claudia. "I've surprised you," he said.

She shrugged, fought for composure. "A little," she said. "I get Addison, sort of. But the mayor. . . ."

"He's a Judas."

Lane vigorously shook his head, but Hendricks brushed him off with a wave. "I've been his biggest campaign contributor—not directly, of course, but that's neither here nor there. The point is, he's profited politically and he could've continued to." He gestured at Claudia with his wine glass, already nearly empty. "I've put more people in positions of power than you can imagine."

"I have no doubt." And she didn't.

"But this little son of a bitch—would you believe he had the audacity to come here and whimper about the negative impact *I'm* having on *him?*" Hendricks's eyes flashed. "I gave him Willow Whisper. I gave him my dickhead stepson to run it. But the minute there's pressure? He folds, and . . . well, you've heard the adage that a little knowledge is a dangerous thing?"

She said yes.

"Well, that's the situation with Lane. He knows just enough to be dangerous. I can't have him shooting off his mouth about things."

"Like the building inspector. Frank Tinnerman."

Hendricks snorted. "There's another loser."

"You mean 'was.'"

"I stand corrected."

"He's under the patio, isn't he? It's why no one dared let Hemmer tear it up."

"It was expedient. In business, you learn to do what's expedient. Tinnerman was squeezing us for more money."

"Why didn't you just stay with the town's original building inspector?" she asked, although she already knew the answer.

Hendricks scoffed. "Because, Detective, we needed someone with a less critical eye. The state's gone way overboard on building requirements. They're expensive. That old guy—what's his name?"

"Edgar Wiles."

"Right. He would've held us up for months, dickering over every board, every nail, every pipe. Time is money."

"Ah. That's where Mayor Lane came in. He eased Wiles out for you and eased Tinnerman in. Then Tinnerman got too pricey."

The delight on Hendricks's face seemed genuine. "You're bright and straightforward. You would've been an asset in business, Detective." He glowered at Manning. "Pay attention, Boyd. You could learn something from this woman."

Claudia watched Hendricks pour himself another glass of wine. He never offered one to his stepson, and his stepson didn't ask. Manning wouldn't even meet Hendricks's eyes.

"So did you do Tinnerman yourself?" she asked.

"It's a long story."

"In that case, top me off." Claudia willed her hands not to shake as she held out her glass. She needed him to keep drinking. He would if he had company. "I could use a good story right about now."

The wind had eased, but rain continued to fall steadily. Hendricks watched it for a second. "Why not. We've still got time." He gave her an amused look. "It'll be interesting to see how much you knew, how much you guessed, and how you react when you learn how wrong you were."

CHAPTER · 35

IN THE BUSINESS WORLD nothing mattered but results, and you didn't achieve them by poring over the latest management book on the bestseller list or leaving them up to committees under the guise of empowerment. No. You didn't do that. You used money and threats to get results. Anyone who told you different would be lying.

Hendricks's unwritten mission statement for AfLUX? Kill or be killed. Eat or be eaten.

That's what he told Claudia, and he told her in the same matter-of-fact tone he'd used to inform her that she would die in a tragic accident later. Of course, the "kill or be killed" philosophy wasn't intended literally, but if push came to shove . . . well, you did what you had to do. In all matters you reacted swiftly and decisively. And you never, ever panicked.

But Boyd didn't get it. He waffled on day-to-day matters. He panicked on big ones. Hendricks saw it coming—*predicted* it would come—and that's why he sent Farina to baby-sit. He'd used Farina before. Hell, he'd even bought the man a clean identity just so he'd be available when needed. Farina was a business expense, and so was the house and car he gave him cash to buy. All of that, just to make sure Boyd didn't screw up.

Claudia listened to Hendricks's recitation with only an occasional interruption. The thing with Manning, for instance. Why give him Willow Whisper to develop at all? Why not give it to one of his sons? His *blood* sons. It made no sense, and she asked him about it.

Hendricks had switched to scotch on the rocks. He rattled ice cubes in his glass and took a swallow before answering.

"I got complacent. First and only time that ever happened. Last time, too." He laughed bitterly. "Boyd's mother was rich. *Very* rich. That was attractive to me, enough to marry her after her first husband died. Boyd was seven and as whiny then as he is now."

Claudia didn't have to look at Manning's face to know what it would show.

"My businesses were doing well before she came into my life, but they really took off with her money behind it. She never challenged me, and why should she? I built an empire. She never wanted for anything, and neither did Boyd. Imagine my surprise when she died four years ago and I was presented with a last-minute codicil to her will. It dictated that the bulk of her estate would be held in escrow until Boyd was given a business of his own to develop. I would receive an annual stipend in the meanwhile, but it would expire within five years of her death if by then her son's business wasn't up and running. She had pancreatic cancer. It's brutally fast, and she knew that." He clucked. "She didn't trust me to look out for him. Imagine that." Then he sighed. "The good news is that the language in the codicil was hastily assembled and vague enough for liberal interpretation. Lawyers can tie it up in court for a while, but in the end, 'develop' doesn't necessarily mean 'own.' It's why I'm majority owner, and jerk-off here isn't."

Now Claudia did turn to look. Manning's face was contorted with shock and rage; but Hendricks saw it first, and with chilling speed he pivoted and aimed his .45 at Manning before the younger man could say a thing. "Not a word, Boyd. Not one. You didn't know and now you do. So what? It changes nothing."

But it did, thought Claudia. Manning had an expiration date on his head. Hendricks had complied with his late wife's estate provisions—and in less than the requisite five years. Who could call Willow Whisper anything less than successful? Hendricks was positioned to collect. She wondered if Manning understood.

The rain drummed steadily and Hendricks returned to his story.

It was all very simple. The Tinnerman confrontation could've occurred anywhere; it just happened to take place behind the house that Hemmer was having built. What made the whole damned thing complicated was how Manning handled it. Instead of meeting Tinnerman's demands and dealing with him after Willow Whisper was finished in some five or six months, no, Manning had to panic and whack him on the head with a piece of rebar. How unbelievably pedestrian could you get?

But wait, it got worse. With the light beginning to fade but before darkness settled in, the body could draw attention. And that's when Manning panicked again. Hemmer's patio had been framed, but not yet filled with cement. Wonder Boy scrabbled at the dirt with a shovel and buried Tinnerman without even checking for a pulse. But then you could tell the earth had been turned, or at least Manning thought you could, and he got it into his head that cement had to be laid now. *Right now.* He remembered a kid from one of the concrete crews, a Mexican who needed money and wouldn't ask questions because he was an illegal and so you just knew he'd do it and not say a word because immigration would ask *him* questions and then he'd be deported.

With trembling hands Manning had used his cell phone to make a call. The pour for Hemmer's patio wasn't scheduled for another day, but he was the boss and he could divert a load if he wanted, and he could pick who he wanted for the job, and that's what he did. Juan-Carlos Santiago came out, driving that big cement truck like he did it every day, even though he didn't. He told Manning the cement wasn't ready, the mix was rushed, it would come out wrong, but he poured it and he didn't ask why mesh hadn't been laid or why the ground looked uneven. Right there in the waning light he poured the cement and smoothed it over with a rake and a trowel, and made it look good, and when he was done, Manning hit him with the rebar, too.

"So what's he got now, this whiz kid?" said Hendricks. "He's got another body *and* a cement truck *and* Tinnerman's car to explain away. Can you *believe* it?" He laughed. Ha, ha, ha. What a silly predicament.

Claudia didn't dare appear distracted. But she could hear the rain tapering—and with it, her confidence. She forced herself into another round of slow breathing.

"Well, to make a long story short, Boyd finally called Farina, which is what he should've done to begin with. Farina's no genius, but he gets the job done. And he did."

With the two of them working together, playing lookout and digging a new grave, they got Santiago buried. Farina forged Tinnerman's signature on blank permits that he got from the inspector's car. Then he told Manning to call the concrete contractor and raise holy hell about Santiago's abandoning the job before it was done, making like the kid all of a sudden got cold feet—thought the job was an INS setup or something. Hey, guys up and quit all the time, especially the illegals. But Farina told Manning to make it look good. Rant. Rave. And before anyone even thought about questioning the plausibility of Santiago's abandoning the job midstream, ram it all home with threats of pulling the plug on any more work. Santiago wasn't important, but more work was. The contractor sent some-

one out to retrieve the truck. Farina got rid of Tinnerman's car. Hoo, boy!
What a day.

"So you *weren't* involved in the murders," said Claudia. "What happened to—"

"Oh, please. Farina reported to me. He told me what went down. And you know what? I think he *liked* that they happened. He was numb with boredom in your little town. Plus he had something to hold over Boyd, which gave him some kind of perverse kick. And of course Wonder Boy didn't have the balls to—"

Manning screeched a profanity and launched at Hendricks, cutting off his words but not his reactions. With rocket-like speed, the older man spun and shot out a fist. Manning caught the punch in an eye and pinwheeled back a few steps before thudding to the floor. Claudia moved a half-second later, but her legs failed her, and before she was off the couch, Hendricks snatched his gun and pointed it dead center at her chest.

"Good instincts, bad idea," he said quietly.

She reclaimed her position, trying to appear less shaken than she felt. Wine had slopped onto her hand, but amazingly she'd never let the glass go, her fingers so tightly clamped to it that it seemed like an extension of her hand. She took an unsteady sip. An opportunity had presented itself and she'd blown it.

Manning rocked on the floor, his hands clutching his face. He moaned and shuffled backward to rest against a wall. Hendricks regarded him disdainfully, then set the gun back down, drained his glass, and poured another drink.

"Where was I?"

Just like that.

"Farina." She cleared her throat. "Right after he told you what went down at Willow Whisper."

"Ah, yes. Farina." Hendricks tapped his glass with a fingernail. "The interesting thing about him is that when he's cleaned up, he looks like a stand-up kind of guy, the ideal neighbor. So I told Boyd to install him on the homeowners association. I couldn't do anything about the property itself without raising questions. Hemmer had already bought the house and would be living in it soon. All I could do was monitor things from a distance, and I figured with Farina in place we'd be all right. Farina wasn't about to jeopardize his 'Bonolo' alias. Well, you'd think not, but I imagine you've already guessed what happened next."

Claudia took a sip of her wine to show she was still a party girl, and now she told the story. Farina's boredom didn't fade. He quietly started dabbling in porn again. Not a lot. Just enough to feel some action, maybe get something going of his own. But then . . . Hemmer. He wouldn't quit about his house, so Farina orchestrated the scheme to turn him into a monster before Hemmer even took hostages and became one.

"Exactly," said Hendricks. "He tried for a preemptive strike." In retrospect, he told Claudia, he supposed Farina's campaign to make Hemmer look like a deviant made sense. Who better than Farina knew what kind of heat that could bring? But the hostage thing—even though it appeared to come out all right with Hemmer's death, it only gave Farina new concerns.

"Right in front of you, Detective, Hemmer insinuated he knew what Farina was all about. Farina took it for fact. They'd just had an encounter outside that stupid little bookstore." He laughed. "By the way, I love that you took Gloria here down, even for a while."

Addison sat zombie-like in her chair, her eyes unfocused, her body slack. Claudia thought she had probably gone into shock, and almost wished she could follow her into the same oblivion. But Hendricks had moved on, reciting details in a voice that deviated from matter-of-fact to sarcastic only when talking about his stepson.

During Hemmer's brief flirtation as a hostage-taker, he'd hinted not only about having knowledge of Farina's porn activities, but about having additional homeowners association files in the house. Even if it was all talk, it was too risky to let sit. Farina's idea? Eliminate anything even remotely incriminating and plant a video to reinforce the image of Hemmer as a pornographer. Manning contributed the key for Farina to get in, then moved to buy the house from Sandi's grandparents. They could save their asses and come out looking good.

"Sloppy, sloppy, sloppy," said Hendricks, shaking his head. "But it still could've worked out if Wonder Boy hadn't panicked all over again when you started asking questions, the gist of which the good mayor was only too happy to pass along. Boyd got it into his head that you would mysteriously find the Mexican's body—and no offense, Detective, but there wasn't a damned thing in the world that would've led you in that direction, no matter how insightful you might be."

He was right and Claudia didn't bother with a denial. Hemmer had copies of the forged building department papers. From those, she might've eventually unearthed Tinnerman. But maybe not even that. She glanced at Manning. He'd stopped moaning but continued to rock slightly, his hands at his face, his back pressed against the wall. He was down for the count.

"Boyd, though, he apparently thought you had some kind of divining rod that would lead you to the Mexican, so he took it upon himself to remove the body."

"Which he couldn't pinpoint some two years after the fact," Claudia supplied.

"*And,*" said Hendricks, "which would've been efficiently plowed under when the final phase of Willow Whisper got under way."

"It would've been soon," she said.

"Very soon."

"No one had to know."

Hendricks nodded. "Too bad that so many people do now." He looked meaningfully toward Lane and Addison.

"One thing," said Claudia. "I know this sounds like a cliché, but you'll never get away with all this. Never mind the 'loose ends' in this room. You've still got Kurt Kitner, Jennifer Parrish, Farina—"

"Parrish I'm not worried about. I had Farina do away with Kitner, and then I did away with Farina myself." He saw the shock in her eyes. "Just business."

"Wow."

Hendricks took it as flattery. He shrugged modestly. "It's like I told you, Detective, in business you move swiftly and decisively. And though an investigation might be messy, here's another cliché to keep in mind: Dead men tell no tales."

CHAPTER · 36

THE RAIN HAD STOPPED and it was time. Not all roads would be passable yet, but Hendricks believed enough water had receded for his purposes. Manning owned a Corvette and a Dodge Ram. Claudia didn't need to guess which one they'd use. Hendricks ordered her to her feet, not even a shadow of regret in his eyes.

She seized wildly for an opportunity—a hint of hesitation, a moment of distraction—anything. Hendricks had downed three drinks to her half glass of wine. If he was affected, though, he didn't show it in slurred speech or sluggish behavior. He was all about business—and this was business—and that's all he showed. She rose unsteadily with her glass and tried to work the pinch from her muscles.

"Can I pee first?" she asked.

Hendricks smiled. "In the end, people facing death will do absolutely anything they can to postpone it."

He nonchalantly picked up his gun and strolled toward Lane and Addison. The mayor trembled uncontrollably, his face contorted with fear. Addison merely closed her eyes. Claudia wondered how he intended to do away with them. He'd only spelled out his plans for her, though she was sure he had theirs carefully drafted as well.

"It's instinctive, of course," Hendricks continued. "To delay death, people will endure the most horrendous pain. They'll invoke the name of every saint. They'll tell you about their children and fumble through their wallets to pull out family pictures." He stopped behind his captives and, with his free hand, toyed with Addison's hair, lingering in a way that under other circumstances would seem affectionate. "The walking dead will cry and scream. They'll beg. And," he said pointedly, "they will ask to pee. Sorry, Detective, but no."

He moved to Manning and barked at him to get up and fetch what they needed. Manning didn't protest, but when he moved too slowly Hendricks gave him a sharp kick in the ribs. Claudia winced and looked away, her gaze falling on the bank of windows behind them all. They stood floor to ceiling; on a bright day they were altars to the quiet splendor of the outside. Now they loomed cold and black, colossal gaps against the monotony of the walls, sinister in the absence of rain. In full throttle the rain had been her enemy. Then her friend. Its demise meant her own now, and indeed the only remaining evidence of a storm at all announced itself in weak flickers of lightning far away. The windows were tinted and the night so black she could barely see even that, and a second later she realized that she hadn't. The lightning was just an illusion.

Manning hobbled off and she caught Hendricks watching her.

"You're wishing for more rain?" he asked, amused.

"It's just . . . yes." She exhaled. "One more drink?"

"I'm afraid not." He tsked. "You've heard the whole story, most of which you already knew."

"Except I'd figured Farina for the killer." She rolled her neck, tensed her muscles. "I knew Manning had to be involved, but maybe not all the way."

"It's a minor detail. Farina would've killed them, too. Boyd's panicky nature simply got them dead faster."

Claudia moved slowly to avoid alarming him, and held out her wine glass. "Come, on. You're way ahead of me, you know."

"Your delay tactics are unimaginative and beneath you."

"Okay." She paused, letting him know she was thinking. "Umm . . . well, how about this one? Someone's got a weapon trained on you through the window."

"What, like this?" Hendricks swiftly leveled his .45 at her.

"That's about right."

He snorted. "That's the oldest one in the book, Detective." He waggled the gun at her. "Enough, already."

"No, really. Look."

She pointed and Hendricks must've thought it was funny, really funny, because he started to laugh outright, laughed until the window exploded in a boom and bits of glass cascaded everywhere, sparkling like diamonds in the glare of the flashlight behind them.

Claudia lurched for her gun, rolled once, and came up with it in her hands. From the corner of her eye she caught Suggs clambering through the shattered window, his flashlight erratically splaying light against the walls.

She swiveled into a crouch, sweeping the room with frantic eyes, the .38 frozen in her grip. No one had screamed. Lane and Addison couldn't. But someone had been hit. Blood flecked her right arm and blotched her eyeglasses. She could taste it on her lips. Not her, though. Not the chief; he was in and frozen in his own crouch, an uncertain expression on his face.

Hendricks, then. Where was he? He couldn't have—

She glimpsed movement to the right. Heard a muffled gasp. The chief, too. He saw it. He heard it. They exchanged glances and looked to the source in the precise second Hendricks burst from behind Lane's arm-chair. Claudia stood and aimed. Suggs stood and aimed. But Hendricks was just as fast and jammed his .45 beneath the mayor's chin, the muzzle of the gun sunk so deep that it looked like a magician's trick, like any second it might come out the top of his head. Lane gurgled and shook violently, his eyes so wide they looked inhuman.

"Drop your weapon!" Suggs shrieked. "Do it now!"

Blood ran from Hendricks's right shoulder, his shooting arm, but he held the weapon steady in his left, this ex-Marine who understood pain—how to give it; how to receive it; how to weather any storm. His eyes flicked to Claudia. "Tell him not to be stupid," he hissed. "Tell him!"

"Shut up and drop it!" Suggs yelled. "Let Lane—"

"Chief," Claudia said, her voice quiet but urgent.

"I'm not gonna negotiate on—"

"Please!" She locked eyes with him and shook her head slightly. "Let's all just settle down a minute, think this through."

"You better listen to her, 'Chief,'" said Hendricks. He sneered at Suggs. "Fire on me and I'll kill Lane, maybe have time to shoot Gloria, too." His right arm spasmed and he flinched, but his gun didn't waver from the mayor's chin. He took a breath and said, "Ask her. She knows I'll do it."

He wouldn't hesitate. Not for a second. Claudia nodded reluctantly, calculating distance. Suggs was closer than she was, but at an angle that put Addison in the same line of fire. The young woman sat unblinking in her chair, so lifeless that if her eyes weren't open she would appear dead. Claudia's position gave her a shot that wouldn't pose an unacceptable risk to Addison. But the mayor—no matter who fired at Hendricks, Lane was in jeopardy. If Hendricks didn't kill him first, a shot from her gun or the chief's might. And then there was Manning. He might've fled at the sound of Suggs's gun. Or he might be ready to spring from the hallway with his own gun.

Claudia felt the skin on her neck tighten at the unknown behind her. "What do you propose, Hendricks?"

"Put your weapons down. I use Lane to get to my car, then release him and go. Nobody has to—" Hendricks briefly shuddered. Sweat ran into his eyes. He blinked it away and licked his lips. "Nobody has to die."

"No way! *No way!*" Suggs settled deeper into his stance, gun held steady. "Let Lane go! Let's end this!"

"Not gonna happen! Now *lose the weapons!*"

Neither man moved, but primal rage gripped them with an intensity that shook Claudia more than any of the threats either of them had verbalized. Her heart banged wildly. They had seconds to make this end. Inaction was a death sentence.

Had Suggs come alone? She didn't know, couldn't ask, heard nothing but the moody strain of violins—Hendricks's classical music still floating through the room as though the world had not tilted on its axis. Lane's eyes pleaded with her.

Think, think, think.

They had to back Hendricks off. They could do that only if they defused the moment.

Or ratcheted it up.

Her eyes darted from Hendricks to Suggs, back again. Nothing had changed, except that Hendricks's mouth twitched with the trace of a grim smile, and he pushed his .45 farther into the mayor's neck. He lived and died by making decisions. He was making one now. Claudia saw it in his eyes, knew it in her gut. She was out of time. They were out of time.

She took a lungful of air, because she couldn't recall ever screaming in her life and right now her life—all of their lives—might depend on her ability to do it convincingly. One chance. One more lungful of air, and. . . .

She shrieked, "Get down! The window! *The window!*"

The first time she'd told Hendricks to look at the window, he'd laughed it off. It had been his mistake. This time he whirled instantly, aiming his .45 toward the newest danger, his attention off Lane for a nanosecond, and Lane, God love him, he scrunched into the armchair and never even saw the flame from Claudia's gun.

Suggs sprinted toward Hendricks so fast that he almost reached him before the man collapsed completely. Claudia simultaneously scissored toward the hall and yelled, "Look out, Chief! Manning's still—"

"Stand down, Hershey! It's okay. It's all over. I brought company with me. The boys radioed they caught Manning outside a second before Hendricks drew on you and I fired. Dropped my damned portable outside, but I 'spect they'll be burstin' in here any second." He stood and inhaled shakily. "The paramedics won't be far behind, not that it's gonna matter for this son of a bitch." He toed Hendricks's lifeless body, then holstered his sidearm and brushed glass crumbs from his shirt and pants. "Timely shot, Hershey. Good one, too."

The adrenaline after-burn was fading fast. Claudia gripped the wet bar for support, unable to respond. She watched Suggs as he freed Lane and Addison. From beginning to end it had happened so fast—forty seconds? A minute? She could barely process events. She could barely find her voice.

"You all right?" Suggs asked.

She cleared her throat. "I think so. You okay?"

"You're standin'. The bad guy's down. Yeah, I'm good."

With the gag removed from his mouth, Lane's teeth rattled like castanets. He would be incapable of coherent speech for a while, maybe for the first time in his life. Addison made no effort to speak at all. The femme fatale had shriveled to a lifeless doll. Suggs murmured reassurances to them both. A second later three uniformed officers burst into the room, guns drawn. He barked orders at them, then told one of them to fetch blankets for Lane and Addison. He looked at Claudia, asked her if she wanted one, too.

She shook her head and said, "You know, I was starting to wonder if you'd ever get here."

"I was starting to wonder if you'd ever notice me through the window."

"I thought you were lightning."

"Nah. Fast as it, though."

"Faster." She declined an officer's offer to bring her some water. Nothing would sit well in her stomach for a while. "So the radios are working okay again?"

Suggs waved a hand back and forth. "They've been on and off all day. Communications were down when Richardson came out to check on you. Took him nearly an hour to manage his way back to the station. He was waterlogged and scared witless because he couldn't figure out if he should be worried about you or not. I wouldn't know to be worried, either, except for the bandanna he brought back with him."

"Bandanna?"

"He found it stuck against a tree, wondered was it maybe yours."

The festival bandanna had been in her car. Claudia pictured it caught on her jeans, maybe snagged on a pocket rivet and dragged into the storm when she bolted from the Imperial to check license plates.

Suggs grinned crookedly. "Apparently you impressed on him the value of details. I think he would've brought the mailbox back if it'd looked bent to him."

"Richardson," she said softly. "Wow." And then she sank to the floor, dimly aware that her hands stung from minute glass cuts and that the gash on her head had begun bleeding again. She wished she had accepted the water. She half wished she hadn't spilled the rest of her wine.

Suggs looked at her. "Hey, you gonna help, or what?"

She thought "or what" but wobbled to her feet and got back to work.

CHAPTER · 37

THE INSTRUCTIONS had obviously been translated from some other language, and when Claudia scanned them she laughed out loud. But that was before she fully understood that "some assembly required" meant chipped nails, nicked knuckles, and forfeiture of an entire morning—at least if what you'd purchased was a gas grill. She surveyed the parts on her lawn and vowed that in the future she'd pay the assembly fee for anything larger than a toaster oven.

The sun made the repair work on her head itch maddeningly. She had anticipated stitches, but no, the ER doctor had used some kind of waxy substance to close the wound from Hendricks's gun. The cut wasn't very deep, and over time the wax would comb out with her hairbrush—kind of like dandruff, he had informed her. She probed the laceration gingerly, feeling a slight crust at its edges, but no evidence that unseemly flecks threatened. Good. No doubt Tom Dixon could handle a few flakes, but it wasn't the visual she cared to present on his first visit over. Neither was an unassembled grill, for which he was bringing steaks. She put her hands on her hips and cursed the pieces, which sprawled across the lawn like junkyard debris.

"Nice talk, Hershey."

She turned at the chief's voice and reminded him she was on vacation, just three days into a two-week stretch.

"So does that mean I should go," he said, "and let you read the latest developments in tomorrow's paper?"

"Not a chance. Pull up a grill lid and sit."

"Hell of a project to be startin' so late," he muttered, his eyes scanning the grill parts. "It's hotter than . . . wait a minute."

Claudia saw his gaze on her feet and she swore again, this time silently.

Too late to stuff them in shoes.

"Hershey, is that *nail* polish I see on your toes. It *is*, isn't it. You went back and had your toenails done all on your own. Son of a gun."

"It's . . . more like a protective coating than polish per se."

"Per se."

She sighed. "Yeah."

"Well, I like it."

She braced for a punch line, but instead he snatched the grill instructions off the ground and squinted at the tiny text. Then he looked at her work so far. "You got the damned heat shield all wrong, Hershey. It's not gonna fit to the support brackets that way. Give me a Phillips-head."

"You don't have to—"

"Come on, come one, come on. I don't have all day."

She handed him the screwdriver. "Morons write the instructions, you know."

"Yeah, yeah. Why don't you see about puttin' the wheels on the base while I fix this. We can talk while we work."

Claudia fetched some iced tea from the house, then bent to the task with Suggs. He told her some details she'd already learned from furtive conversations with Carella, her ally against the chief's order that she "relax, damn it, and think about anything except the job." So she knew that Moody came through with enough of Santiago's personal effects for a DNA match, and she knew that Tinnerman's body had been unearthed from beneath Hemmer's patio. Manning hadn't thought to remove the building inspector's wallet; no one worried about a positive ID.

But Suggs had a few surprises. Kitner wasn't dead; never knew he'd been targeted. Farina couldn't be bothered, although he was happy to tell Hendricks later that he had. They went out on Hendricks's yacht to talk about that and other matters. Farina never made it back. The expectation that his body would be recovered from the Atlantic Ocean was nil.

"Damned good thing I nailed Hendricks and not Manning," said Suggs. "If Hendricks was still alive he wouldn't give us nothin' but a load of lawyers that'd make the O. J. trial look like kids' play. But Manning can't shut up. He knows the state attorney's office has him solid for Santiago and Tinnerman, so he's givin' up everything on his stepdaddy, lookin' for a break in sentencing. Between his statement, the stuff Hemmer stashed away, and what you figured out, the state's already callin' it the case of the century. Course, these days that's what they call every case with more'n one body."

"They giving Manning murder two?"

"Probably. But he faces a boatload of other charges and won't see the light of day for a long, long time. Maybe never. Give me a hand here for a second."

Claudia helped the chief wrestle the control panel onto the heat shield, then held it while he tightened screws. He grunted approvingly, then took a long drink of his iced tea. "You ever get your A/C fixed?" he asked.

She nodded. "They came on time, made a lot of noise, and charged me $300. But it's cool inside."

"Good."

The sun shined brightly from a cloudless blue sky, its presence so commanding that to imagine it vanquished by an even greater force seemed preposterous. But Claudia knew she would never again trust it fully. It had turned traitor, eclipsed her judgment, drawn her into jeopardy. . . .

If only.

She looked at Suggs, fumbling with a plastic bag of flat washers. "I could've got them all killed," she said quietly.

"Damn packaging," he said, using a fingernail to pry staples from the top. He paused and caught her eye. "Hershey, there's a couple ways to look at things. If you hadn't gone out to Manning's place when you did, at least two more people would damned sure be dead today. So you went and it turned out all right. On the other hand, if it were me, I guess I'd do a little head check to see if my motives were pure as the head on a fresh beer. Then you know what I'd do? I'd let it go, because, Hershey, you think way too much for your own good." He tore at the package with his teeth, then grunted with satisfaction when it opened.

"I'm just grateful that—"

"Did you know Hendricks was an FBI target? Short-listed by the IRS, too. One way or another they'd been lookin' at him for years. Possible racketeering, fraud, tax evasion. But no one could ever get close enough to pull together an indictment. I talked to one agent said he'd never met such a smug bastard."

Claudia pushed aside her personal torment. There would be time for recrimination later. There always was.

"Yeah," Suggs said, "his problem with Manning wasn't just that Manning screwed up with Willow Whisper. Turns out that Hendricks had an affair with Gloria Addison before his stepson did, but she dumped the old boy in favor of the young stud, which of course Hendricks wasn't supposed to find out."

"Except that would've been too good for Farina not to pass along."

"You got it. Addison met both of 'em in the Miami law office where she temped. It's where Hendricks and Manning took care of legal matters."

"I wondered. I never could quite tie all the threads from Addison to everyone else. How's she doing now?"

"Not good. She's either in some kind of catatonic state or she's fakin' one good."

"Lane?"

Suggs snorted. "I don't think he should look for Christmas cards from the people who used to suck up to him. But probably no one's gonna get him on more than misfeasance in office. Ambitious as he was, it doesn't appear like he really knew what was happening with Willow Whisper, and no one can prove he's the one who snuck in and stole files from the building department. Meanwhile, the deputy mayor's stepped in to take his place for now. He's about 12 years old, but I get along with him all right."

Claudia smiled. She thought about sharing her opinion on the deputy mayor, but Suggs had his face back in the instruction sheet, muttering something about an air shutter and the valve orifice. The latter brought to mind a joke he would probably appreciate, but Claudia thought sharing it with Sydney later might be more appropriate. Hard to tell with the chief. Hard to tell with Sydney, for that matter. Her relationships with both of them were still evolving, and it may be that's the way it always would be.

Then again, so what? She had air-conditioning in the house, and family and friends to share it with. She looked at her watch. In a few more hours, maybe one more. Obviously she wasn't ready to share *that* with the chief yet, but boy howdy, the thought of a cowboy coming over was enough to tweak the playful side she didn't let loose very often.

She looked at Suggs. He was really into the grill now, cursing it with some of the same words he'd badgered her about using. What the hell. She interrupted him and told the joke.

TAKE A STAB AT THESE MYSTERIES COMING SOON

The death of her mother-in-law was accidental. But it didn't matter. Deidre knew if the secret got out, she would end up in jail, leaving her two young daughters without a mother. Her friends were willing to help, but could such an ominous secret stay hidden forever?

The Secret of Fairwind Estates

by Lisa Church

Three Dirty Women and the Shady Acres

by Julie Wray Herman

When Three Dirty Women Landscaping Inc. is hired to landscape the grounds of Shady Acres Retirement Center, Korine McFaile finds she has to think twice about her decision to place her mother-in-law there. Someone seems determined to lower the median age of Pine Grove, and the results are murder.

Someone wants Bitsy and Matt to stay out of the dark, abandoned fort—and is making sure they do. Is it because valuable jewels really are hidden inside? Or is someone afraid Bitsy and Matt will discover more than just buried treasure?

Bitsy and the Mystery at Tybee Island

by Vonda Skinner Skelton

SILVER DAGGER MYSTERIES